DON'T MOVE

Margaret Mazzantini was born in Dublin in 1961. *Don't Move* is her second novel. It has won numerous awards, including the prestigious Italian Strega Prize. She has three children and is married to the actor Sergio Castellitto, who stars alongside Penelope Cruz in the film of the book. She lives in Rome.

DON'T MOVE

Margaret Mazzantini

DON'T MOVE

TRANSLATED FROM THE ITALIAN BY
John Cullen

V

VINTAGE

Published by Vintage 2005

8 10 9

First published in Italy in 2001 as *Non ti muovere* by
Arnoldo Mondadori Editore S.p.A.

First published in Great Britain in 2004 by
Chatto & Windus

Vintage
Random House, 20 Vauxhall Bridge Road,
London SW1V 2SA

www.rbooks.co.uk

Addresses for companies within
The Random House Group Limited can be found at:
www.randomhouse.co.uk/offices.htm

The Random House Group Limited Reg. No. 954009

A CIP catalogue record for this book
is available from the British Library

ISBN 9780099462033

The Random House Group Limited supports The Forest Stewardship
Council (FSC), the leading international forest certification organisation.
All our titles that are printed on Greenpeace approved FSC certified paper
carry the FSC logo. Our paper procurement policy can be found at:
www.rbooks.co.uk/environment

Printed and bound in Great Britain by
CPI Antony Rowe, Chippenham, Wiltshire

For Sergio

You went through the stop sign. You had your imitation wolfskin jacket on, your headset was plugged into your ears, and you never even slowed down. The rain had just stopped, and soon it would start again. The sky was the colour of ashes, and above the branches of the plane trees, above the TV aerials, it was filled with great, twittering, feathery flocks of starlings. They looked like giant blotches, black against the grey of the sky, veering and swerving in tight formations, packed so close that they were touching one another, but harmlessly; and then they would open up and spread apart and almost disappear from sight before coming together again, as densely as before. Down on the ground, the pedestrians were covering their heads with newspapers, even with their bare hands, to protect themselves from the hail of droppings raining down from the sky, sliming the pavement, mingling with wet fallen leaves in viscous clusters, and giving off a heavy sweetish smell everyone was in a hurry to get away from.

You came flying along the avenue, heading for the intersection. You almost made it – the guy in the car almost managed to miss you. But the street was slick with starling guano. The car wheels skidded a little on that slippery surface, not much, but enough to graze your motor scooter. You flew up towards the birds and then down into their shit, and your backpack with all the stickers on it came down with you. Two of your notebooks landed in the gutter, in a puddle of black water. Your helmet, which you'd neglected to fasten, bounced off the street like an empty head. Someone ran over to you right away. Your eyes were open, your face was filthy, you'd lost all your front teeth.

Your skin was peppered with asphalt cinders that darkened your cheeks like a man's beard. The music had stopped; your earphones were tangled up in your hair. The man in the car sprang out, leaving the door wide open, and ran to where you were lying. He looked at the big gash in your forehead and reached into his pocket for his mobile phone, but it slipped out of his hand. A boy picked it up – he's the one who reported the accident. Meanwhile, the traffic was at a standstill. The guy's car was where he'd left it, straddling the tram tracks, and the tram couldn't pass. The driver got out, along with a lot of his passengers, and they all walked over to where you were. Total strangers stood in a circle around you and stared. A little groan came out of your mouth, followed by a bubble of pink froth; you were sliding into unconsciousness. All the blocked traffic delayed the ambulance, but you weren't in a hurry any more. You were closed up in your fake-fur jacket like a bird with folded wings.

At last, the emergency team got to you, put you in the ambulance and sped away through the traffic with their sirens wailing. Some cars pulled over to the side of the road to let you pass, but the ambulance driver had to go up on the pavements along the river, and all the while the IV bottle was swinging above your head and a hand was squeezing a big blue bag, again and again, pumping breath into your lungs. In A & E, the doctor who took charge of you slipped her finger into your mouth and down between your mandible and your hyoid bone. That's an extremely sensitive pressure point, and your reaction was abnormally weak. She took some gauze and wiped away the blood that was running out of your forehead. She examined your pupils; they were fixed and asymmetrical. And you were bradypnoeic, you were breathing too slowly. They put an artificial airway into your mouth to reposition your tongue, which had slid to the back of your throat, and then they inserted the suction catheter through your nose to clear your airway passages. They pulled up blood, tar, mucus and tooth fragments. They put a pulse oximeter clip on one of your fingers to measure the oxygen saturation of your blood. Your oxyhaemo-globin percentage was eighty-five, dangerously low, and so they intubated you. The doctor slid the blade of the laryngoscope, with its cold light, into your mouth. A nurse came into the room, pushing the trolley with the cardiac monitor, but when she plugged the machine in, it didn't start. She struck the monitor a gentle blow on the side, and the screen lit up. They pushed up your T-shirt and pasted the electrodes on to your chest. The CAT-scan room was in use, so you had to wait a little before they put you into the scanning tunnel. The scan showed that you had a head trauma affecting your temporal lobe. On the other side of the glass window, the emergency physician asked the radiologist to make new, more detailed cross-sections. They revealed the depth and extension of a haematoma outside the cerebral parenchyma. On the opposite side of your skull, the contrecoup haematoma, if there was one, wasn't visible yet. But they didn't inject you with the contrast medium, because they were afraid of renal complications. They quickly called the third floor and had them get the operating theatre ready. The casualty physician asked, 'Who's the neurosurgeon on duty?'

In the meantime, they had started preparing you for surgery. A nurse carefully undressed you, cutting off your clothes with a pair of scissors. No one knew how to notify your family. They were hoping to find some kind of identification on you, but you didn't have any. Then they looked in your backpack and found your diary. The casualty doctor read your first name, then your surname. She stared at it for a few seconds before returning to your first name. All at once she felt hot, her face was burning, she needed to breathe and couldn't; it was as if a stubborn mouthful of food were obstructing her windpipe. She forgot about her sanguinary profession and looked you in the face like an ordinary laywoman. She studied your swollen features, hoping to prove herself wrong, to drive away her awful thought; but you look like me, and Ada couldn't help seeing the resemblance. The nurse was shaving your head; your hair was falling to the floor. Ada gestured at your dark brown locks. 'Careful. Be careful,' she whispered. She went over to the intensive-care unit and spoke to the neurosurgeon on duty. 'That girl, the one they just brought in . . .'

'You don't have a mask on. Let's step out.'

They left that aseptic environment, where relatives aren't allowed, where the patients lie naked and breathe artificially. They went back to the room where the nurse was prepping you. The neurosurgeon looked at the monitor, checking your heart rhythm and your vital signs. 'She's hypotensive,' he said. 'Have you excluded thoracic or abdominal injuries?' Then he gave you a sidelong, furtive look. With a quick movement of his fingers, he opened your eyelids.

'Well?' Ada asked.

'Are they ready in the operating theatre?' the neurosurgeon asked the nurse.

'Not yet. They'll be ready soon.'

Ada was insistent. 'Don't you think she looks like him?'

The neurosurgeon turned round and held your CAT-scan results up to the light that was coming in the window. 'She's got a subdural haematoma.'

Ada wrung her hands and raised her voice: 'She looks like him, doesn't she?'

'It could be intracranial, as well . . .'

It was raining outside, but Ada took the exterior walkway that led from the emergency wing to the main hospital building. Wearing her short-sleeved tunic, her arms tightly folded, she stepped silently in her green rubber medical clogs. Instead of taking the lift up to the surgery floor, she climbed the stairs. She needed to do something, to keep moving. I've known her for twenty-five years. For a brief time, when I was still single, I used to flirt with her, half seriously, half in jest.

Ada opened the door to the physicians' lounge, where a nurse was clearing away some coffee cups. Ada took a plastic cap and a surgical mask from their containers, hurriedly put them on and entered the operating theatre.

I must have noticed her after a little while, when I shifted my eyes to the nurse to pass her the clamp. I thought it was strange

4

to see Ada there. She works exclusively in intensive care, and our rare encounters generally take place in the snack bar on the basement floor. But I didn't pay any particular attention to her; I didn't even nod a greeting. I removed another clamp and passed it to the nurse. Ada waited until my hands were away from the operating field. Then she whispered, 'Doctor, you must come.' The nurse was taking the suturing needle out of its sterile wrapping; I heard her tearing the plasticised paper as I looked up at Ada. She was standing very close to me – I hadn't noticed how close. She wasn't wearing any make-up, and I found myself staring into a pair of naked, tremulous, glittering female eyes. Before she was transferred to A & E, she'd been one of the best anaesthetists on the hospital staff, and she'd pumped nitrous oxide into many a patient of mine. I'd seen her remain calm and unemotional even in the most crucial moments, and I'd always admired her for that, because I knew how much effort it cost her to bury her feelings inside her green hospital tunic.

'Later,' I said.

'No, Doctor, it's urgent. Please come.'

Her voice sounded different, filled with a strangely intense authority. I believe my mind remained blank – I suspected nothing – but my hands suddenly felt heavy. The nurse presented the needle holder. I'd never left an operation unfinished. I closed my hand, realising as I did so that I was reacting too slowly. I started sewing the abdominal wall back together, but then I took a step backwards, trying to put some distance between myself and the patient, and I collided with someone standing behind me. 'You finish up,' I told the surgical registrar. The nurse passed him the needle holder. The metal instrument struck his gloved hand with a dull slap that sounded amplified in my ears. Everyone in the room looked at Ada.

Behind our backs, the door of the operating theatre closed silently and firmly. We stood facing each other in the waiting area. 'Well?' I said.

Ada's chest was heaving under her tunic, and her bare arms were blotchy from cold. 'Doctor, we've got a girl with a cranial trauma down in intensive care . . .'

Automatically, almost without noticing it, I stripped off my gloves. 'Go on.'

'I found her diary. Doctor, her last name is the same as yours.'

I raised a hand and removed the surgical mask from her face. Her voice wasn't agitated any more; her courage was at an end, and what remained was a calm, breathless plea for help. 'What's your daughter's name?' she asked.

I think I leaned towards her so that I could see her better, so that I could search her eyes for a name that wasn't yours.

'Angela,' I murmured into those eyes, and I saw them flood with tears.

I ran down the stairs, I ran through the rain outside, I ran past an arriving ambulance that jerked to a dead stop a few feet away from my legs, I ran inside the glass doors of the emergency room, I ran across the nurses' station, I ran into a room where someone with a broken limb was screaming, and I ran into the next room, which was empty and in disorder. That's where I stopped. Your brown hair was on the floor. Your wavy brown hair and some bloodstained gauze, all swept up into a little mound.

In an instant, I'm turned into dust, walking dust. I drag myself to the intensive-care unit and go down the hall to the glass wall. There you are, shaved and intubated, with bright white bandages around your bruised, swollen face. It's you. I enter the room and stand beside you. I'm a father, a poor father like any other, sweaty, dry-mouthed, shattered by grief. My scalp is cold. I can't get my mind around what's happening; it's looming over me, ready to crush me, and I remain in a kind of blurry stupor. My sorrow dazes me, cripples me like an embolus. I close my eyes and reject my sorrow. It's not really you lying there; you're at school. When I open my eyes again, I won't see you. I'll see another girl, any other girl, some ordinary girl in the world. But not you, Angela. I open my eyes and it's really you, some ordinary girl in the world.

There's a box on the floor with DANGEROUS WASTE written on it. I discard a part of myself: the man, not the physician. I must do this. It's my duty; it's the only thing left for me to do. I must look at you as though you're a stranger to me. I move the electrode that's rudely touching your nipple to a more seemly position. I look at the monitor: fifty-four heartbeats per minute. But going down: now it's fifty-two. I raise your eyelid. Your pupils are anisocoric. The right one is completely dilated; the intracranial trauma is in that hemisphere. You need immediate surgery so your brain can breathe. The mass of tissue displaced by the haematoma is pressing against the hard, unyielding inner wall of your skull, smothering the centres that control all the nerves in your body, depriving you with every passing instant of a bit more of yourself. I turn to Ada. 'You've given her cortisone?'

'Yes, Doctor. And medication to protect the lining of her GI tract.'

'Does she have other injuries?'

'Possibly a ruptured spleen.'

'Haemoglobin?'

'Twelve.'

'Who's in neurosurgery?'

'Me, I am. Hello, Timoteo.'

Alfredo puts a hand on my shoulder. His white coat is unbuttoned; his hair and face are wet. 'Ada telephoned me. I had just left the hospital.'

Alfredo is the best surgeon in his department, and yet nobody gives him any special consideration. His manner is tentative, his behaviour is frequently off-putting, he has no visible merits; he works in the shadow of the chairman of surgery, who stands around watching while Alfredo wears himself out. Many years ago, I gave him a few words of advice, but he never listened to me; his character's not as highly developed as his surgical skills. He's separated from his wife, and I know he has a teenage son more or less your age. He wasn't on duty, he could have opted out, no surgeon likes operating on a colleague's relative. Nevertheless, he jumped into a taxi and had the driver drop him off in the middle of the traffic outside. He ran through it as fast as he could, darting past the cars in the rain. I'm not sure I would have done the same.

'Is everything ready upstairs?' Alfredo asks.

'Yes,' replies the nurse.

'Let's go up.'

Ada approaches you, takes you off the respirator and hooks you back up to the Ambu bag for your trip to the operating theatre. Then they get you under way. As they're loading you into the lift, I see one of your arms slip off the trolley. Ada leans down, reaching for your hand.

I stay downstairs with Alfredo. We sit in one of the rooms near the intensive-care unit. Alfredo turns on the trans-illuminator, puts up your CAT scan, and examines it from a few inches away. At one point, he stops, furrows his brow, gazes more intensely. I know what it means to search the nebula of an X-ray for some helpful clue.

'See here,' he says. 'This is the main haematoma, near the dura mater. I won't have any problem getting to it. We'll have to see how much damage the brain has suffered – that's something I can't predict. Then there's another area here, deeper down. I don't know, maybe it's an effusion caused by the contrecoup . . .'

We exchange glances, standing in the lurid light that projects the image of your brain on to the wall behind us. We know we can't lie to each other. 'Ischaemic complications could have started already,' I whisper.

'I have to open her up; then we'll understand.'

'She's fifteen.'

'That's good. Her heart is strong.'

'She's not strong – she's little.'

My knees buckle, and now I'm crying without restraint, pressing my hands against my wet face. 'She's going to die, isn't she? We both know it. Her head is flooded.'

'We don't know shit, Timoteo.' He goes down on his knees beside me, takes my arm and shakes me hard, shaking himself at the same time. 'We're going to open her up and take a look. I'll aspirate the haematoma, give her brain a chance to breathe, and we'll see what happens.'

He gets to his feet. 'You're going to be in there with me, right?'

8

Before I stand up, I wipe my nose and my eyes with my forearm. A shiny trail of mucus clings to the hairs. 'No, I don't remember anything about the brain. I wouldn't be any help to you . . .'

Alfredo gives me one of his imperturbable looks. He knows I'm lying.

In the lift, we don't talk; we look up at the illuminated numbers of the floors we're passing. We separate without a word, without even touching each other. I take a few steps and sit down in the doctors' lounge. Alfredo is scrubbing for surgery. In my mind, I follow each of his movements as he goes through a ritual I'm quite familiar with. I see him thrust his arms up to the elbows in the big stainless-steel sink; I watch his hands unwrap the sterilised sponge. I've got the smell of antiseptic in my nose. The nurse passes him the sterile towels so he can dry himself off; the scrub nurse ties his surgical gown . . . It's unusually quiet around here – everyone's been reduced to silence. A nurse, someone I know very well, passes in front of the open door, our eyes meet, and his immediately shift to the floor and his rubber shoes. Now Ada's at the door. Ada, who's never been married, who has a ground-floor flat with a garden that her upstairs neighbours' laundry falls into.

'We're starting,' she says. 'Are you sure you don't want to come?'

'Yes.'

'Do you need anything?'

'No.'

She nods and tries to smile.

'Listen, Ada,' I say as she moves away.

She turns towards me again. 'Yes, Doctor?'

'If the worst should happen, ask everyone to leave. Then, before you come to call me, before I see her, disconnect the respirator, remove all the needles and all the tubes, clean up everything, and cover up the – well, just try to give her back some dignity.'

★

9

Now Alfredo has finished scrubbing, and he enters the operating theatre with his hands in the air. The registrar approaches him and slips on his gloves. You're lying under the theatre lamp. I've got one thing left to do, the most terrible of all: I've got to notify your mother. You remember, she left for London this morning. She was supposed to interview somebody, a Cabinet minister, I think. She was very excited. Her cab drove away from the house just before you left. Earlier, I heard the two of you talking in the bathroom. You came home at 12.15 on Saturday night, fifteen minutes later than the time you'd agreed to, and she was very upset. In certain areas, she's not at all indulgent. She can't stand it when you break the rules; she takes it as a personal attack on her serenity. Generally, though, she's an easy-going mother; when she's inflexible, it's a kind of self-defence, sure, but believe me, it oppresses her, too. I know you're not doing anything wrong. You meet your friends after school and talk in the twilight, in the cold, you pull the sleeves of your sweaters over your hands and shiver under all that graffiti. I've never been strict with you. I trust you; I even trust your mistakes. I know you from the way you are at home and from the rare moments we spend together, but I don't know you as you are with other people. I know you have a good heart, and I know you give it all to your great friendships. And so you should; it's wonderful to have that sparkle in your life. But your mother doesn't see it that way. She thinks you don't study enough, that you waste your energy, and she's afraid you'll fall behind in school.

Sometimes you and your friends walk down the block and descend into that subterranean bar on the corner, that smoke-filled underground cavern. I looked down in there once. I was standing outside, peering through the pavement-level windows. I saw you all laughing, kissing one another, stubbing out cigarettes. There I was, an elegant fifty-five-year-old gentleman out for a nocturnal stroll, and there you were, sitting on the other side of one of those little grated windows the passing dogs like to mark. You were all so young; you were sitting so close together. And you're all so beautiful, Angela, you and all your friends. Beautiful. I've been meaning to tell you that. I was almost ashamed to be spying on you, watching you all so curiously, like an old man watching a child unwrapping a gift. But so I did, and I saw you down there, unwrapping your life in that smoky bar.

I just spoke to my secretary. She's managed to get word to the people at Heathrow Airport. They'll meet Elsa as soon as she gets off the plane, take her to a private room and explain the situation. It's terrible to think about her sitting up there in the sky with a lapful of newspapers and no clue at all. She thinks we're safe down here, my poor daughter, and I wish her flight would never end – I wish her plane would go round the world indefinitely. Maybe she's looking at a cloud right now, one of those clouds that hide the sun almost but not completely, and a golden beam is passing through the little window and lighting up her face. She's probably reading an article written by some colleague and reviewing it by adjusting the contours of her mouth. I know all her involuntary expressions; it's as if every emotion has a tiny indicator on her face. I've sat next to her on many aeroplane flights. I know the creases in her neck, that little pouch that forms under her chin when she lowers her head to read; I know the fatigue in her eyes when she takes off her glasses and lays her head back against the seat. Now the air steward's offering her a meal on a tray and she's refusing in perfect English and asking for 'Just a black coffee' and waiting for the smell of pre-packaged food to go away. Your mother always has her feet on the ground, even when she's in the air. Now she's probably sitting back with her face turned towards the window; maybe she's pulled down the stiff little shade for her half-hour of rest. She's thinking about all the things she has to do today, and, on top of that, I'm sure she's determined to go into town to buy you something. The last time she came back from a trip, she brought you that great-looking poncho, remember? But no, maybe she won't buy you anything; maybe she's still angry with you . . . What's she going to think when the people from the airline meet her on the ground? Will her knees give way? What will be the look on her face as she stands there in the midst of all that international coming and going? How much terror will be in her eyes? This is going to age her, you know, Angela; this is going to age her a lot. She loves you so much. She's a liberated, highly civilised woman, she's a model of social grace, she's extremely knowledgeable, but she knows nothing about grief. She thinks she knows, but she doesn't. She's up there in the sky, and she doesn't yet know what grief is like down here on earth. It's an atrocious wound, a hole in the heart, and it's sucking in everything at top speed, like a whirlpool: cassettes, clothes, photographs, tampons, marking pens, compact discs, smells, birthdays, nannies, armbands, nappies. Everything's gone. She'll need all her strength in that airport. Maybe she'll run to the window overlooking the runway and fling herself against that transparent wall like an animal swept away in a flood.

My secretary spoke to one of the airport managers, who assured her that they'll proceed with extreme caution; they'll try their best not to alarm your mother too much. Everything's been arranged: she'll be on the next plane home. There's a British Airways flight that leaves London shortly after her arrival. Everything's been arranged: they'll give her a seat in some quiet corner, they'll bring her some tea, they'll offer her a telephone. I've got my mobile in my pocket, turned on and ready for her call. I've checked it; it's got good reception and good signal strength. I'm going to lie; I'm going to try to tell her you're not in critical condition. Naturally, she won't believe me, she'll think you're dead. I'm going to be as convincing as I can.

You were wearing a ring on your thumb. I'd never noticed that before. Ada managed to get it off – it's here in my pocket. I try to put it on my own thumb, but the ring's too small. Maybe it'll fit on my middle finger. Ah, don't die, Angela, don't die before your mother's plane lands. Don't let your soul fly up to the clouds she's looking at so calmly. Don't cross her flight path, dearest daughter. Stay where you are. Don't move.

I'm cold. I'm still in my scrubs; maybe I should change. My street clothes are in the metal locker with my name on it. I carefully put my sports jacket on the hanger over my shirt, I left my wallet and my car keys in the upper compartment, and I closed the little padlock. When was that? Only three hours ago, perhaps even less. Three hours ago, I was a man like any other. How devious grief is, how quickly it sets in. It's like a corrosive acid, deep down inside, eating away. I'm leaning over, resting my arms on my knees. On the other side of the accordion curtain, I can see a portion of the oncology wing. I've never spent any time in this room before; I've only walked in and out of it. I'm sitting on an imitation-leather sofa. In front of me, there's a low table and two empty chairs. The green floor is covered with small dark spots that move frenetically before my eyes, like microbes under a microscope. Because now it seems to me that I've been expecting this tragedy to happen.

We're separated by one corridor, two doors and a coma. The distance between us is like a prison, but I'm wondering if it might be possible to break free of it, to imagine it as a kind of confessional, and to request an audience with you right here, my child, right on this floor with the dancing spots.

I'm a surgeon, a man who has learned to divide things, to separate healthy parts from diseased ones. I've saved many lives, but not my own, Angela.

We've lived in the same house for fifteen years. You can recognise my smell, my footstep. You know how I touch things; you know the even sound of my voice. You know both sides of my character, the gentle side and the irritating, indefensible, hostile side. I don't really know what you think of me, but I can imagine. You think I'm a responsible father, not without a certain sardonic sense of humour, but too aloof. You and your mother have a solid bond; sometimes your relationship is stormy, but it's always very much alive. I've hung around in the background, like an empty suit in a wardrobe. You've learned more about me from my absences, my books, my raincoat in the hall, than you have from my flesh-and-blood self. And I don't know that other story, the one you and your mother have written about me with the help of the clues I've left here and there. Like your mother, you've come to prefer missing me, because having me around requires too much effort. Many a morning, I've left the house with the sensation that the two of you, bursting with all that energy, were pushing me towards the door to get me out of the way. I love the natural rapport between you and your mother, it brings a smile to my face; to some degree, you two have protected me from myself. For my part, I've never felt 'natural'. I've tried hard to be – I've made some pretty drastic attempts – but when you have to try to be natural, you're already defeated. So I've long since accepted the blueprint you made for me, the carbon copy that responded to your needs. I've been a regular guest in my own house. I've never got angry, not even when it's rained on my day off and the maid has spread out the drying rack with your clothes on it, yours and your mother's, next to the radiator in *my* study. I've grown accustomed to these damp intrusions; I never complain. I remain in my armchair, unable to stretch my legs out completely, I place the book in my lap and I stare at your laundry. I've found company in those wet clothes, perhaps more so than with the two of you in person, because I could catch in their thin, gleaming fabrics the brotherly fragrance of nostalgia. I've thought of you two, of course, but I've felt nostalgia principally for myself, for the days when I was a fugitive from justice. Angela, I know that my hugs and kisses have been stilted and awkward for too many years. Every time I've put my arms around you, I've felt your body quivering with impatience, if not downright discomfort. You could never feel at ease with me, that's all. It was enough for you to know that I was there, to look at me from a distance, as though I were a traveller on another train, standing at the window, with his face blurred by the glass. You're a sensitive, sunny girl, but your mood can change in a second; you often fly into a blind fury. I've always suspected that that mysterious rage, which leaves you baffled and a little sad, has grown inside you because of me.

Angela, there's an empty chair right behind you, behind your innocent back. And there's an empty chair inside of me. I look at it, at its back and its legs, I wait, and I seem to hear something. It's the sound of hope. I know about hope. I've heard it busily throbbing in dying bodies, I've seen it dawn in the eyes of a thousand patients, I've felt it sputter and stall every time I've moved my hands and decided the course of someone's life. I know exactly how I'm deluding myself. I stare at the dark flecks on this floor – they're moving slowly now, like soot – and I delude myself into thinking that I see a woman in that empty chair, even if only for a moment, filling it not with her body, no, but with her pity. I see two low-cut wine-coloured shoes, two bare legs, a forehead that's too high. And already she's there in front of me, come to remind me that I'm a plague-spreader, a man who marks others for misfortune, carelessly including those who love him. You don't know her – she passed through my life before you were born, but her passage left an indelible imprint, like a fossil. I want to reach out to you, Angela; I want to join you in that tangle of tubes where you're lying, where the craniotome is about to break your head open, and tell you the story of that woman.

I met her in a bar, one of those bars you find on the outskirts of big cities. The coffee was as bad as the smell coming from the half-open door of the toilet, which was located behind an old table football whose players had been decapitated by the competitive zeal of the bar's patrons. The heat was suffocating. As I did every Friday, I had been driving to join your mother at the beach house we rented by the sea south of the city. On the way, without so much as a tremor, my car had died; it had gone out like a match on the deserted highway that ran between some parched, dirty-looking fields and a few industrial sheds. I was on the outer fringe of the outskirts, and the only buildings I could see were off in the distance. I had to walk to them in the broiling sun. It was early in July, sixteen years ago.

By the time I got to the bar, I was quite sweaty and unhappy. I ordered a coffee and a glass of water and asked where I might find a car mechanic. She was off to one side, bent over and rummaging in the fridge. 'There's no whole milk?' were the first words I ever heard her say. They were addressed to the boy behind the bar, a boy with a pimply face and a small discoloured apron tied tightly around his waist. 'Dunno,' he said, serving me my water with one hand and carefully sliding a dripping pewter saucer under the glass with the other. 'It doesn't matter,' she said, and she placed a carton of skimmed milk an inch or so away from me on the bar. She slipped her hand into a tiny purse, a child's purse made of flowered plastic and closed with a catch. She took out some money and put it down next to the milk. 'There's a mechanic,' she said, picking up her change, 'but I don't know if he's open.' I turned round at the sound of that voice, as toneless as the mew of a cat. Our eyes met for the first time. She was neither beautiful nor very young, with badly bleached hair and a thin but strong-boned face. She was wearing too much make-up, which made her bright eyes look sad. She left the milk on the bar and walked over to the jukebox. Despite all the sun outside, the place was dark, it smelled like a backed-up sewer, and soon it was filled with the tedious sounds of an English rock group that was very much in vogue in those days. She stood against the jukebox, practically clutching it, closed her eyes and began to move her head slowly from side to side. She stayed like that, a quivering shape in the shadows in the back of the room. The bartender glided out from behind the bar and stood at the door to give me directions. I went all the way round the block, but I couldn't find the mechanic's shop. The streets were empty of people. Up above my head, an old man on a balcony was shaking out a tablecloth. I went into the bar again, sweatier than before.

'I couldn't find it,' I said. I took some paper napkins out of a metal container and dried my forehead.

The jukebox had fallen silent, but she was still there. She was sitting on a chair, a dazed expression on her face, staring into space and chewing a piece of gum. She got up, took her carton of milk from the bar and bid the bartender goodbye. When she reached the door, she stopped. 'I'm passing right in front of the shop. If you want . . .'

I followed behind her in the scorching sun. She was wearing a purple T-shirt and a short lizard-green skirt, and on her feet she had a pair of high-heeled sandals, narrow strips of multi-coloured leather, above which her thin legs exerted themselves clumsily. She carried her milk in a patchwork bag with an extremely long shoulder strap, which almost reached her knee. She walked quickly, paying no attention to me, never turning round, dragging her feet along the uneven pavement, hugging the walls.

She stopped in front of a rolling shutter pulled all the way down. According to a small piece of yellowed paper taped to the metal, the shop was closed and would reopen in a couple of hours. I thought about your mother; I had to call her and tell her of my plight. Perspiration was running from my head, behind my ears, along my shirt collar. We stopped in the middle of the street. She turned towards me, just her head, and looked at me. Her eyes were half closed because of the sultry air and the bright sun. 'You have a bit of paper on your forehead.'

I felt around on my sweaty skin for the remnant of that bar napkin. I asked her, 'Is there a telephone booth around here?'

'You have to go back, it's in the other direction. I don't know if it works. They break everything here.'

Still chewing her gum, working her jaws vigorously, she kept one hand raised to ward off the sun. Her eyes, which turned out to be pale grey now that we were out in the open, ran over me swiftly, taking me in. She didn't look like a person who was afraid of strangers, but perhaps my tie and the wedding ring on my finger reassured her.

'If you want, you can use my telephone. I live back there,' she said, stretching her neck out towards an unspecified location on the other side of the street. She crossed over without looking. I followed her along a dirt path leading downhill, then through a labyrinth of increasingly spectral edifices, until we came to a block of flats that was still under construction, though some of its flats were already occupied. There were naked steel girders where terraces should have been and gaping holes that opened on to the void and were blocked by upended bedsprings.

'We'll take the shortcut,' she said, heading for the unfinished building.

We walked among the concrete pillars of what seemed to be an enormous abandoned car park, where we finally found some respite from the sun. Then we stepped into a dark lobby covered with spray-painted graffiti. It stank like a public urinal, and the stench was mingled with a fried-food smell coming from who knew where. The lift door was wide open. The panel with the buttons was uncovered, the wires exposed.

'We'll walk up,' she said. I followed her up several flights of stairs. Sudden screams occasionally pierced the silence, and the light of television sets flickered in the darkness like signal flashes from hellish lives. The filthy stairs were littered with used hypodermic needles. She stepped over them casually, lifting her bare feet in their flimsy sandals. I wanted to go back, Angela. I whirled round at every noise, expecting someone to jump me from behind, someone who would rob me or maybe even kill me, some accomplice of the vulgar woman who was leading me on. Her bag thudded against the stairs, raising a cloud of dust, and from time to time her smell, a warm, stale mixture of make-up and perspiration, reached my nostrils. I heard her murmur, 'It's disgusting, but it's the fastest way,' as though she had read my fearful thoughts. She spoke with a slight southern accent, lingering gloomily on some syllables and aborting others.

She climbed up one more flight, then walked rapidly through the dirt covering the floor and stopped in front of a metal door. Thrusting a finger into the hole where the lock should have been, she pulled the heavy obstacle towards her. Light struck me in the face so violently that I had to raise an arm to protect myself; the sun seemed very close. 'This way,' she said, and I saw her body drop out of sight. *She's nuts. I'm following a woman with a diseased mind. She picked me up in that bar just so I could watch her commit suicide.* I found myself standing at the top of an exterior stairway. It was a fire escape, a plunging iron spiral. She was descending the steps fearlessly; from where I stood, I could see the dark roots of her blonde hair. Now she looked unbelievably agile in her high heels, like a small boy, like a cat. I ventured into the coils of that spiral staircase, holding tightly to the rusty tubes and bolts of the handrail. My jacket caught on something; I pulled at it and heard the fabric rip. I was startled by a sudden roar, and there before my eyes, very close, was a gigantic viaduct. On the other side of the crash barrier, cars were whizzing by. I couldn't figure out where we were, so I stopped and looked around. The woman was below me, standing on an embankment some distance away. With her peroxided blonde hair, her painted face and her multicoloured bag, she looked like a clown left behind by the circus.

'Here we are!' she shouted.

And, in fact, there was a structure behind her, an old pink wall that didn't seem to belong to any visible house. She turned towards that wall, and now I saw that it was part of a free-standing dwelling, a sort of minuscule villa crumbling away right under the piers of the viaduct. We walked through a small thicket of dusty shrubs, then climbed two steps to a porch. The door was made of green staves, the same colour as her skirt. She stretched an arm towards the rows of bricks above the door and detached a key stuck up there with a piece of chewing gum. She opened the door, took the gum out of her mouth, stuck it to the key and pressed the whole wad back into place over the door. While she was stretched out like that, I looked at her exposed armpit – not shaved, but not bushy, either. Just a tuft of long, fine hairs, plastered together by sweat.

A diagonal beam of sunlight cut through the air inside the room. That was the first thing that struck me, together with a mixture of odours that reminded me of a house in the country: the smell of soot, overlaid by the sour tang of bleach and rat poison. The room was square, with a coffee-coloured stone floor. On the far wall was a fireplace like a big sorry black mouth. The interior of the room was dignified and orderly, though somewhat indistinct because the light came from a single window. The shutters were set ajar, and one of the columns of the viaduct showed through the opening. Three Swedish-style chairs were pushed under a table covered by a patterned oilcloth. Next to this was an open door, through which I could glimpse a kitchen cupboard with an imitation-cork veneer. She said, 'I'll put the milk in the fridge,' and stepped into the kitchen.

She had claimed to have a telephone. I looked for it in vain on a low table with an ashtray in the shape of a seashell, on a lacquered chest of drawers littered with knick-knacks, on an old couch rejuvenated by a cloth covering with a floral design. I noticed a poster hanging on the wall. It was a studio photo-graph, artificially lit and decorated with little plastic umbrellas, and it captured for posterity a monkey wearing a baby's cap and holding a baby's bottle.

She came back quickly. 'The telephone's over there, in the

bedroom,' she said, gesturing at a curtain made of plastic strips right behind my back.

'Thanks,' I murmured, looking at this bit of bar-room decor and once again fearing an ambush. She smiled, revealing a row of small defective teeth.

On the other side of the curtain was a narrow room almost entirely occupied by a double bed with no headboard and a tobacco-coloured bedspread. A crucifix, slightly askew, hung against the wallpaper. The telephone was on the floor, sitting next to its connection socket. I picked up the receiver, sat on the bed and dialled Elsa's number. In my mind, I followed the ringing of the phone as it penetrated the beach house. It ran over the coconut-fibre rug in the living room, climbed up the bright stairs to the first floor, entered the large bathroom with the mirror fragments set into the indigo-blue plaster, brushed over the linen sheets of the still-unmade bed, over the desk piled high with books, drifted through the gauze curtains into the garden and over to the pergola, which was overgrown with white jasmine blossoms, then to the hammock, and then to my old pith helmet with the rusty eyelets; but there was no response. Maybe Elsa was swimming, or maybe she'd already come out of the water. I thought about her body, stretched out on the beach, and about the water licking at her legs. The telephone was ringing away, unheard. I ran my hand over the chenille bedspread, and at the same time I spotted a pair of worn fuchsia slippers tucked under a cheap-looking dresser. Leaning on the mirror was the photograph of a young man, obviously taken long ago. I felt uncomfortable in that room, sitting on a stranger's bed, in the sleeping quarters of the deranged clown who was waiting for me a few feet away. One of the dresser drawers was partly open, revealing a swatch of red satin. Almost without noticing it, I slipped a hand into the crack and touched the slippery fabric. The clown's face poked through the plastic strips.

'Would you like some coffee?'

I sat down on the sofa in front of the monkey poster. Something in my throat was bothering me; it felt dry and grainy.

I gazed around me, and that modest setting seemed to augment my physical discomfort. On a bookshelf, a porcelain doll holding a sheer parasol pressed her frightened face against the first in a row of identical volumes, one of those general encyclopaedias you can buy in instalments. The dreariness was all of a piece, well cared for, honourable. I looked at the woman, who was coming towards me with a tray in her hands. Considered against the background of her house, she seemed less lively; she took on a shabby decency that was perfectly in keeping with her surroundings. They depressed me. For one thing, there was that collection of knick-knacks next to my arm. I hate furniture cluttered with trinkets, Angela, as you well know. I like an unencumbered surface, with maybe a lamp in one corner and a book or two, nothing more. My shoulder twitched with a sudden impulse to fling out my arm and knock all that trash to the floor. She served me the coffee. 'How much sugar?'

I attached my lips to the cup and took a sip. The coffee was good, but my mouth was deadened by fatigue and ill humour, and so the liquid left a coating of bitterness on my tongue. The woman came and sat at some little distance from me on the sofa. The light was behind her, but her frayed fringe failed to hide her high forehead. It was too high, too prominent for the rest of her face, which gathered around the furrow between her nose and her heavily painted mouth in a single fixed grimace. I looked at the hand she was holding the espresso cup with. The flesh around her short fingernails, which she no doubt chewed, was red and swollen. I thought about the smell of stale saliva on those fingertips and shuddered. As I did so, she bent forward. I saw a dog's muzzle appear from under the sofa. A sleepy middle-sized dog with a dark, wavy coat and long amber ears. He licked her hand, including those nibbled nails, as happy as though he'd received a reward.

'Heartbreaker,' she whispered, rubbing her big forehead against the dog's. He noticed me, but he seemed to look at me without interest, and I saw that his eyes were strangely clouded. She gathered up the tray and the dirty cups. 'He's blind,' she said in a lowered voice, as though she didn't want the beast to hear her.

'Would you give me a glass of water?'

'Do you feel all right?'

'No, I'm hot.'

She turned round. As she walked to the kitchen, I observed her buttocks. They were as thin as a man's. My gaze slid over her entire retreating body: her narrow, curved back, the empty space between her legs where her thighs should have met. This was not a desirable body. Indeed, it looked downright inhospitable. Swaying on her high heels, she came back to where I was sitting and handed me a glass of water, then stood there and waited for me to give her back the glass. 'Do you feel better?'

Yes, I did; the water had cleaned my mouth.

She didn't accompany me to the door. 'Well then, thank you,' I said.

'Don't mention it.'

The heat was still there, hanging heavy in the air, imperceptibly shifting things. The asphalt felt soft under my feet. I took up a position next to the closed shutter and started waiting for the shop to reopen. I was sweating again, and I was thirsty again. I went back to the bar. I asked for a glass of water, but when the young bartender with the pimply face stepped aside, I got a good view of the row of bottles behind his head, changed my mind, and ordered a vodka. I had him pour it into a tall glass and requested some ice, which he doled out from the bottom of an aluminium container. Maybe as it melts, I thought, it'll give off the same smell as the rest of the place, rancid mayonnaise and sour floorcloths. I walked over to the far side of the bar room and sat down next to the jukebox. I took a long, noisy swallow; the alcohol penetrated me like a sharp pain, like a hot flash that turns at once into an intense, protracted chill. I looked at my watch – I still had more than an hour to wait.

I wasn't used to intervals, Angela. I was barely forty, and already I'd been a senior surgeon for five years, the youngest in the hospital. My private practice was growing, and with some reluctance, but more and more often, I performed operations in private clinics. I caught myself appreciating those places, where the patients had to pay and where everything was clean, well organised and silent. I was barely forty, and maybe I had already fallen out of love with my profession. When I was a young man, I was impetuous, always in motion. After my internship, my first years in practice were febrile, vigorous, like the time I punched a nurse because he hadn't waited for the steam autoclave, which sterilises the instruments, to complete its cycle correctly. Then, almost without my noticing, a veil of peacefulness, accompanied by a mild feeling of disenchantment, came over me. When I talked about it with your mother, she said that I was simply slipping into the habit of adult life, making a necessary and by and large agreeable transition. I was barely forty, and I'd given up taking offence some time ago. It wasn't that I would have sold my soul to the devil; it was just that I hadn't offered it to the gods. I'd kept it in my pocket, and there it was now, in the pocket of my lightweight summer suit, inside that ugly bar.

The vodka gave me a spark of life. A tall young man, filthy with dust and mortar, glared at the fan and its motionless blades. As he headed for the table football, followed by his stocky friend, he blurted out, 'It's hot! Turn on the fan!' With a brusque yank, he pulled the cylindrical handle on the table, and the balls started to roll in the wooden belly. The stocky boy threw in the first ball, dramatically letting it fall to the playing field from high above his head, apparently some kind of ritual, and then the game began. The two of them said little to each other. Their hands gripped the handles tightly as they flipped their wrists, striking hard, precise blows that made the metal rods vibrate. The bartender slouched out from behind the bar, drying his hands on his towel, and turned on the fan. As he was walking back, I handed him my glass and said, 'Bring me another one, please.' The fan blades began moving, sluggishly stirring up the hot air in the bar. A napkin fluttered to the floor, and I bent over to retrieve it. I noticed a few revolting piles of sawdust and, a bit further away, the legs of the two table-football players. By the time I straightened up, my head was heavy with

24

blood, and the sudden movement made my brain reel. The bartender brought the glass of vodka to my table. I drank the whole thing in one gulp. My eyes floated towards the jukebox. It was an old model, speckled blue in colour, with a little window. When a song was playing, you could look into the jukebox and see the metal tone arm gliding across the record. I thought, I'd like to hear a song. Any song at all. That woman's face came back into my mind. Wearing too much make-up, looking dazed and coarse, she was swaying in the light that came from the lower part of the music machine. A ball leaped off the table football and rolled across the floor. On my way out, I left the young bartender a handsome tip. He laid aside the sponge he was using to wipe off the bar and gathered the money into his dripping hands.

I walked back to the mechanic's shop. In front of me, a group of half-naked children were laboriously hauling a cart containing a large plastic bin bag filled with water and leaking from many holes. The mechanic had finally hoisted his rolling shutter, but only partway, and I had to duck to enter the shop. Inside, under the oiled breasts of a calendar girl, I found a powerfully built man of about my own age, wearing overalls too tight for him and black with grease. He and I climbed into an old Citroën Dyane with blazing hot seats and drove to where I'd left my car. It needed a new oil pump and a cylinder sleeve. We went back to the shop to pick up the required parts. The mechanic discharged me in front of the shop, tossed what he needed into his boot and drove away.

I loafed about aimlessly for a while. My shirt was drenched with sweat and my glasses were fogged, but I didn't care about the heat any more. This calm indifference was due to the alcohol, but it also happened to correspond to one of my most secret desires. I'd been driving myself hard during all those years of success; I was always where I should be, always traceable. Now, purely by chance, I was flying under the radar, and I assented to my temporary freedom, which I saw as an unexpected reward. Now I would offer no further resistance; I'd let myself explore my new situation, like a tourist. I went back to the unfinished block of flats. The children, having poured the water from their rubbish bag on to a mound of pozzolana, were moulding the stuff into a sort of hut that looked like a big black egg. I stood there stupefied and watched them under the hammering sun.

My mother never wanted me to go out into the courtyard and play with the other children. After her marriage, she'd had to adjust to living in a poor neighbourhood. It wasn't a sad part of the city at all; it was crowded and lively, and it wasn't even very far from the centre. But your grandmother refused to look out the windows. In her view, our neighbourhood wasn't sad – sadness was something she knew how to bear. No, it was much worse than that; it was one step above absolute penury. She lived a sequestered life in that flat, as though it were a cloud where she had reconstructed her life, where she had settled in with her piano and her son. During certain languid afternoon hours, I would have liked to join all that teeming life I saw going on downstairs, but I couldn't bring myself to humiliate her. I pretended that the downstairs world didn't exist for me, either. She would hustle me on to the bus that took us to her family home, to her mother, and in that setting, amid all those trees and those elegant houses, I could finally open my eyes. When my mother was there, she was radiant; she was another person altogether. We'd lie down together on the bed in her old room and laugh and laugh. She was filled with new energy; she shone with new beauty. Then she'd put her overcoat back on and assume her normal look. We'd catch the bus back home long after dark, when everything was pitch black outside. She'd run from the bus stop to our front door, terrified by the abyss that surrounded her.

My mother's face passed before my eyes – or rather, her faces, one after another, all the way to the end of the sequence, when her face was closed in death and I asked the sexton to leave me alone with her for a moment so that I could look at it one last time. I chased away that image by angrily shaking my head.

Now I'll go back to get my car. I'll pay the mechanic, turn on the

engine and drive home to Elsa. Her hair will still be wet, along with her
gauzy primrose-coloured shirt. We'll go to that restaurant and sit at that
table in the back and look at the lights of the gulf shining through the
darkness. I'll let her drive so I can lay my head on her shoulder . . .

She didn't look surprised. In fact, I got the feeling she'd been expecting me. She blushed when she stepped back to let me in. I entered awkwardly, inadvertently stumbling into the book-shelf on the wall. The porcelain doll fell to the floor. I bent down to pick it up. 'Don't worry about it,' she said, swaying towards me. She was wearing a different T-shirt. This one was white, ornamented with a gaudy paste flower. She murmured, 'How's your car?'

Her voice was uncertain, and so was her mouth, with all the lipstick gone. I looked past her shoulder at her tidy, wretched house, and it seemed even drearier than it had a little while ago. But this didn't bother me. In fact, I took a mysterious pleasure in the sensation that everything around me was incontestably dismal. 'They're fixing it,' I said.

Her hands were behind her back, and I could hear her rubbing them together. She lowered her eyes, then raised them again. It seemed to me that her whole body was quivering imperceptibly, but maybe I was only drunk.

'You want to use the telephone?'

'Yes.'

Once again, I went into the bedroom; once again, I stroked the tobacco-coloured chenille bedspread. I looked at the telephone. I looked at it as though it were made of plastic, a toy that wouldn't put me in touch with anybody or anything. I didn't even touch it. I closed the dresser drawer. I straightened out Jesus on the wall. Then I stood up and walked towards the door. I just wanted to get out of there. The vodka had left me with a dull headache and no manners. *Maybe I won't go to the beach house; maybe I'll go back to the city and get into bed, I don't want to do anything or see anyone.*

'No answer?'

'No.'

There's that cold fireplace behind her, empty and black as a toothless mouth. I catch her by the arm and hold on. She breathes through her mouth; her breath is like a rat's breath. Suddenly, her face is quite close to me, and it changes shape. Her eyes with their dark shadows look huge; they dart about under her eyebrows like two imprisoned insects. I'm twisting her arm. She's so alien to me, and so close. I think about hawks, about how frightened of them I was as a little boy. I raise my hand to knock her far away from me, her and her knick-knacks and her poverty. But instead, I grab the paste flower on her shirt and pull her against me. She tries to bite my hand, working her jaws in the air. I don't yet know what she has to be afraid of, I don't know what I intend to do. I only know that my other hand is pulling that coarse hair of hers very hard, I've got a handful of it, and I'm holding it like an ear of corn. Then I go at her with my teeth. I gouge her chin and her hard, frightened lips. I let her groan, because now she has a good reason, now that I've torn that paste flower off her chest and seized her skinny breasts and started to knead them. And now my hands are between her legs, between her bones. She averts her eyes from my fury, lowers her chin to her neck, raises one vague arm above her head. And that arm trembles, because I find her sex, as lean as the rest of her, and I've already got mine in my hand. I thrust her quickly against the wall – no, more than quickly – and her yellow head jerks downwards. She's a loose-limbed puppet, slumped backwards against the wall. I pull her up by the jawbone, drooling into her ear. My saliva runs down her back while I thrash inside her bony cavity like a raptor in a captured nest. And thus I make an utter ruin of her, of myself and of that muddled afternoon.

I don't know if she was panting afterwards; maybe she was crying. She lay on the floor, clasping her body. Quite beside myself, I retreated hastily to the other side of the room. The blind dog's muzzle, resting on one paw, protruded from under the sofa. I could see his hanging ears, his clouded eyes. The unmoving monkey on the wall kept sucking his bottle. My glasses were on the floor near the door; one lens was broken. I took a few steps and bent to pick them up. Then I stuffed my wet shirt tails back into my trousers and left the house without a word.

The car was parked in front of the mechanic's shop with the key in the ignition. I started the engine and drove away. Soon I was going down the long, straight road, past stands of wild pine and thickets of withered reeds. I hit the brakes but failed to come to a full stop, then opened my door and vomited while the car was moving. I fumbled around under the seat and brought out my bottle of water. The plastic container was hot, and so were its contents. I rinsed out my mouth, stuck my head out the window, and poured what was left in the bottle over my head. The road ran on, as did the smell of great heat, mingled now with the odour of the sea, which was very close. I let go of the steering wheel and raised my hands to my face so I could sniff them. I was looking for a trace of my brutality, Angela. But all I could detect was the odour of rust, perhaps from the fire escape. I spat on my hands. I spat on those creases: my life line, my head line, my heart line. Then I rubbed my palms together until they burned like fire.

The beach house, built in the 1950s, was low and square and rather plain. Outside the kitchen window stood a tall palm tree, and next to the tree was a pergola, where a jasmine vine clambered, diffusing its overpowering perfume. The rest of the yard was bare, enclosed by a fence of little iron spears corroded by salt. The gate, which opened directly on to the beach, screeched on its hinges at every gust of wind, emitting a sound identical to the cries of the frightened seagulls. The house faced a strip of comparatively unfrequented shoreline. The bathing establishments were located further down the coast, beyond the mouth of the river, beyond the fishing boats riding at anchor, their trawls hanging idly in the air like famished mouths.

Your mother was the one who picked out that place, that summerhouse. She said it made her think of a tent in the desert, especially at sunset, when the glare coming off the sea seemed to move the walls. There was also a cat that influenced her decision. He was drowsy and docile, and he let Elsa pick him up, then stayed with her all the while the girl from the estate agent's was opening the shutters and getting rid of the musty odour that accumulates in houses when they're closed up all winter long. She showed us the house on a weekday near the end of March. Your mother was wearing a coat of Casentino wool, as violently orange as the sun we'd enjoy there later that summer. On the way back, we stopped to eat at a restaurant that was too big for just the two of us. Its windows overlooked the rocky seashore, but sea salt had made them opaque. It was cold, and we both got drunk, though we didn't drink very much: one carafe of wine, followed by one *amaro* apiece. Elsa and I left the restaurant embracing each other, staggering a little, and carrying a souvenir plate. We hid in a nearby pine grove and made love. Afterwards, I laid my head on her belly. We stayed like that, on the lookout for the future that we expected. Then your mother got up and walked around, gathering a few shrivelled pine nuts. I stayed where I was so I could watch her. I think that was the happiest day of our life together, but naturally we didn't realise it.

Almost ten years had gone by since that day in March, and I drove past the pine grove without turning round. The road under my wheels was getting covered with sand. I parked the car by the side of the house, under the thatch. I had to duck so I wouldn't run into the clothes line, where Elsa's beach towel and swimsuit were hanging. It was a plum-coloured one-piece suit made from some elastic waffle-weave material; she'd roll the top down to her waist when she was sunbathing. The swimsuit was hanging there, inside out. As I passed, my shoulder grazed the white lining of the crotch, the piece of Lycra that snuggled up between my wife's legs.

I walked around the house and went in through the living room, which featured a big sky-blue angled sofa. The sand on the soles of my shoes made a grating sound. I took them off – I didn't want Elsa to hear me. I walked barefoot over the stone floor, which was always cool. I spread my toes and stretched my heels to get more of my feet on that cool surface as I stepped into the kitchen. The tap hadn't been turned off all the way and was dripping on to a dirty plate. There was a knife lying on the table, and next to it a piece of bread abandoned among crumbs. I picked up the bread and started to eat it.

Your mother was upstairs, taking a nap. The bedroom door was half open, and I gazed at her as she slept there in the dark: her naked legs; her silk camisole with the thin shoulder straps; the sheet, crumpled up at the foot of the bed, where she had kicked it off of her; her face, covered by the thick mass of her hair. I thought, Maybe she was already asleep when I called, and that's why she didn't hear the telephone. And that thought soothed me, the thought that she was sleeping while I . . . as if in a dream. I was chewing my bread; my wife was asleep. Her breath was as calm as the sea outside the window.

I threw my underwear into the laundry basket and got into the shower. Then I went back downstairs in my bathrobe, leaving wet footprints on the stairs. I found my sunglasses and went outside to sit in the pergola. Through my dark lenses the blue of the sea looked more vibrant and intense than it really was. I was at my house, surrounded by the fragrance of familiar things; fear was somewhere else, far away. I had run away from a fire – I could still feel the flames on my face. I looked around and tried to bring things slowly into focus. I had to reaccustom myself to the man I believed myself to be, the one who'd got lost inside a glass of vodka, melted away like those filthy little ice cubes and given in to a sordid impulse. I put a hand in front of my mouth to smell my breath. No, I didn't stink of alcohol.

'Hello, sweetheart.' Elsa put her hand on my shoulder. I turned round and kissed her immediately. My kiss was badly aimed and partially missed her lips. She was wearing her gauze shirt; a hint of her nipples, darkened by the sun, showed through the fabric. Her eyes were still full of sleep. I pulled her close again for a better kiss.

'You're late.'

'I had to do a really difficult operation.'

I'd lied instinctively, and now there I was, stuck in my lie. I took her hand and we walked on the sand along the seashore.

'You want to go out to eat?'

'If you want to . . .'

'No, it's up to you.'

'Let's stay home.'

We sat down at the water's edge. The sun was beginning to show a little mercy. Elsa straightened her legs, thrust out her toes, and watched her toenails disappear and reappear in the wet sand. We were used to being together like this; neither of us objected to sitting side by side in silence. But after being apart for several days, we were spoiled by solitude and we had to reactivate our intimacy. I picked up your mother's hand and stroked it. She was thirty-seven years old; perhaps she, too, missed that girl in the orange wool overcoat, the one who swayed tipsily out of the restaurant and sat on the breakwater, doubled over with laughter, while the wind blew the spray around. Maybe she was searching for her younger self there, at the tip of her toes, where the white foam ebbed and flowed over her feet. But no, I was the one who had gone missing. It was me, with my long, unpredictable working hours, my niggardly giving, my hasty taking. In any case, we certainly didn't start digging about in search of our reciprocal shortcomings, in the sand or anywhere else. We no longer had the courage for that. Courage, Angela, belongs to new love; old love is always a little cowardly. No, I wasn't her boyfriend any more; I was the man who waited for her in the car while she went into a shop. Elsa slipped her hand into mine. Her hand was soft, like the muzzle of a horse that recognises its fodder.

'Shall we go for a swim?' she asked.

'Yes.'

'I'll put on my bathing costume.'

I watched her go back to the house; I watched her strong, solid, wilful legs as she walked up the beach. I thought about those other, scrawny legs, flaccid on the inner side, where I'd squeezed them so hard. And once again, I relished the taste of her sweat, of her fear. 'Help,' she'd murmured at one point. 'Help.'

Now Elsa was going through the gate to the yard, smiling the way we smile at things that belong to us. I turned to look at the sun, which was going down into the sea in a shimmer of pink light, and I thought that I was a stupid man. This was one of the splendid evenings of my life. In such a moment of serenity, I thought, I should fold up my embarrassment and put it aside.

She returned, wearing her plum-coloured costume and carrying a towel under her arm. She was still incredibly beautiful, thinner than when I'd first met her, maybe a little harder, but more open. Her well-kept figure corresponded perfectly to her soul.

'Shall we go in?'

The lining inside her swimsuit, the white gusset before which

33

I had trembled as though before a judge, had disappeared between her thighs. With a sudden movement, I sprang to my feet. She was standing still at the water's edge. I gazed at the curve of her back. I was the love of her life, the old man who'd wait for her, double-parked, outside the shops. Maybe she desired someone else; maybe she'd already had him. When you've reached a mature, rational age, fidelity isn't so valuable. But infidelity is, because it requires precautions, frugality, discretion and various other attributes of senility. We two together were starting to resemble an old overcoat when it's lost its original shape, together with any uncomfortable stiffness, and this very collapse, the natural wear and tear of its fabric, makes it unique and inimitable.

I opened my bathrobe and let it fall on the sand. Elsa's head snapped round in surprise. 'You're naked!'

She laughed as she waded into the sea, following my white arse, which was really too broad to be a man's arse. Did she still like it? Surely she preferred me with my clothes on, camouflaged under pieces of cloth. My belly stuck out; my arms had no muscles. I wanted her to look at me without indulgence; I wanted to let her measure objectively the imperfections of the man with whom she proposed to spend the rest of her life. I dived into the sea and swam underwater until I felt my chest swelling and hardening. I turned over on my back and floated while wavelets lapped at my mouth. Before I saw your mother, I could feel her arms displacing the water, and then suddenly she emerged at my side. Her wet hair made her face look bare. No, even if I had told her the story of my erotic adventure, she wouldn't have believed me. I thought about some of the sexy scenes we'd watched at the movies, risqué images that came rushing down upon us from the screen in the darkness of the theatre. Your mother would sit as though thunderstruck, holding her breath, while I felt irritated and shifted about in my seat. *She can't be stupid enough to believe people screw like that in real life, can she?* But when we left the cinema, she'd look as dreamy as the face on a playing card.

She spat a little sea water in my face, then kicked out and

started swimming ahead of me. I listened to the sound of her body moving through the water, further and further away. I lay still, floating with my eyes half closed and my legs a little apart, letting the current rock me along. Maybe some little fish below me was observing the keel of my body. I turned over and dived, keeping my eyes open in the blue underwater glimmer. I went all the way to the bottom, where the water was cold, and I lingered there for a while on the slowly shifting sands. I opened my mouth, shouting into the deafness of the water: 'I raped a woman!'

And then, with my arms spread wide, accompanied by my air bubbles, I swam back up like a big white fish towards the light that suffused the surface of the sea.

When I was a medical student, Angela, I was afraid of blood. During anatomy classes, I used to duck behind the other students' backs. I'd listen to the sounds of intense surgical activity and the voice of the professor as he explained the details of the operation. In the room where the cadavers were dissected, blood wasn't grey, as it was in our textbooks; it had its real colour and its real smell. Yes, I could have altered my plans and schemes: I could have opted for a career as an untalented doctor of general medicine, like my father. He wasn't any good at diagnosis, and I would never have been any good at it, either. I had no intuition. And I wasn't interested in treating sicknesses hidden behind a wall of flesh. I wanted to open, to see, to touch, to cut away. I knew that I'd do good work only if I could get to the bottom of things, only there and nowhere else. I fought tenaciously against what seemed to be my destiny; I struggled against my natural reaction with all my strength, because it was killing my dreams and forcing me to go in the wrong direction.

And then, one morning in the students' toilets, I deliberately cut myself. I used a razor blade and slowly made an incision in the adductor muscle of my left thumb. I felt the wound grow wet and the blood seep out. I had to endure it, had to open my eyes and endure the sight of it. And at last, I succeeded. I watched my blood drip into the sink and felt slightly faint, nothing more. That same day, I stood close to the operating table in class and finally looked. My heart remained calm. It also remained calm the first time I pressed a scalpel into living flesh. Before newly incised flesh begins to bleed, time passes in a special way. The blood doesn't flow immediately; for a fraction

36

of a second, the wound remains white. I've performed thousands of operations, and it's only then, at the moment of the incision, that I feel a slight dizziness, because the revulsion I used to struggle against is still alive in me. I raise my hands and leave the cauterisation of the wound to my assistant. Except for those first moments, though, I've always remained clear-headed and calm, even in the most desperate situations. I've always done everything I was capable of doing, and when I've had no other recourse, I've let people die. I've taken off my mask, I've washed my face and hands and forearms, and, without asking myself useless questions, I've looked in the mirror to see how my efforts have marked my features. My child, I don't know where people go when they die, but I know where they stay.

Alfredo must have already started by now. The cutaneous layer is detached, the bleeding stanched. They're probably cutting into the fascia of the temporal muscle. Then they'll saw away a section of your skull. It's a difficult operation; if they apply too much pressure, they run the risk of nicking the dura mater. Afterwards, if they have to, they'll sew the bone section into your abdomen to keep it sterile – but later, at the end of the procedure. Now there's no time for frills; they have to go straight to the blood. And here's hoping that the haematoma hasn't compressed the brain too much. I'd like to be an ordinary father in this situation, one of those trusting men who put their faith in anyone wearing a doctor's coat and bow before it as before a sacred garment. But I can't pretend I don't know how little the goodwill of even the best surgeon can accomplish against the workings of fate. A man's hands are rooted firmly in the earth, Angela. God, if He exists, is behind our backs.

You know, sweetheart, it's my sense of decency that stops me from entering the operating theatre. Because if you don't make it, I don't want to remember you like that; I don't want to watch while your heart stops beating in such undignified circumstances. I want to remember you like a father – I don't want a memory of your naked, pulsing brain, I want to remember your hair. The hair I stroked at night, bending over

37

you as you frowned in your sleep. The sight of your little face filled me with fantasies about your future. One was about your wedding day: I imagined your white arm on my dark sleeve; I pictured that long walk, at the end of which I'd turn you over to another man. I'm ridiculous, I know. But the truth about men is often ridiculous.

Out here there's a lot of silence. There's silence in these empty chairs in front of me; there's silence on the floor. Out here, I could pray; I could ask God to enter into Alfredo's hands and save your life. I've prayed only once before, a long time ago, when I realised I had lost and I didn't want to give up. I raised my stained hands to heaven, and I summoned God to help me, because I knew that if the creature under my scalpel died, everything else would die with her: the trees, the dogs, the rivers, even the angels. Everything in creation.

I saw them too late, when there was no more chance of escape. I felt afraid, and then I saw them. Halfway down the corridor, just a few steps from Radiology. Two policemen standing next to a door. Arms in grey uniform shirts, pistols in holsters. They were listening to a third man, who was in street clothes. He was speaking in a low voice, barely moving his lips, which were so dark, they looked as though he'd been eating liquorice. It was summer; the hospital was empty. The man's eyes moved towards me. They looked like little glass spheres; they pounced on me there in the corridor. He was practically taking aim, staring at me, and then one of the policemen turned and looked at me, too. The lift was at their backs, a few steps past them on the other side of the hall. I kept walking, but I felt hollow, like a puppet. A week had passed since the atrocities of that other afternoon, when I'd had too many drinks on an empty stomach.

I didn't have a clear memory of what had happened – it was as though everything had taken place under a layer of glue. But she couldn't have forgotten. Not her. I'd left her huddled up against the wall in the darkness, a heap of beaten limbs. Used and tossed aside, like a condom. I thought, Maybe she's behind that door the cops are standing in front of. Maybe they've brought her here to identify me. Now, when I'm just about to walk past that repulsive person with the olive skin, she'll come out into the open. Short, faceless, with hair like a raffia basket on her head, she'll stretch out her arm towards me: *It's him. Grab him.* Her cockroach legs have carried her out of the distant suburbs, scurried through the better neighbourhoods and brought her to me. The cops are going to arrest me. They'll do it unobtrusively, the way it's done in a public place, so as not to create panic. A tight grip on my arm, and a calm voice saying, *Please come with us.*

But instead, Angela, nobody so much as glanced at me. With my finger on the red button, I waited for the lift doors to open. The others were still there; they hadn't moved. I didn't look at them, but I saw them, three dark shapes in the corner of one of my eyes. By the time the lift arrived, I was no longer myself. With my shirt sticking to my back, I smiled at a lady and a little girl who were going up with me. 'After you,' I said, like a stupid brute. *I haven't done anything, madam. Can't you see that? I'm a nice man. Please go downstairs, walk up to those nasty-looking fellows, and tell them so.* Meanwhile, we were flying up past the floors in a metal box.

While I made my usual rounds, visiting the beds of the patients I'd recently operated on, I avoided looking directly at anyone. Eyes down, squinting professionally through my bifocals at the medical charts, at the gold Mont Blanc pen I used to adjust sedative levels. Then I headed for the operating theatre, and on the way my shoulders trembled like wings. I made my customary entrance, kicking the door open, holding up my sterilised hands to a nurse, who slipped on my gloves. I've got my hands up like a criminal, I thought, and I managed a small smile. Then peace descended, the serenity of work. Iodine solution, cold scalpel, blood. My hands were as calm and precise as always — no, even more so. It's just that they weren't mine; they were the hands of a man I was looking at, an impeccably professional man whom I no longer admired. I looked at myself the way an entomologist looks at an insect. Yes, now I'm the one that's the insect, I thought, not her; she's just a poor woman, a victim of chance, whom I violated, whom I bit, whom I sucked dry. I saw the rubber hands down there, not mine, and yet thoroughly mine, gleaming white hooks at work in a world where I knew how to handle myself and where I was a doer of good deeds.

Electric scalpel. Cauterise the blood vessels. *They're still out there, waiting for me. I'll be wearing my scrubs when they arrest me —*

what an absurd way to go to jail. Kocher forceps. Swabs. *They're leaving me a little time for remorse. That's why they didn't grab me before; they want me to go through this torture. Pure cruelty. Yes, she was in that room; she saw me pass and nodded her head. Then she collapsed in her chair like a broken reed. They brought her a glass of water and told her, Don't you worry, the bastard won't get away from us. We'll get him and his dirty little dick, too. I didn't look into the room when I passed it. I didn't have the nerve. Too bad.*

I made an effort, but I couldn't recall what that room was used for. *The first door is the one you go through to get to the blood-sample room. But what's behind the open door the policemen in the grey uniforms were standing next to?*

In my mind, I rushed into that empty, unknown space, where I thought the woman I couldn't remember any more was hiding. And it seemed to me, Angela, that this memory loss was enough to erase what I had done.

Why didn't I go back and caress her and persuade her that nothing had happened? When I want to, I know how to cajole a fragile heart. I could have begged her pardon; I could have offered her money. I could have killed her. Why didn't I kill her? Because I'm not a murderer. Murderers kill. Surgeons rape. Vascular clamps. Aspirator. *She's filed charges against me. She picked up her patchwork bag and went down to the local police station.*

I felt as though I could see her, sitting on a chair in one of those rooms that smell like rubber stamps and torturing her fingernails to keep her courage up. While she was pressing her pale legs together and describing the distinguished-looking man who had assaulted her, someone was typing at a desk behind her back. Who knows what she told them . . .

What part of me stayed with her? I'd like to know what trace I left on her uninviting body. I was crazy with drink, with heat, with perverted lust. But she was sober. She looked at me; she suffered me. Whoever suffers remembers. Autostatic retractor. *Maybe they gave her a gynaecological exam; she lay on the narrow white bed and turned her face to one side and submitted to yet more humiliation. And there, with her legs spread wide apart, staring into space, she decided to ruin me for ever.* Kelly forceps. *Maybe they got a sample of my seminal fluid*. Kelly forceps again. *No, she couldn't possibly have found me. She doesn't know a thing about me; she doesn't know where I live or what I do. On the other hand, maybe she does. When I went into the bedroom to use the phone, I left my bag on the sofa and she went through it. You bitch, you ragamuffin bitch. They'll never believe you.* Swabs. *I'll defend myself. I'll say it was her. I'll say she used some excuse to lure me into her house and rob me, maybe even kill me. Wasn't I afraid when I was following her inside that unfinished apartment building, with the darkness and the stench and the squatters? It was fear that put me in such an altered state. I attacked her to protect myself from the fear.* Isolate the choledoch duct. *She was behaving obscenely, I'll say. She tricked me; she gave me drugged coffee . . . Yes, maybe there was something strange in the coffee she gave me. It stinks like poison in that shack, Mr Commissioner. You should go there and inspect the place.* Cystic duct. Thread. *Maybe there are some bodies buried in that dusty garden. The cars passing overhead on the viaduct rattle the windowpanes, and all the noise drowns out the screams of the poor victims. It's a miracle I'm alive! Arrest that hag!* Drainage tube. *How could you, you wretch? What made you think you could ruin me? Who did you think would believe you?* And then in my mind I slapped her hard across the face; her raffia-basket head jerked back and forth. *Surely they'll believe me. The policemen will apologise, and I'll leave them one of my cards. It's always useful to know a surgeon.* Tampons. *The man with the dark lips has a face like someone suffering from liver disease. I'll be magnanimous. I'll pick up the telephone; I'll call a couple of colleagues and arrange for a complete check-up. I'll skip the usual procedure and move him to the top of the waiting list, the way I do for only my closest friends. He'll thank me; he'll make a bow as he thanks me. He'll send me a bottle of liqueur and a police calendar, which I'll give to a nurse.* Recheck haemostasis. *You, on the other hand, are going to get shoved out of here in handcuffs, little slut. You're illegal, like your neighbours. I'll send a bulldozer to knock down your house.* Count the sterile towels. *My word against yours.* Needle holder. *And we'll see who wins!* Suture thread.

The operation was over, and I looked up again. I could feel defiance colouring my eyes, and contempt. Standing next to my registrar, a junior doctor in a white coat too big for him was staring at me as though in a trance. I hadn't noticed that he was there – he must have approached the table just a moment before. His face had the look of one who has used too much will-power on himself. Maybe he was just trying to remain on his feet. Maybe he was afraid of blood. Imbecile.

I stripped off my gloves, left the operating theatre, and went into the locker room. I sat down on a bench. Looking outside, I could see the usual view of the adjoining wing of the hospital, the low windows along the interior stairways, the people going up and down. Only steps and legs were visible; faces were hidden by the wall. First, a pair of men's trousers passed, then a nurse's white legs. I remember thinking that nothing can save us from ourselves, and that indulgence is a fruit that's already decayed when it falls to the ground. I'd given free rein to all those indecent thoughts, and now I was as useless as a dead sniper.

The doors to the operating theatre were wide open, and the room itself was in disorder. A man in a dressing gown, carrying a roll of toilet paper in his hand, was walking down the corridor towards the bathroom. I said goodbye to the nurses and got into the lift. Inside of me, there was nothing but what I had struggled against. I got out on the ground floor. There wasn't anybody standing next to that door any more, and beyond it was an ordinary room, a waiting room for dialysis patients. Two women with yellow faces were sitting in there, waiting their turn. No, Angela, she hadn't ever been in that room, or in any other room in the hospital. She'd stayed in a heap against the wall, under the poster with the monkey. She hadn't even raised her head.

Something unexpected had already happened that year, Angela; on Easter night, I lost my father. It was painless – I almost never saw him. After my mother died, our meetings had become more and more infrequent. I knew he lived in a home, but I didn't even know its address. He'd agree to meet me from time to time in a bar, which was a converted houseboat floating on the river, near some tennis courts. Our appointments were always at dusk, when the light was the softest. He liked appetisers, glasses rimmed with sugar, little saucers of olives. He held his stomach in and sat so as to present his best profile. He enjoyed feeling like a young man. The only thing I remember from those rare meetings is the sound of tennis balls struck by rackets and bouncing off the dusty red surface of the court.

On the day of my father's funeral, I stood listening to the priest give the homily. Elsa was next to me, wearing an embroidered black veil over her face and crying. I'm not sure why – perhaps just because it seemed to her like the right thing to do. A thickset man with white hair moved out from behind a column and walked past me. He was wearing a shabby velour tie with its label half off and dangling against his shirt. He stepped up to the microphone and read a little page he'd written himself. Flowery, useless words; my father would have liked them. This must have been one of his best friends. Clutching a snotty handkerchief in one hand, he read in a voice drenched with authentic grief. He had a peculiar manner, affable and repellent at the same time, and his whole face, from his hair to his collar, was yellow with nicotine. Afterwards, he stood in front of the church, smoking a cigarette. He shook my hand and tried to embrace me, but I recoiled. Nobody in the family seemed to know him. He went away, hopping down the church steps, his sturdy body stretching the seams of his iridescent jacket. In that unknown man and the mixed impression he left, I thought I recognised my father's only legacy.

One day, driving towards the sea, towards your mother, I thought about my father. In the months following his painless, sudden death, it had tormented me more than I would have expected it to. Sometimes I'd wake up at night and go to the kitchen and realise, between the fridge and the table, that I was an orphan. Not because I'd lost *him,* but because I'd lost any chance of having the father I wanted; whatever remote possibility there might have been had died with him. Maybe it had always been there, that possibility, and my pride would never let me see it. Remorse, sombre and silent, had crystallised inside me. Now it was summer, and I was still lying awake at night, brooding over my strange sadness. I thought that maybe the arrival of cooler weather would get me back on track. As I drove to the beach, I thought Elsa and I might go to Norway for the August break. I wanted to walk along the precipices of huge rift valleys, sail into fjords, cross the Vestfjord to the Lofoten Islands. And then I wanted to stay there and catch giant codfish in the cobalt-blue ocean while the wind turned my skin red.

A middle-aged woman was driving the car ahead of me – I'd been behind her for some time. I could have turned on my indicator, sounded the horn, pulled out to the left and zoomed past her, but instead I leaned on the steering wheel and bided my time. Her short hair was pinned up with a comb; there was something pensive about the back of her neck. She was a woman who was coping, stiffening her girlish back, but she'd lost her bearings. *That's enough; now I'm going to honk the horn and rattle her backbone.* But then I thought about my mother. She got her driver's licence late in life, a gift from herself. She would climb into her little runabout – it smelled like furniture polish – and drive away to parts unknown. Her herringbone overcoat, carefully folded, was on the passenger seat. She drove the same way as the woman in front of me, clinging to the steering wheel for dear life, afraid that the car behind her would honk its horn. Angela, why does life come down to so little? Where's mercy? Where's the sound of my mother's heart? Where's the sound of all the hearts I've loved? Give me a basket, my child, give me that little basket you used to take to nursery school. A few bright lights have shone on my life, like fireflies in the dark, and I want to put them inside.

The woman in front of me slowed down, and I slowed down, too. I let myself be led along, as docile as a newborn in a pram. The roadside fields were dirty. It was somewhere around here that my car had broken down a few weeks earlier.

The green door was bolted shut. I knocked several times, but there was no response. Up above on the overpass, the cars went whizzing by. I wondered how many times I had passed overhead on my way to the beach, completely unaware of the life down below. Beyond the piers of the viaduct, there were other dwellings: rusty sheds, caravans. The lugubrious carcass of a burned vehicle showed through a patch of grass. Maybe it had fallen from the viaduct and nobody had ever bothered to haul it away. Nearby, there was an area of bare clay, dried and cracked by the sun. A snake with gleaming black skin slithered over it before disappearing back into the grass. She wasn't home. As I walked away, the shadow of her house spread over that depressing landscape and buried me.

I went the long way back to my car and put the key in the ignition, but I didn't turn it. Instead, I manipulated the radio dial in search of some music, and then I laid my head against the back of the seat. I was in the shade; outside, there was that great buzzing heat and, as usual, little else. Every now and then, an isolated scream rolled down from some unidentifiable hole in the wall. I turned off the radio. I stretched my legs out past the pedals, half closed my eyes and saw her through the slit between my eyelids, like a wide-screen film. She was walking among the cement columns on the basement floor of the big unfinished block of flats. I'd been right to wait for her there. She'd gone that way, as she had before, because it offered some shelter from the sun. She seemed to walk faster when she stepped into the light, and then slowed down and almost disappeared when she reached the long black shadows of the columns. I'd been afraid I wouldn't recognise her, but I recognised her as soon as I saw her. Far off, tiny, half hidden in the darkness. With her scare-crow head and her thin bandy legs. I spotted that disoriented way of walking she had – maybe there was something wrong with one of her hips. She was heading for me without knowing it, walking a little sideways, like a suspicious stray dog. She was carrying a large shopping bag in each hand – her arms were stretched and taut. These weights, however, failed to stabilise her as she advanced; in fact, they pulled her off balance. Now she's going to fall, I thought; now she's going to fall. And I grabbed the door handle, ready to get out and go to her. But she didn't fall, and then another shadow hid her. I let go of the handle and stayed where I was. Her broad forehead came back into the light, and with it the sensation that it wasn't her I was spying on; it was myself.

While she continued to come my way, moving through that chequerboard of darkness and light, I went over in my mind – frame by frame, like a film – the obscene moments I'd spent with her. I slid down in my seat, inert and sweating in sexual apnoea. Because all of a sudden I remembered: her lifeless body, extinguished like her cold fireplace; her bowed white neck; that sad, enigmatic gaze. No, I hadn't done it all by myself. She'd wanted it as much as I had. More than I had. And the wall, and the chair that fell over behind us, and her wrists, pinned to that glossy poster above her head – they all passed before my eyes. The memory was in the pit of my stomach. Even the smell of the two of us together came back to me: the smell of delirious passion, overpowering the smell of ashes. Ours had been a desperate embrace, and the desperation was all hers, riding on those skeletal legs that now were walking towards me. I was not used to making love like that, but she was. She dragged me down with her. And here she was, walking with her shopping bags. What was in them? *What did you buy? What do you eat? Drop those bags, leave them in the dust and come with me, little dog.*

47

With the light behind her, she was thin, very thin. She looked like one of those little invertebrates with anaemic exoskeletons that come out of the ground in the spring. In the same way, she seemed to be surfacing after a struggle. She was going home undismayed on an ordinary day in her wretched life. What was she like? Why did she wear so much make-up? The patchwork bag hung on its long shoulder strap and beat against her legs. I had to leave. She stopped inside a cone-shaped shadow. She put one shopping bag on the ground and touched her overheated neck and fumbled with her peroxide hair. I stayed so I could capture that gesture, remembering the scent of her sticky neck. I hadn't had anything to drink. My stomach felt fine, my head was clear . . . and in that sober, normal, clear-headed state, I desired her. I couldn't trust myself any more; already, while I watched her, I was violating her. It was all a lie. I hadn't waited for her so I could apologise; I'd lurked around like a hawk, ready to swoop down on her and do her in again. She was close to the car now – she was going to pass by without noticing me. I thought I'd look at her in the rear-view mirror until she was out of sight, and then I'd go away and never come back again. I lowered my head, looking at my hands. They were resting on my thighs, as if to remind me that I was a respectable man.

Her belly came to a stop outside the passenger window. I raised my eyes, and though I expected to find two wells of terror in hers, I saw instead a look of slight confusion. I got halfway out of the car and leaned on the open door, with one foot still inside. I said, 'How are you doing?'

'Fine, sir. And you?'

'Don't call me "sir".'

'What brings you to these parts?'

'I forgot to pay the mechanic.'

'He told me that, sir. He wanted to know if I knew you.'

'Don't call me "sir".'

'All right.'

'What did you tell him?'

'I said I didn't know you.'

She didn't seem angry; she didn't seem anything. Maybe she's used to it, I thought; maybe she's a woman who goes with anyone who turns up. And now I looked at her, and all my fears were gone. The dark rings around her eyes made them sink even deeper into her bony skull. Bluish veins showed in her neck and ran down under her black-and-yellow-checked shirt. It was made of some stretchy material that sparkled in the sun, two-bit stuff stitched together on a sewing machine by some Asian juvenile. She brought a hand up to her fringe and began to pull at it, spreading it out in little tufts to give her oversized forehead some cover from my stare. The full sunlight exposed every flaw in her face, and she knew it. She must have been well past thirty – there were already tiny webs of wrinkles around the corners of her eyes. All her skin looked wan and sickly. But in her openings, in her eyes, in her nostrils, in the narrow gap between her lips, wherever her breath passed, there was a rustling, a gentle calling, like a heavy wind wedged in the thickest part of the woods.

'What's your name?'

'Italia.'

I received this improbable name with a smile. 'Look, Italia,' I said, 'I'm sorry about . . .' I shoved my free hand deep into my pocket. 'I wanted to apologise to you. I was drunk.'

'I have to go; I've got frozen food in this heat.' And she bent her head to peer inside the shopping bag she had never put down.

'I'll help you.'

I bent to take the bags from her, but she resolutely held on to them. 'No. They're not heavy . . .'

'Please,' I whispered. 'Please.'

There was nothing left in her eyes except that absence I'd already seen there, as though she were emptying herself of all will. In the palms of my hands, I felt the sweat in hers, which were still clutching the handles of the shopping bags. We went through the block of flats and down the rusty fire escape and came to earth in front of her house. She opened the door, and I closed it behind us. Nothing had changed; everything was enveloped in the same desolation: the flowered cloth on the little couch, the poster of the monkey with the baby's bottle, the same odour of bleach and poison. I felt something shift inside of me, a sort of interior landslide, slow and soft and warm. My sexual impulse seemed to be in no hurry; it was languid, plodding. I put down the shopping bags. A can of beer rolled under the table. She didn't stoop to pick it up. She was leaning on the wall, looking out of the window through the slats of the closed shutters. As I moved closer to her, I loosened my tie. My testicles felt like a painful weight between my legs. This time, I took her from behind. Her eyes worried me, and besides, I had an agenda. I wanted to be able to enjoy her bowed neck, the twin rows of her ribs. I might have scratched her back; I couldn't avoid doing that. Afterwards, I rummaged in my trouser pockets for my wallet. I left some money on the table. 'For the frozen food,' I said.

She didn't reply, Angela. Maybe I had finally managed to offend her.

Your mother was in the garden with Raffaella, who rented a cottage not far from us every summer. They were laughing. I bent down and grazed Elsa's cheek with a kiss. She was sitting in a lounge chair, and she reached up and tousled my hair with a limp hand. I straightened up at once. I was afraid she'd smell something strange. Raffaella got to her feet.

'I'm leaving. I promised Gabry I'd take her some of the mousse I made.'

Raffaella passed a good part of the day in the water, wearing a terry-cloth cap on her head. She'd float a few yards offshore, waiting for someone on the beach to decide to go for a swim. You'd make a few strokes, and there she was in front of you, like a buoy. She loved to gossip while she soaked, and since she travelled all the time, she had plenty of stories to tell. Now Elsa was turning purple next to her, but Raffaella never suffered from the cold; her bathing costume was permanently wet, even after the sun went down.

I gazed, for no particular reason, at Raffaella's sturdy thighs. She laughed, overcoming my look with her usual irony. 'What do you expect?' she said, pointing at Elsa. 'All skinny women have a fat bosom buddy.' She picked up her pareu. 'You look pale, Timo. You should get some sun.'

She died three years ago, you know. I operated on her twice. The first operation was on one of her breasts. The second time, I cut her abdomen open and sewed it back up again in the course of half an hour. I went through with it because she was a friend, but I had known all along there was no hope. She'd never come in for a single check-up after the first operation – she went to Uzbekistan instead. She gave her sarcoma the opportunity to metastasise undisturbed. Raffaella was a tolerant woman. Live and Let Live was her motto, and it applied to everybody.

At the time I was talking about, of course, she didn't have cancer. She was wearing a pair of clogs, and they made an unbearable clatter on the brick pavement as she walked away. I stayed tense until her annoying shuffle reached the silence of the sand.

Elsa's feet and calves extended past the end of the chair she was stretched out on. I sat down next to them and started to stroke her from her toes to her knees. Her skin was smooth and fragrant with sun lotion. Every time I arrived at the beach house to meet her, every time I thought about arriving there, it made me happy. And now there I was, huddled at the foot of her lounge chair, not happy at all. I had recently become aware that something was out of balance. There were some slight oversights: nothing cool to drink in the fridge, my bathing costume left to fade in a sunny corner after the last time I'd gone swimming, my favourite shirt not yet ironed. And, most of all, there was Elsa herself, her impassive face. I didn't feel waited for; I didn't feel loved. I knew I wasn't being fair. Elsa loved me, but with the reasonableness that I'd reduced her to; in the beginning, she'd been far more passionate than I was. She'd adapted herself, for love's sake, to my caution, my reserve, but since my father's death, I'd been regressing. I felt doubts; I felt internal struggles and rebellions. Feelings I'd avoided during my adolescence were emerging intact. Now she was my entire family, and I expected her to notice me. But your mother never did love weak people, Angela, and unfortunately, I knew that. That was the reason I'd chosen her.

I stroked her legs, but there was no answering tremor. All I got was the sweetish scent of her sun lotion. I loved her, but I was no longer able to attract her attention. I loved her, and I had turned off into that suburb, into the bones of that other woman. She didn't disappoint me; her flesh held no memories; I was screwing nobody. When I made those euphoric, pathetic detours, I became the reckless boy I'd always wanted to be but never was. I'd go down and play in the courtyard in spite of my mother, in spite of her pale hands resting on the piano keys. I'd tear frogs apart. I'd spit into the plates. And afterwards, I was alone, just like before. But the fragrance of crime stayed with me, and now it was rising up from the darkness and keeping me company while a clump of reeds next to the garden began to move. Their rustling harmonised with the soft sound of the wind.

'Do you remember that man at my father's funeral?'

Elsa was propped up on her elbows. She turned her head towards me a little. 'Which one?'

'The one who read.'

'Yes, vaguely . . .'

'Did you think he was genuine?'

'Well, some poor devils bluff their way into strangers' funerals because they have nothing better to do.'

'Right, but I don't think he was one of those. He knew Dad's nickname, and besides, he was crying.'

'Everyone's got plenty of reasons to cry. Funerals just provide a good excuse.'

'So why were you crying?'

'For your father.'

'You hardly knew him.'

'I was crying for you.'

'But I wasn't sad.'

'Exactly.'

She slid her legs out from under my hands and decided to laugh. 'It's late. I'm going to have a shower.'

Right, go and have a shower! I'll stay here a little while longer. I'm going to watch the sun lower itself into the sea from the purple edge of a sky so beautiful, it makes a man believe in God – and also in a world where his dead are waiting for him to tell him that nothing will be lost. And all the while I'm thinking about my father, there's a burning sensation in the tip of my cock. I'll tend to it by myself (it seems only right) under this cardinal red sky. And then maybe I'll get one of the beers out of the fridge – or get pissed off if I find them under the kitchen table, still warm.

★

53

There was a whole raft of people at Gabry and Lodolo's place, completely surrounded by a circle of torches whose flames stretched out in the wind. Suntanned faces came towards me; white teeth flashed in the dark. I was wearing my white linen suit but no tie. The hair on the back of my head was still wet, giving me a little chill, a shiver that slipped down under my shirt. As usual, I hadn't shaved all weekend. With a glass in my hand, docile as an apostle, I said hello to people here and there. Over by the drinks table, talking to Manlio and his wife, Elsa was moving her hands, tossing her hair, smiling. Her full lips kept parting to reveal her slightly prominent upper teeth, as though she knew the powerful attraction of that small flaw. Her satin dress, the same crimson red as her lipstick, caressed the tremors of her full breasts as she laughed. At parties, we always went our separate ways; that's the way we liked it. Every now and then, we'd brush past each other to make some whispered comment, but most of the time we waited until we got home, until after she kicked off her high heels and slipped into her espadrilles. Our friends made us laugh; the more tragic they were, the more they made us laugh. We spoke very badly of them, but with great affection, thus absolving ourselves. Elsa had a talent for getting to the kernel of every relationship. She'd toss away the peel and dig into the most succulent part of the fruit. She had performed an autopsy on every marriage in our acquaintance. Thanks to her, I knew that all our friends were unhappy.

At the moment, however, they seemed quite content. They were eating, drinking, looking at one another's spouses. Evidently, their unhappiness was nimble enough to evaporate after a few glasses of *prosecco* and drift away, past the edge of the roof garden, down to the sea below, over Lodolo's motorboat with its gleaming white fenders and out into the black water. No, I didn't feel that I was surrounded by souls in pain.

Manlio was talking to Elsa, and only now and then did he shoot a quick glance at his Swiss wife. Martine moved her head in little jerks, following the movements of her eyes, which protruded too much and opened too wide. She was tiny, thin and wrinkled: a tortoise, wearing a necklace of brilliant stones. She drank. She wasn't drinking now, because Manlio was there, keeping an eye on her. But she drank when she was alone and Manlio was performing his operations. Uterine prolapses, deliveries, D and Cs, egg implants and extractions – all carried out, preferably, in private clinics. Manlio was very fond of Martine; he'd been taking her around with him for twenty years, like a jack-in-the-box. It really seemed as though he'd bought her in a toyshop. All his friends said, practically in chorus, 'What does he see in her?' I, for my part, saw nothing special in him. Martine kept an excellent house, she could cook *gigot d'agneau* and *pasta all'amatriciana* with equal skill, and she had no opinions. You'd pig out to your heart's content and then forget to thank her; you don't thank a jack-in-the-box. Naturally, Manlio cheated on her. 'Naturally' was what Elsa said. 'Such a brilliant, red-blooded man, stuck with that anorexic alcoholic.' I looked over at Martine past the crowd of faces between us, and I thought, Yes, if she were my wife, I'd gladly cheat on her with Elsa. Naturally. Elsa was so desirable, with her beautiful thick hair, her firm flesh, that slightly imprecise smile, those nipples sticking out there like an invitation. She was acting a little too giddy with Manlio this evening. He was her gynaecologist. He gave her her Pap tests; he'd put in her IUD. Had she forgotten that? He certainly hadn't. His cigar was clamped between his teeth, and his eyes burned like two embers. The jack-in-the-box bobbed up between them, inhaling the smoke from her menthol cigarette.

I went to get another glass of wine, and in passing, I brushed against Elsa's red satin. Manlio raised his glass to me in what was supposed to be a gesture of mutual understanding.

Do what you must, Manlio. And get stuffed while you're at it. You wear tailor-made shirts with monogrammed pockets, but there's that protruding belly underneath. You've certainly managed to grow yourself a spare tyre since we were at the university together. And what do you want? Do you want to screw my wife, fatso?

Manlio was my best friend. Was and is, as you know. My

heart has saddled me with a lifelong affection for him, though I couldn't tell you the reason why.

Now, Raffaella was in full party mode, moving her broad hips inside her heavily embroidered Turkish kaftan. Standing next to her was Lodolo, the host; with his narcotised stare and his rumpled shirt, he looked like some poor house guest. Livia was far gone; her hair covering her face, her arms in the air, she was shaking her ethnic jewellery, totally focused on Adele, who was wearing a tight lobster-coloured sheath dress and swaying by herself, twitching her head and shoulders back and forth like a schoolgirl at her first dance. Their husbands, standing a little off to the side and embroiled in one of their formidable political discussions, ignored them. Livia's Giuliano, tall and prematurely grey, was bending over Adele's Rodolfo, a brilliant civil-law expert who performed with a troupe of amateur actors in his spare time. During another summer that was still to come, he would divorce poor Adele, cutting her off with lawyerly ruthlessness, putting an end to all her privileges practically overnight, without pity and without shame. But life is gradual; it unwinds itself over a length of months and years, and it leaves us time for everything. That evening, Adele was far from her future, and she shook her head and displayed the triangular-shaped ornaments that adorned her earlobes.

'Come on, Doctor!' she shouted at me.

My eyes found a way through the wall of heads in front of me and met, just for a second, the eyes of your mother. She, too, must have been at least one glass past her limit, because she was blinking myopically. She put her hand to her mouth, too late to cover a little yawn. I don't like to dance. At a party, I generally try to stay well away from the music, which I always find aggressive and loud. But if I've got to dance, I plant myself inside my own square yard of floor space, and I never leave it. I closed my eyes and started bobbing and weaving, my arms hanging limp at my sides. The music got inside of me and stayed there, deep and hollow, like the sound of the sea inside one of those big shiny conch shells. I had recently seen one, but where? Oh, right, it was next to the jade elephant on top of the little chest, the one with the chipped lacquer, at that woman's house. Several times, when I opened my eyes briefly and peered through the sweat, I had found myself staring at that vulgar conch shell, at its curled opening, pink and smooth as a woman's sex. Now I was bobbing and weaving more stubbornly, bending forward, far forward, and then straightening up and throwing my head back. Overhead, the sky, brimming with stars, was full of forgotten light, like the darkness left behind at the end of a fireworks display. My drink had slipped out of my hand, and I could feel pieces of glass under my shoes. I lost my balance and nearly fell into Raffaella's arms. 'Watch out, Timo,' she said. 'I might say yes.' She laughed, all the way up to her ears. Livia laughed, too, and so did Manlio, who was hopping around behind me in an attempt at solidarity. The expression on his face was wild. I put my arms around Raffaella's thick waist and pulled her into a tottering pas de deux. Her feet got tangled up in her kaftan, which was too long, and her fat belly gurgled against mine as I catapulted her here and there among the crowd. *Let's dance, Raffaella. Let's dance. In a few years, your belly will be under my hands, an isolated piece of flesh surrounded by cloths, and your head will be on the pillow with the blue health-unit logo. You'll say, 'What a shame. I was finally losing weight,' and burst into tears. But for now, laugh, dance, let yourself go!* And I'm dancing, too, Angela, in the samba of my memories. Completely clueless, like everybody else. Like your mother. She'd taken off her shoes, and she held them in her hand as she danced, arching her feet and frantically squashing her toes against the floor as though she were trampling grapes. The music was under her bare soles. 'Watch out,' I said. 'I broke a glass.'

And I slipped away from the dance floor.

The garden, laid out over a broad terrace, was filled with exotic, fearful-looking plants. Some of them were very tall, with abnormal excrescences on their stalks and stiff, pointed leaves; others were studded with needles, each of them culminating in a dusty little flower cluster. The moon drenched them in whitish light and made their anaemic pigment look even paler. I walked through the garden, and it seemed that I was strolling among a colony of ghosts. When I came to the wooden fence, I stopped and looked out. The water was deep blue and utterly calm. I fixed my eyes on the bottom of the horizon, watching the consternation of the sea in the darkness. My father was dead, gone away for ever. He had a heart attack, and he fell over in the street. And I wasn't a son any more. Wearing my white linen suit, staring into the dark, I was a spectre now, too. I turned and faced the direction of the party, spying on my friends through the curtain of that ghostly garden. We'd known one another for a long time, since the fragile days when we had ideals and little goatees. What had changed? The space around us, the wind that flung us about everywhere, exposed to the elements. One morning, we closed the windows; spring was coming to an end, and a dead sparrow was floating in the roof gutter. All of a sudden, we withdrew into ourselves. When we shaved, we looked into the mirror and saw our father's face, the face we used to make fun of. Out in the world, we were ties, honoured professionals, business consultants and disjointed conversations. Up until that evening last winter, on the sofa – a fine long designer sofa – in Manlio's new house. I started estimating its size, and I realised that his house was twice as big as ours – or was it Elsa who pointed that out to me? I joined in the conversation, tossed back a few drinks. Appetisers were passed around. I kept talking, and I glanced at Elsa out of the corner of my eye. Sitting on one arm of the sofa with her legs crossed, my wife was looking outside. Not at the sky, no; there was a terrace overlooking the river, and she was estimating that terrace's square footage. Without realising it, I started talking too loud; I became aggressive. Manlio was staring at me in astonishment; his red cashmere tie hung down into his crystal wine glass. In the car on the way home, without taking her eyes off the street – it had just rained – your mother asked, 'How much money do you suppose someone like Manlio makes?' I mumbled some figure. Later, after we got home, I was pissing in the bathroom, and as I stood there holding my dick, I cried, because all at once I understood: we had grown old.

But back then, back at the party, I was clinging to the wooden fence at the far end of that hellish garden and laughing, laughing like a madman, all by myself. Down below, half hidden by a rock on the shore, little Martine, blissfully drunk, was nibbling something.

I wake up in the middle of the night and look out of the wide-open window to where the palm tree is rustling its dark leaves. Your mother's asleep; her crimson dress lies across a chair. A knot of tension clamps my arm, then penetrates my back, deep down between my shoulder blades. I stick one elbow under the pillow, raise myself a little and kick my legs out. Elsa turns around in the darkness. 'What's wrong?'

Her voice is breathy, weary, but considerate. I've lost the feeling in my arm. I'm afraid I'm having a heart attack. I feel around for her hand and clutch it. She's wearing her silk camisole with the shoulder straps like shiny little ribbons. She's lying on her side, facing me. One of her breasts leans gently on the other. I move closer to her. I bury myself in her perfume. Slowly, I pull the sheet away from her body. A stripe of light runs along her legs. 'You can't sleep?' she asks.

I don't answer her; my lips are already on her legs. Without saying anything else, she thrusts a hand into my hair and strokes my head. She understands; she knows me; she knows how I make love. She doesn't know that I do it when I'm afraid. I know I can't surprise her, but that doesn't seem so terrible. The absence of surprise reassures us, and we progress together towards an evenly distributed sense of well-being. Our movement is an adagio, precise as the ticking of the clock on the chest of drawers. Our bodies are warm; our genitalia throb moderately, like well-bred muscles. But I think there's a false note in this score, my love. Your hair's in my mouth as I think that, and I squeeze you tight, because tonight I'm afraid. We reach our climaxes with our eyes closed, crouched like punished children inside our sexual organs.

Afterwards, your mother gets up because she's thirsty. She crosses the room in the darkness, and I hear her go downstairs to the kitchen. I think about her naked body, dimly lit by the fridge light, and I wonder if she still loves me. Then she comes back, carrying a Coke. 'Do you want a sip?'

She climbs up on to the window sill; she wants to look out as she drinks her cola. Now she's perched there, framed against the palm tree's dark leaves, with her back against the wall and her legs slightly bent. Her naked body against the night, against my ghosts. She's higher than I am, still and gleaming, like a bronze statue. And the thought that comes to me seems to be the only one possible. 'Let's have a baby.'

I've taken her by surprise. She smiles, snorts through her nose, lifts an eyebrow, scratches a leg: a series of small manifestations of discomfort.

'Have your IUD taken out,' I say.

'Are you joking?'

'No.'

I can feel that she doesn't want to understand. We've been together, man and wife, for twelve years, and we've never felt the need of any addition.

'You know, I don't believe in it.'

'Don't believe in what?'

'I don't believe in the world.'

What are you saying, Elsa? What do I care about the world, about all that anonymous flesh? I'm talking about us. About my little thing and your little thing. I'm talking about a speck, a firefly in the darkness.

'I wouldn't feel right about bringing a child into this world . . .'

You press your legs together; you make yourself small. You'd like to metamorphose into a cockroach and scurry away along the wall. Where will you run to? You don't want to have children because the world is violent, polluted, trivial? Come back here; get down and come lie next to me. I'm naked on this bed, waiting for you. Give me a better answer.

'Besides, I don't think I'd be able to hold an infant in my arms. I'd be afraid.'

Or are you afraid of giving up the woman you're holding on to? The one you like? I know, my love, but there's nothing wrong with that. Egoism consoles us; it keeps us company. You're already tired of feeling that you're under scrutiny, and maybe now you're cold, too. You're fidgeting; you're worrying. You're afraid you're no longer enough for me.

'How about you? Why do you want to have a child?'

I could tell you it's because I need a cord to bind up the strange thoughts I have, to hold them together. Or because I'm losing pieces, and I'd like to see a new little piece in front of me. Or I could tell you it's because I'm an orphan.

'Because I'd like to see a kite flying,' I say, and I don't know what I've said.

But at last, the tension slackens. It was a game, a joke. Your mother once again looks on me without suspicion. 'Jackass,' she says, laughing, and tosses back a slug of Coca-Cola. 'We're fine just as we are, don't you think?'

But I'm thinking of a length of cord vibrating in the wind, of a little wrist keeping me attached to the earth. It's me, Elsa, I'm the kite, I'm flying in the sky: a trapezoid of rags up here, down below its big shadow, and chasing them my kid, my missing piece.

Why didn't I drive you to school? It was raining, and I often give you a lift when it rains. My first operation was scheduled for nine o'clock, but I could have made it. I could have dropped you off a little early. You would have stayed under the portico, chatting with your friends and waiting for the bell to ring. You like getting to school early, and I like having you next to me in the car when it's raining outside. Our breath fogs the windows, and you stretch out an arm and wipe the glass with your hand. You're never drowsy in the morning. You're always awake and alert; you check out everything that moves. We don't talk much. I look at the ends of your fingers. They're barely sticking out of your sleeves, which are too long. You're constantly pulling them down even further. You wear those strange tops, short in the waist but extremely long in the sleeves. Isn't your stomach cold, Angela? No, it's your hands that are cold; it wouldn't be cool to have a cold midriff. You're all bundled up in your heavy jacket, but underneath, you really don't have enough clothes on. For you and your friends, summer and winter are the same thing. You don't adjust to the change of seasons; that's not done any more.

'How are things going at school?'

'Fine.'

You always say things are going fine. Your mother says you're not doing as well as you should, so she goes to your school and talks to your teachers. You study with the radio on. I used to study with the radio on, too; I never told you that. Your behaviour's normal. Kids today all have the same problem: you don't know how to concentrate. But your mother says I'm too lenient with you. It's true; I've left the job of your upbringing to her. She's the one who insists that you make your bed; she's the one who requires you to leave the bathroom in order after you have a shower. I, on the other hand, indulge your disorder without reproaching you. This morning, you left a used tampon on the bathroom sink; I threw it away for you.

'So long, Daddy.'

I like it when you call me that. You're a good girl. You've got an amusing face, full of irony. I watch you getting out of the car and running through the rain. Maybe you'll fail your courses; who gives a damn? You're my hook in the world, Angelina, in this world that turns and turns without changing seasons.

It's only recently that we've begun sniffing around each other, you and I, since about the time when you and your mother started squabbling. You know, I'd been waiting a long time for that to happen, standing on the sidelines and waiting with folded arms for so many years. I smiled at you through the bathroom door – the bathroom, where you two do most of your quarrelling, both of you in your underwear, the eyeshadow spilled in the sink – I smiled at you, and you saw me. So you smiled back, and your mother got annoyed. 'At last,' she said. 'You're both the same age!'

She didn't want me to buy you that scooter. I didn't want to, either, but I didn't want to tell you no. You'd been lobbying for that thing for so long. You were determined, methodical, indefatigable. So I said to Elsa, 'She'll just jump on someone else's moped. She won't have a helmet, and she'll probably climb on behind someone who goes too fast.' Your mother said, 'I don't even want to talk about it.' I kept quiet after that, and she left the house without telling me goodbye. But the truth is, I wanted to see your eyes shine; I wanted to feel you throw your arms around my neck and say, 'Thanks, Daddy.' I wanted it like a little boy. And when it happened, the person who got most emotional was me. But your mother and I both knew that we'd already lost. We can't tell you no. We can't tell ourselves no.

63

She caved in faster than you thought she would. Then came the exchange of warnings and promises. I leaned on the counter at the motorcycle shop and wrote out a cheque. We picked the most expensive helmet. Your mother rapped it with her knuckles, testing its hardness in a final, futile defensive gesture. Then she felt the padding that was going to protect your head. *Her* head.

'It'll keep you warm, too,' she said, and she gave you a sad smile. You grabbed her by the shoulders, shook her, assaulted her like a gentle storm. Your happiness drove away her gloom.

And for the first time, we went back home without you. You were behind us on your new scooter, following our car, which was moving very, very slowly. I saw your red helmet in the rear-view mirror. I remember saying, 'We can't live in fear for her. We have to let her grow up.' And I was afraid of thinking, We have to let her die.

I threw the keys on the hall table and immediately took off my shoes. I'd been seeing patients in my office all afternoon. The last one was a woman, obviously a well-to-do person. Her eyes seemed to be moulded into one single expression, much like the buttons on her tailored outfit. The designer's initials stamped on those buttons – the final vexation of the day – were still floating in front of my eyes. I started undressing on my way to the bathroom. I stepped into the shower, and the telephone rang. It was your mother, punctual as always. 'Did you get yourself some groceries?'

'Of course.' Naturally, I was lying. That summer, I lived on *arancini,* balls of fried white rice, stuffed and tasty. I used to eat them in a speciality shop that's gone now. There was a big marble counter, and a skinny man who served me my portion in silence. Three *arancini* on a heavy crockery plate, the kind they use in pubs. You know, sweetheart, life's like a big roll of adhesive paper. It fools you; the glue looks strong, looks as though everything will stick to it, but when you unroll it, you see that a whole lot of stuff is missing, and there are just four things left. Four crappy little things. Well, in my case, one of those crappy little things is a thick pub plate with three *arancini* on it.

When I stayed in the city, I missed your mother's dinners. At the same time, I liked the feeling of absence as I stood there naked in my own little puddle. I savoured the taste of solitude, the touch of a familiar hand in my crotch. Walking from one room to another, I realised that nostalgia's a very elastic sentiment; you can fit into it anything you want. I turned on the television set. There was a summer programme, so attuned to the season that the master of ceremonies was in a swimming pool, floating on a polystyrene island and accompanied by a black Siren. I muted the volume and let the artificial light from the screen reverberate around me. I went into the bedroom, took the book I was reading from the bedside table, went back to the living room, and sprawled out naked on the sofa, just as I used to do sometimes when I was a boy. Some summers, when my parents went away on holiday, I stayed home to study. I'd help my father load the last suitcase into the inaccessible boot of his Lancia coupé, then pass my days throwing the house into disorder. I scattered books, underwear and leftover food everywhere, including the carpets. I liked to desecrate the modest rooms my mother kept tidy all winter long. And at the end of the holiday, when my parents returned and everything resumed its normal order, I found I was better able to endure our home life by conjuring up the memory of my summer transgressions. I think I felt the very same pleasure a degenerate waiter feels when he spits clandestinely on to an overly demanding customer's plate.

A dull, distant rumbling came in through the window of the flat and penetrated the silence. Maybe the weather was changing. I'd left a chair out on the terrace the previous evening; slipping on my bathrobe, I went outside to retrieve it. A bird of passage had apparently gone off course and flown into the courtyard. Now it was terrified, fluttering among the plants down in the garden and looking for a way out. I watched it stop and hover, as though it had to struggle against the weight of the sultry air. Darkness had fallen all of a sudden, and soon it would start raining. I stayed outside, waiting for the cooling breeze I thought might be on the way. Despite its padded surfaces, the chair wasn't comfortable at all. A black sound of beating wings passed over my head; the bird had finally succeeded in making good its escape. The air in the courtyard was as inert and heavy as before. The storm must have stayed away. I went back inside and brushed my teeth.

★

My dear wife, what can I do? I feel like inserting myself into the body of a certain little woman tonight. I feel like rubbing her raffia-basket head against me. I want to feel hot breath on my body. I want a dog to lick my hand in the dark. I swear an oath to you while you sleep: This is the last time. I was about to betray her again, but it didn't seem right to spoil my evening. Little by little, as I drove out of the city and into that shantytown, I became more and more euphoric, because it was like entering another world, a city across the sea, a collection of huts built on piles, a little Saigon. And all that unsightliness I was approaching, all those trembling lights, leaped out to meet me as though they were part of an amusement park that was being kept open for me alone.

It was the first time I'd gone to her house at night. I liked recognising things, fingering them in the dark, like a thief. The unhealthy odour of those surroundings seemed familiar, and once again I sucked it into my lungs like a perfume. The part of me that I feared was there; I had invoked it. The dubious stairs, the filth under my shoes, the long shadows on each floor – everything was silent, except my wolfish heart. The iron spiral of the exterior staircase was like a perpendicular black shaft engulfed in night. I rushed down those stairs, spinning faster and faster, more and more excited. I reached the final stage, the embankment under the viaduct. The ground was hard and dry, like the bottom of a vanished sea. I took the final steps towards her pile dwelling, towards the little madam of my Saigon.

There was no light coming from the window on the other side of the porch. I made a fist and knocked on the green door. I had tripped on the stairs, and my ankle was hurting me. I rolled my fist sideways and hammered on the door insistently. Where could she be at this hour? Out with her friends? Why shouldn't she have friends? Maybe she was in one of those nightclubs that look like industrial warehouses, with a searchlight outside pointed at the sky. She was in the midst of the throng, dancing with her eyes closed, as she was when I first saw her leaning on the jukebox. Why shouldn't she dance? Maybe she had a man, a sloven like herself, a man who was holding her close right now, and I didn't exist for her, even in her thoughts. Maybe she was a prostitute; after all, she'd accepted my money, it didn't seem to offend her. At that very moment, her skeletal legs were pounding the dark pavement somewhere, pacing up and down some remote avenue on the fringe of the city. Leaning on a car and talking to the driver through his window, she negotiated the price of herself, with her sickly face, her sunken eyes, her smeared make-up. Maybe Manlio was inside that car. Every now and then, he liked to dredge up some creature of the night, so why not her? No, not her. I stopped knocking; I'd exhausted my arm so much, it was trembling. She wasn't good-looking. She was pallid, depressing. Her meagreness struck me as a form of protection; no one could possibly imagine how she behaved when her torpid body caught fire and she became another person. But maybe she was that way with all of them. Who was I to deserve anything more? I lifted my aching arm and knocked again. She wasn't home. The whore wasn't home. Defeated, I turned round, leaned back against the door and looked at the night. The deserted viaduct, and below it the shacks, from which there came a few faint signs of life. *Maybe that's where she goes. She goes to the Gypsies. She gets drunk in their caravans, and then she gets her raggedy fortune told.*

I heard a little moan, a rustling sound on the other side of the door. I thought about her body, her hands, and once again I surprised myself by not remembering her as clearly as I wanted to. 'Italia,' I whispered. 'Italia . . .'

And it was like putting a cloak over her, limiting her to a single place, inside the four walls of her name, hers and no one else's. 'Italia,' I whispered again, and now I was stroking the wooden door.

I heard a whimper, a scratching paw, and I realised it was the dog. He started barking, the blind beast, as wretched as his mistress. It was a smothered bark, the bark of an old dog that soon grew tired. I smiled. *She'll be back. If she's left the dog here, it means she'll be back, and I'll wait for her. I'll have my way inside her body for the last time.*

Headlights bathed the wall of the house as a car passed on the viaduct. Among the bricks above my head, something glinted in the darkness, and then I remembered the key. I reached up and found the key attached to one of the loosened bricks with a used piece of chewing gum. I closed my hand, and it was just as if I were taking hold of her. I knew I shouldn't do it, but already I was feeling the door, clutching the key in my other hand and searching for the keyhole.

It was pitch black inside, and there was the usual smell, only staler. I was in her house, and she wasn't there; the transgression excited me. And now I had the pleasing thought that the key hadn't been stuck up above the door by chance. She had left it there for me. I felt my way along the wall and found the light switch inside a chipped ceramic apple. An energy-saving lightbulb came on in the middle of the room. The blind dog stood blank-eyed before me, one ear straight up, the other flopping down. Truly a miserable watchdog. I flipped the switch off. No, no light; I'd wait for her in the dark. The darkness would hide me from myself. I took a few halting steps and collapsed on the sofa. Silence permeated the house. Apart from the few small sounds made by my intruder's body, there was only the breathing of the dog, which had taken up its position under the sofa. I began to grow accustomed to the darkness; now I could distinguish the shapes of the furniture, the groups of bric-a-brac on the various flat surfaces, and the outline of the fireplace against the wall. In the dark, the house had a sacredness and a desolation all its own, and the fireplace seemed like a dismantled altar.

She was there. In her absence, she was all the more there. The last time, we had never looked each other in the eye; I'd pushed her face down on to the sofa. Now I fell to my knees in front of it, looking for the spot where she'd braced herself as she bucked under me. Still kneeling on the floor, I rubbed my face in the darkness. Italia had been like this, pinned in this corner. I searched with my nose, with my mouth – I was trying to feel what she must have felt when I took her. I wanted to be her, so that I could feel the reaction that I provoked in her flesh. I didn't even try to resist. I ran full speed towards the precipice almost

69

without realising it. Pleasure, deep and warm, spread through my belly, entered my shoulders, my throat. Just like a woman's pleasure.

But I soon became a man again, Angela, and all the sweetness was gone, replaced by the smell of my breath after the last spasms died away on that sofa. I felt uneasy, unexpectedly sad, and in the violated darkness, everything seemed worse. My legs were stiff, and I was soiled like a teenager. The dog lying next to my knees hadn't missed any of my passionate tremors. I pulled myself to my feet, running into things as I looked for the bathroom. I found a door and an electric wire running along the wall, then followed the wire until my hand came to a switch. My face appeared in the mirror in front of me; the sudden, malevolent light dazzled my eyes. I was in a kind of niche, covered with old tiles. I turned on the tap. While I bent forward to bathe my face over the sink, I saw a glass hanging inside an iron ring, and in the glass was a toothbrush long past its prime. Together with the disgust I felt at the sight of those squashed, frayed bristles, I was assailed by a feeling of disgust for myself. There was a small bathtub — a hip bath, really — and a rubber mat was draped across the edge of it. The bottom half of the plastic shower curtain was spotted with mildew and slung over the curtain rod. The bar of soap had been neatly stored in its container. On the shelf under the mirror, there was only some hand cream and an opaque glass jar of the foundation make-up Italia used on her face. A wicker basket was on the floor. I lifted the lid and saw a little pile of dirty clothes. I fixed my gaze on a pair of crumpled knickers, and I heard a coarse voice inside me begging me to stuff them into my pocket immediately and bear them away. I looked into the mirror again and asked my lupine eyes what kind of man I had turned into.

I turned off the light and went back into the other room. As I passed the sofa in the darkness, I leaned over to adjust the flowered cloth. In doing so, I stepped on the dog's paw, and he let out a yelp. I went out the door, locked it, and tried to push the key back into its hiding place, but the gum had lost its elasticity. I tried to soften it by rubbing it between my fingers – I couldn't bring myself to do the job with saliva. I heard a sound, a distant clicking. Heels on metal steps. I tossed the gum into my mouth and chewed it hard. I dropped the key and bent down to look for it. When the heels reached the bare ground, the clicking stopped. I found the key, jammed it with my thumb against one of the chinks in the bricks, and pressed as hard as I could until the gum stuck. I crouched down, creeping away through the grass, and hid behind the house, near the carcass of the burned vehicle. She appeared almost at once. Two black legs, unhurried, accustomed to the darkness. And between the legs, the usual bag. She seemed tired; her spine was curved even more than I remembered. She stretched out an arm, reaching for the ledge above the door, but the key fell into her hair. I flattened myself against the wall while she rummaged in her hair. Peering with only one eye, I saw her fingers brush the key, then seize it, and as she did so, her face changed. I could barely see her, but I sensed that a precise emotion was rising in her. She detached the key from the gum and stood still for a while, holding the gum in her fingers; she'd noticed that it was wet. She looked around in the darkness, turned her eyes in my direction, and stared. *Now she's going to discover me; now she's going to come over here and spit in my face.* She took a few steps, then stopped. She was barely visible in the pale moonlight. I squatted down behind the skeleton of the burned car. She looked into the dark where I was skulking, and maybe she could see me. Her eyes were fixed on emptiness, but it was as if she knew I was there; the thought of me was reflected on her face. She went no further. She turned round, slipped the key into the lock and closed the door behind her.

71

The next evening, I had dinner with Manlio at one of those trattorias in the city centre where the outside tables rock back and forth on the uneven pavement and you have to stoop down and slide a shim under what seems like the proper leg, and then when you sit up straight again, you discover that now another leg's too short and the table's still wobbly. Just like life. Manlio was joking – he was making his chest expand under his jacket – but he wasn't happy. He'd had some problems in the delivery room. He was muttering a few set phrases for effect, he was feeling sorry for himself and, naturally, he was lying. Against his will, he was insincere; he'd never been one for self-scrutiny, and he had no intention of starting now. He fell in with other people's moods and impulses and ended up making them his own. And so, that evening, with the zeal of a true friend, he was trying to climb down into the deep burrow where I was apathetically wandering. His effort had been going on for some time. I was silent and distracted; I'd attacked the antipasti violently at first, wielding my fork like a weapon, but then I'd left them unfinished and hadn't ordered anything more. Manlio was trying to follow me, borrowing my mood, but meanwhile he was nibbling at everything in sight: grilled peppers, fried ricotta, sautéed broccoletti.

I asked him, 'Do you go with whores?'

He didn't expect such a question, not from me. He smiled, poured himself a drink, made a clucking sound with his tongue.

'Do you or don't you?'

'How about you?'

'Yes, I do.'

'Come on.' He didn't know where this was leading; maybe he was thinking about Elsa. It didn't seem possible to him that a man with such a wife would pay for sex. However, the shift in the conversational tone didn't displease him; he could handle it, and it went with the wine. 'Me, too, from time to time,' he said, and now he seemed like a little boy.

'Do you always go with the same one, or do you change?'

'It depends.'

'Where do you take them?'

'We stay in the car.'

'Why do you go with them?'

'So we can pray together. What a stupid question.' He laughed, and his eyes disappeared.

It's not a stupid question, Manlio, but you realise that too late, while you're looking at a passing tourist with her arm around a giant in Bermuda shorts. Now you have a bitter look on your face.

Later, I told him it wasn't true, I didn't go with whores. He was annoyed, but he kept on laughing. His cheeks grew flushed; he said that I was being an arsehole – 'an arsehole, as usual' is what he said. In the meantime, however, our boredom had vanished. The evening had taken a turn; we'd entered more intimate territory, where there was a flicker of something that resembled the truth, and as Manlio walked to his car, he looked like a sincere man, a desperate man. We said goodbye quickly – a pair of claps on the shoulders – took a few steps in the dark, and already we were far apart, each on his own pavement, free of any residue left by the other. Ours was a sanitary friendship.

I could tell you, Angela, that the shadows of the street lights seemed to fall on my windscreen like dead birds, and that in their falling, I saw everything I didn't have raining down on me; I could tell you that the torrent of shadows came down faster and faster as I sped along, and that I felt a growing desire to fill that absence with something, anything. I could tell you many things that might sound true now but maybe aren't true at all. I don't know the truth; I don't remember. I only know that I was driving in her direction without any distinct thought. Italia wasn't anything. She was like the black wick in an oil lamp. The flame burned beyond her, in that greasy light that enveloped the things I needed, all the things I didn't have.

I turned on to the long, tree-lined road and drove past the indistinct commercial figures standing by the roadside. The beams of my headlights struck bodies floating in the night like jellyfish, painted them for an instant with dazzling light, and then returned them to the darkness. Near one of the last trees, I slowed down and stopped. The girl who came over to my car had legs covered with black net and a perfect face for her line of work: sour and infantile, agitated and gloomy – the face of a whore. She croaked something, perhaps an insult, as I pulled away and watched her disappear in the rear-view mirror.

She was home. That night, she was home. The door opened slowly. The dog came round the side of the house and approached me, sniffing hard and wagging his tail between my legs. He seemed to recognise me. And now Italia was there in front of me, standing with one extremely white hand on the door. I pushed her inside with my body. Maybe she'd already been sleeping, because her breath was stronger than usual. I liked it. I grabbed her by the hair, forcing her to bend her neck, to stoop down. I rubbed her face against my stomach. Right there, where the thought of her caused me pain. *Heal me, heal me* . . . I bent down and ran my mouth all over her face. I stuck my tongue into her nostrils, into the corners of her eyes.

Later, she sat on the sofa, pulling down the front of her T-shirt with one hand to cover her sex. She was waiting for me like that when I came out of the bathroom. I had washed myself in there, sitting on the edge of the tub, next to the mouldy shower curtain hanging down from its rod. I walked over to her, seized a handful of her hair and shook her head as I tried to slip the money into her hand. She went limp; I had to squeeze her hand to make her close it. She accepted what I gave her as one accepts pain. I had to leave; I couldn't recapture myself in her presence. It would have been unseemly, like looking back on one's own excrement.

You want to be alone, too. I'm getting to know you. You do what I want; then you disappear like a mosquito at sunrise. You place yourself among the flowers on your sofa and hope that I won't notice you. You know that you're not worth anything except in the throes of passion; you know that while I'm tying my tie and getting ready to leave, I'm already disgusted by everything. You don't have the courage to move as long as I'm there; you don't have the courage to show your arse while you walk to the bathroom. Maybe you're afraid of getting killed; you're afraid I'll toss you on to the baked clay of that dried-up river bed, like that black car that fell from the viaduct. You don't know that my anger dies when I die inside you, and that afterwards I'm an unlioned lion. What do you do when I go away? What do I leave you with? This cold fireplace, this room I've razed, I who offended you in the heart of the night without even loving you. The dog will come close to you, you'll need that fur, you'll stroke him while your eyes are fixed somewhere else. He's blind, after all. Scenes, obsessions from your past, will rise up before your mind's eye. Eventually, though, your confidence in the present, in what's there, will come back to you. You'll get up and put a few things in order – an overturned chair, for example. And you won't need to pull your T-shirt down; when you bend over, you'll feel the air on your naked buttocks and pay no attention. Without my eyes moving over it, your body's worth what it's worth: as much as a chair, as much as hard work. But when you get up, you'll feel a filament of my semen running down one of your legs, and then – I don't know, but I'd like to know. I'd like to know if you feel disgust, or . . . No. Hurry up and wash, little slut. Stand behind your mildewed shower curtain, grab a sponge and cleanse yourself of this fool's secretions, cleanse yourself of his ghosts.

There were several medlars on the table. I took one and ate it; its flesh was soft and sweet. I took another.

'Are you hungry?' she asked.

Her voice was weak; it proceeded from silence. Italia, too,

must have been having some bizarre thoughts. Before, when I'd stopped squeezing her hand, she had spread her fingers and the money had fallen to the floor. Now she held that empty hand out to me. 'Give them to me,' she said, and I gave her the medlar pips.

'Shall I make you some spaghetti?'

'How do you mean?' I murmured, astounded by this proposal.

'With tomato sauce, or however you want.'

She'd misunderstood my question. Her face, as she scrutinised me, seemed new, different, suddenly vivacious; her eyes vibrated in their sockets like heads just emerged from a shell. I had no intention of staying there, but there was that little shimmer of hope in her expression, a hope quite remote from my own. Because I, too, was hoping for something, Angela. Something that was neither in that room nor anywhere else, something that might have been decomposing with my father's bones. Something of which I knew nothing. Searching for it was a truly futile exercise. 'Do you make a good sauce?' I asked.

She laughed, flushed with delight, and for an instant I thought that maybe my hope was as modest and easy to fulfil as hers. She went to the bedroom, hunching over as she walked, trying to cover herself with her T-shirt, which was too short for the job. She came back quickly, wearing a pair of trousers that looked like overalls and her multicoloured sandals with the straps undone. 'I'm going outside for a minute,' she said. I watched from the window as she reappeared behind the house, where, I now noticed for the first time, she had a little garden. With her heels sinking into the earth and a torch in her hand, she rummaged around in a row of plants supported by canes. She came back inside, carrying a bundle in the bottom of her shirt, and went into the kitchen. I could see her through the door, sometimes all of her, sometimes just an arm or a shock of hair. She reached into a wall cupboard and took out a saucepan and a plate. She washed the tomatoes carefully, one at a time, and then she began mincing the herbs with a large kitchen knife. She worked quickly and skillfully, guiding the knife with her index finger. I discovered, to my amazement, that Italia was a neat, efficient cook, completely in command of her movements and her kitchen. I sat and waited, composed and a bit stiff, like a deferential guest.

'It's almost ready.'

She left the kitchen, went into the bathroom, and closed the door. I heard her turn on the water in the shower. I fluffed up the sofa pillows around me. A fine aroma of fresh tomato sauce was permeating the room and intensifying my hunger. I gazed at the wall, at the monkey clutching his baby bottle. He looked exactly like Manlio. I smiled at him the way one smiles at a stupid friend. In the bathroom, the water pelted down violently for a while, then stopped. I heard a few small sounds, and soon she was out. Her yellow hair looked like wood when it was wet. She was wearing a beige bathrobe. As she tightened the belt around her waist, she sighed contentedly. 'I'll put the pasta on,' she said.

She went back to the kitchen. When she passed me, she left the scent of talcum powder in the air, a doll's scent, as sweet as vanilla. 'Would you like a beer?'

She brought me the beer, disappeared, then reappeared with what she needed to set the table. I got up to give her a hand.

'Please,' she said. 'Don't get up.'

Her voice was as solicitous as her gestures. I kept watching her as she got the table ready. Surprisingly lively for that time of night, she moved swiftly back and forth between the living room and the kitchen. It seemed to me that I was seeing her for the first time, as if I'd never possessed the body under her bathrobe. She knew how to set a table; after laying out the napkins and silverware impeccably, she placed a candle in the centre. Then she came and stood before me. She furrowed her brow, turned up her nose, and moved her upper teeth forward like a little rodent. 'Al dente?' she squeaked.

'Al dente,' I replied. By way of imitating her, I tried to turn up my nose, too, but I discovered it was much less mobile than hers. She laughed; we laughed. She wasn't just cheerful; she was something more. She was happy.

'Here we are,' she said, coming out of the kitchen with a serving dish in her hand. She put the dish down. In the centre, in the midst of the pasta, was a handful of basil leaves, arranged to look like a flower. She served me, then sat down across from me with her elbows on the table.

'You're not going to eat anything?' I asked.

'Later.'

I thrust my fork into my plate. I was hungry. I hadn't been so hungry in a very long time.

'Do you like it?'

'Yes.'

Her spaghetti was really good, Angela. The best spaghetti I ever had in my life. Italia scrutinised me vigilantly as I ate. She followed every nuance of my appetite, encouraging me with her eyes, with little adjustments of her shoulders and arms. It seemed that she was eating, too, that she was savouring every mouthful along with me. 'Would you like some more?'

'Yes.'

I had forgotten the joy of satiety. Forkful after forkful, I could feel that food doing me a world of good. The beer was almost out of my reach, and as I stretched out my arm for it, Italia moved her arm, too, maybe in an effort to help me. I touched the glass bottle, which was still cold from the fridge, and part of her hand, which was surprisingly warm and vibrant. It was an effort to move my hand away from hers. I would have liked to maintain that contact, and not just with her fingers. For a fraction of a second, I was seized by the desire to lay my forehead in that hand, so that it might help sustain the burden of my head. I poured myself some beer, clumsily, without paying attention to what I was doing, and it foamed up and overflowed.

Italia looked at the little puddle of foam spreading under my glass. There was a special light in her eyes; it suffused her skin and surrounded her face with a certain aura, quite delicate and deeply intimate. It seemed to me that she had grown suddenly sad. I followed that sadness past the shadows around her neck and down to her ribs, where I could glimpse her breasts. She saw what I was doing, grabbed the two sides of her robe, and held them together in front of her chest. Now she was in the light, in the dim light of the candle, and she watched me eat. She sat with folded arms, like a Cupid watching in the night.

I pulled over and stopped in front of the row of oleander bushes. The asphalt was sprinkled with sand. Through the bars of the entrance gate, which was standing ajar, I looked at the house, at its slate roof and its bright white walls, phosphorescent in the splendour of the newborn daylight. I didn't go into the house at once; I stayed in the car and let the dampness penetrate me. Some time passed – I don't know how much – maybe I dozed off. Elsa's little runabout was parked under the thatched carport. Her body lay still on the bed, heedless of me. I gazed at things revealed by the dawn – the empty clothes line, our bicycles leaning on the wall.

As the light from the first rays of the sun intensified, so did the deep blue of the sky. In that polished air, everything was extremely visible. If the night had protected me, the daylight, in returning me to everyday things, restored me to myself. I stretched my neck, looked in the little rectangular mirror, and found my old face again. I needed a shave; the stubble of my beard had grown without my noticing it.

I got out of the car, followed the fence, slipped through the reed thicket and came out on the beach. Nobody there; only the sea. I walked across the sand to the shoreline and sat down a few steps from the water on the last dry strip. The house was behind me. If Elsa had opened the bedroom window, she would have seen the back of me, a little dot on the beach. However, she was asleep. She may, perhaps, have been dreaming, searching for a different destiny, plunging into her dreams as precisely as when she dived into the sea and disappeared, without so much as a splash, through a hole in the water.

Can the body love what the mind despises, Angela? That's what I was thinking about as I drove back to the city. Once, I was in a peasant's wine cellar. Because it would have been discourteous to refuse, I tried some of his special cheese, a *formaggio di fossa* with a discoloured, mouldy rind and a cadaverous smell. Inside, to my great surprise, I discovered a flavour both violent and mild; and the aftertaste – the taste of a well, of great depth – caused me to feel longing and disgust, in equal measure, for that cheese and its sharpness.

It was six o'clock in the morning; I had a good while before I had to be back at work. I stopped for a coffee in the usual bar. I thought, This is going to be like returning to a brothel early in the morning to pick up your forgotten umbrella and discovering, instead of the prostitute who satisfied your desires last night, a woman wearing slippers, half asleep and unattractive in every way.

She was surprised to see me. She stood in the doorway, stunned and smiling, and she didn't even invite me inside before asking me, 'What are you doing here at this hour?'

'This.'

'Come on in,' she said, taking one of my hands and pulling me into the house.

She'd stopped being afraid of me. All it took was a plate of spaghetti. She'd already absorbed me into her trashy normality, like the monkey in the poster, like the blind dog. The shutters on the window were open, so the morning light filtered into the room. The chairs were turned upside down on the table. Parts of the floor were still shiny and wet; Italia had already performed her housekeeping chores. She glowed with pride in a job well done; her eyes had the same lustre as the floor. As for me, I was worn out and discontented.

'Let me turn off the iron.' She walked over to the ironing board, which was standing open in a corner. A strip of sky-blue cotton, perhaps part of an apron, hung down from the board. She was already dressed to go out, but she hadn't yet put on her make-up. Her pale eyes caressed me. She could tell by my stubble, by my wrinkled jacket, that I hadn't slept in a bed.

'Do you want a shower?'

'No.'

'Do you want some coffee?'

'I already had some at the bar.'

I sank down into the usual sofa. She started taking the chairs down from the table. Her hair was pulled back in a short, frazzled ponytail that bared her convex forehead. I searched my mind for the only image of her I wanted to conserve: her befuddled, submissive body. But there was too much distance between that image and the woman in front of me. Without make-up, the skin of Italia's face was the colour of dusty alabaster, reddening at the nose and under the eyes. And the black canvas plimsolls she was wearing made her shorter than usual.

She came and sat down across from me. Maybe she was ashamed that I was seeing her unadorned, in her everyday housekeeping normality. She tried to hide her red hands, clutching one of them with the other. I thought she was much more attractive like this, much more dangerous. She was of an indefinite age, like a nun. And now her house put me in mind of one of those churches you find in seaside resorts: modern churches, without frescoes, with a plaster Jesus over the altar and artificial flowers standing in a vase without water. 'Is this house yours?' I asked her.

'It was my grandfather's, but he sold it before he died. I had come up here to give him a hand – he had a broken femur – and afterwards I stayed on. But I have to get out soon.'

'Where are you from?'

'From down south. The Cilento.'

The dog crossed the room and lay down at Italia's feet. She bent forward and stroked the fur on his head. 'He was sick last night. Maybe he ate a mouse . . .'

I approached the animal. When I palpated him, he didn't resist; in fact, he stretched out on his back and spread his paws wide. And when my fingers pressed a painful area, he barely whimpered. 'It's nothing. All you need is some disinfectant.'

'Are you a doctor?'

'A surgeon.'

Her legs were there, just a few inches from me. I had to tug to spread them apart. I kissed her thighs, so white, they were almost blue. I shoved my head in the space between them. They were cold, despite their sweating. Italia bent over me. I could smell her breath; the back of my neck was wet from her mouth. I stood up suddenly, striking her face with my head, and sat down again on the sofa. I brought my hands together and squeezed one with the other, staring all the while at my knotty fingers. 'I'm married,' I said.

I didn't look at her. I sensed her over there, out of focus, at the very edge of my vision. 'I won't be coming here any more. I came back to tell you that.' Her head was bent forward, and she had one hand on her nose. It occurred to me that I might have hurt her. 'And also to apologise.'

'Don't worry about it.'

'I'm not the kind of man who goes around cheating on his wife.'

'Don't worry about it.'

A stream of blood was flowing out of her nose. I stepped over to her and lifted her chin. 'Hold your head back.'

'Don't worry about it. Why do you worry so much?'

An inexpressive smile softened her face. So much indulgence made me feel as though I'd suffered a defeat. I thrust her chin away. I wanted to win; I wanted to beat her.

'Do you often screw people you don't know?'

She didn't get upset, but she'd received a blow. She began staring into space, placing her thoughts somewhere far away. Her eyes seemed to be made of paste, like the dog's eyes. No, I didn't have any right to insult her. I opened my hands and hid my face in them. *Tell me it's not true. Tell me you writhe like that only with me, only with me do you become grey and old, like a dying snake. Only with me do you have the courage to die.* Heartbreaker had stolen one of her fuchsia slippers, and now he was holding it in his mouth without biting it. I said, 'I'm sorry.'

But she wasn't listening to me any more. *Maybe she'll kill herself some day. Maybe she'll remove herself from the world, not for me, but for someone like me, for a predator that will swoop down on her body with the same voraciousness, the same indifference.*

'You have to leave,' she said. 'I have to go to work.'
'What sort of work do you do?'
'I'm a whore.'
And now she was as empty as a sloughed-off snakeskin.

I'm thinking about that iridescent purple scarf you wind around your neck, Angela, the one you steal from your mother. It's older than you are – the wool it's made of resists the passage of time. We bought it in Norway.

When we took the ferry to the Lofoten Islands, she stayed inside, sipping her tea, her hands glued to the steaming cup, while I stayed outside on the deck, in spite of the frigid gusts of wind that were whipping up imposing waves. The ferry, which was cracked and chipped like the fjords disappearing from sight behind us, carried no tourists but ourselves. But it was packed with rough local people, fishermen and fish merchants. The air was white and windy; when I peered through it, I could make out nothing but the tumultuous sea. The change of colours and climate, the two sweaters I had on, and the odour of salted fish that rose up from the hold encouraged me to feel that I was a different man, as often happens when one is on holiday. I was happy to be alone, happy that the bad weather was keeping your mother inside. A sailor wearing an oilskin raincoat struggled past me along the rail. Shouting something incomprehensible, he pointed at the door to make me understand that I had better go back in. With water dripping into the neck of my sweater, I shook my head and smiled. 'It's OK,' I shouted in English.

He smiled, too. He was young, but his face already bore the marks of his windy profession. He stank of alcohol. Raising his arms to the sky, he cried out, 'God! God!' and moved away towards the bow.

★

A bird lands next to me. It takes me by surprise – I didn't see it coming. Its plumage is a dirty-looking colour between grey and green; its webbed feet grip the iron rail like little hands, while its breast steadily rises and falls. It must have braved the rigours of a difficult flight to reach this floating perch. It looks like a strange cross between a kingfisher and a black swan, and there's nothing gentle about it; in fact, it's almost scary. It scrutinises the sea with rapacious red-rimmed eyes, as though choosing a location for its next flight. It's got a beak like a mythical bird, and there's something human about those staring eyes. It sets me thinking: how is it that such a small creature accepts the unremitting challenge imposed on it by nature, while we retreat before a spray of sea water, we with our shoes and our sweaters? Why do we have so little courage?

I think your mother must have noticed something during that trip. I was silent and withdrawn on our long walks, and I could feel her eyes on my back as I moved a few steps ahead of her along one of the cliff-hanging paths overlooking the sea. But she never said anything. In the evenings, we sat close together, crowded by our fellow diners, at a single oblong table in a restaurant constructed of wood and red bricks. We ate fish and potatoes, washed down by a mug of beer. She would reach out her hand, place it on mine, and offer me one of her smiles, overflowing with warmth and grace. I let her gaiety capture me. I hugged her in the midst of those strangers, in that restaurant full of smoke and music.

And later, when I put my hands on her body again, I did it with absolute devotion; my lovemaking was uncharacteristically generous, and Elsa noticed. She repeated 'I love you' again and again as she stroked my hair in the darkness. (Maybe she'd been frightened a few days earlier, when I'd insisted on taking her away from the beach house: frightened at the prospect of the two of us alone together.) Now I gently accompanied her, all the way to the last tremor, and then stretched out beside her. Gratified desire glazed her eyes like a resin. She reached for me with a nerveless arm. 'How about you?'

I caught her hand and grazed her wedding ring with my lips. 'I'm fine as I am.'

My member was already tiny, hidden between my thighs, useless as a little boy's. She looked at me; the glaze on her eyes was thicker than before. Now I was expecting her to ask me something. She passed a reproving hand over my face, trying to alter my intense, needy stare. No, she had no desire to complicate that moment of total abandon, and shortly afterwards, she fell asleep. I lay awake, staring at the wooden ceiling, with no regrets. I had led my wife over the rapids, down through the waterfall of my ghosts, and on to the warm sand, where pleasure flooded her. Now that she was at rest, I went for a walk along the cliffs. The next day, in a crystal morning, we went to a shop where a little woman stood in front of a big loom. Your mother chose violet and purple yarns and watched as the woman wrapped the strands around the beam of her loom. Elsa wore that scarf for the rest of our holiday, and she was fascinated night and day by its changing colours. That scarf became a part of our lives, forgotten for a while, then taken up again, until the day, Angela, when you wrapped it around your neck and permeated it with your fragrance.

At the end of our return trip, as soon as we landed, we found ourselves back in the blazing heat. Elsa left her suitcase in the living room, put on her bathing costume and swam out to Raffaella. In those crucial August days, our sea-coast town filled up indiscriminately, convulsively, with crowds of people, and everybody, including the grocer and the newsagent, was a little short on patience. There was only one bar that stayed practically empty, a shed with a jute roof and a few tables scattered on the sand. This place was on the mouth of the river, where the sea stank, so the beach was deserted – no swimmers, no sunbathers. The proprietor was one Gae, or so he called himself, an old boy with a body like the crucified Christ, wearing only a faded loincloth.

This bar was one of the casual discoveries of that summer. We'd walked along the seashore all the way to the mouth of the river. The shed was actually attached to a shop where boats were laid up and repaired – two oil-stained Poles were busy dismantling motors – and beyond that, the beach ended. Elsa found the shed depressing and not particularly clean; I agreed with her, but then I formed a habit of walking over there almost every day. If it was morning, I ordered a coffee and read the newspaper. If it was evening, Gae indulged himself in the preparation of thick, highly alcoholic aperitifs, which left you dazed after a few sips. There were never many people in the bar. The Poles would get drunk and talk too loud; Gae would sit at my table and offer me a joint, which I'd refuse. For some reason, I liked this place. The sea took on different colours there, maybe because of the seaweed growing on the bottom.

One afternoon, I found myself surrounded by a group of handicapped persons – some supported by crutches, some pushed in wheelchairs – who had appeared on the beach, their arduous progress marked by deep furrows behind them in the sand. They occupied the few tables in the little bar and ordered drinks. One of their minders pulled a radio out of a knapsack, and in the course of a few minutes, the place acquired the atmosphere of a rustic festival. An old woman with a possum's face and fat sunburned shoulders began dancing on the sand.

I felt uneasy, so I got up and walked into the shed, intending to pay for my drink and leave. But then my eyes fell on a young man. He had the look of a halfwit, his exceedingly thin limbs were frozen in a spasm, and his fingers were spread apart like prongs. He was moving his head, insofar as he could, to the rhythm of the music, all the while gazing at his companion. who sat in her wheelchair and smiled at him with sharp, widely spaced teeth like those of a fish. She was a young woman; her face bore the signs of an obtuse, slow-moving life, and she was wearing a pair of plastic earrings. She stared back at her friend the spastic, returning his gaze so lovingly it took my breath away. She paid no attention to his jerking movements; she looked him in the eyes. She loved him, she simply loved him. I had to hurry. The sun had already gone down, and Elsa was expecting me for dinner. I'd drunk at least half a glass of one of

Gae's deadly aperitifs, and I hoped to walk off its effects on the way home. But, with my elbow on the bar and a ten-thousand-lire note in my hand, I thought that I would gladly leave my post in the ranks of the sound and the healthy to be looked at like that, the way that poor, damaged girl was looking at that spastic, at least once in my life. And it was then, my dear daughter, that Italia made a brief foray into my belly, traversing it like a submarine.

It was evening again, and again I was alone in the city. I emptied a large box of photographs on to my desk. I came across a snapshot of myself as a teenager, wearing a pair of shorts and a face full of shadows. I was fat; I didn't remember being fat. Within a few years, I was skinny as could be, as demonstrated by another picture, taken when I was a fresher at university. As I looked at the old photographs, my curiosity was replaced by a strange distress. I realised that I was a fugitive. My life was there; I could follow it with my finger from one glossy surface to another. But I appeared rarely in the most recent pictures, and then never in the centre of the frame: always surprised, always with dazzled eyes. Perhaps the visual record of this gradual but steady flight contained a secret map. I had intentionally escaped from the prison of remembrances. If I should die suddenly, I thought, Elsa would have trouble finding a recent photograph to put on my gravestone. This thought didn't sadden me; on the contrary, it consoled me. I wouldn't leave any evidence behind. Maybe it was my disdain for my father's pathetic self-centredness that had led me into this shadow, a shadow where a much more devious Narcissus lived. Maybe all my life, even in my most intense relationships, I'd been pretending. I'd prepared the image, then moved out of the frame and snapped the picture. The desk lamp was the only light in the room. I took off my glasses and stared into the dark space in front of me. I opened the French windows of my study and walked out on to the terrace. I pissed on the potted plants, watching the warm vapour rise out of the domesticated soil. The telephone rang, and I went back inside.

'Elsa, is that you?'

No reply.

'Elsa?'

Then, deep inside the receiver, I heard a grey, familiar breath.

As soon as I saw her, I threw my arms around her, I imprisoned her in my embrace. She clung to me, breathing heavily, and we stayed like that for I don't know how long: unmoving, clasped tight.

'I was afraid.'

'Of what?'

'I was afraid I'd never see you again.'

She was trembling, shuddering against my neck. I pressed my nose into the dark parting of her peroxide hair; I needed to draw the smell of her head into my lungs. It was the only thing I needed, and at last I felt good again. Her mouth slipped down to my chest. I lifted her by the arms. 'Look at me, please,' I said. 'Look at me.'

She started undoing her shirt. The buttons popped out of their buttonholes, running through her fingers like rosary beads. Her little breasts appeared. I held her wrists. 'No, not here.'

Taking her in my arms, I carried her to the bed in her bedroom. I undressed her slowly, moving around her body with unhurried, judicious hands, as if I were readying a corpse for an autopsy. Submissive, she let me do what I wanted. When she was completely naked, I stepped back to look at her. She smiled, but her smile was full of embarrassment, and she covered her pubes with one hand. 'Please,' she said. 'I'm too ugly . . .'

But I grabbed both her hands and forced them up and back over her head, back past her hair, which was spread out on the chenille bedspread. I said, 'Don't move.'

I slowly moved my eyes over her body, examining her part by part, section by section. Then I got undressed, too, completely undressed, which was something I'd never done in front of her before. I wasn't beautiful, either – my arms were too thin, my belly was too prominent, and then there was that bent tube dangling from my pubic hair – and I felt ashamed. But I wanted us to be like this, naked and not particularly attractive. Each of us exposed to the other, without haste, without heat, immersed in time. Once inside of her, I kept still for several minutes, looking into her frank, faded eyes. We stayed that way, frozen in that field of fire. A tear slid along her cheekbone; I caught it with my lips. I wasn't afraid of her any longer. I lay on top of her, weighing her down, like a man, like a child. I said, 'Now you're mine. Mine alone.'

Later, hunched over at the foot of the bed, she cut my toenails with a little pair of scissors.

'How old are you?'

'How old do I look?'

We fell asleep glued together. I stroked her hair until sleep stopped my hand. But when I woke up, Italia wasn't there. I found a note on the table: *I'll be back as soon as I can. The coffeemaker's ready to go.* At the bottom of the page, there was a lipstick kiss. I kissed that kiss.

I went into the kitchen and lit the burner under the coffee-pot. I opened a cupboard, curious to see what kind of order she kept her things in. There were the stacked plates, the little glasses, the big glasses, the bags of sugar and flour held closed by wooden clothes pegs. I saw a single-page calendar hidden on the inside of the cupboard door. There was writing on the calendar here and there; certain dates from the past two months were marked with little crosses. I ran back over this period in my mind, but I really didn't need to, I knew the truth already: she'd marked the dates of our meetings. I made another discovery on top of the fridge, where I found a glass jar with money inside of it – several banknotes, some crumpled, others simply folded. I counted them; not a lira was missing.

I looked out the window. The sun was broiling the viaduct and searing the scrubland beneath it. A Gypsy woman was hanging out her laundry next to a caravan. Three miniature hens with erect tail feathers were walking in single file near the vegetable garden. Its darkened soil showed that it had recently been watered. *Italia hasn't touched my money since she picked it up and stuck it in that jar.*

I had a shower. Then I put on Italia's bathrobe – the sleeves came to about my elbow – picked up the telephone and sat down on the bed. I told your mother I wouldn't be coming to the beach house that weekend. 'Why not?' she asked.

'I have to be on duty at the hospital.'

The monkey on the wall looked at me, and I looked back. I heard the key turn in the lock.

'Are you still here?'

'Of course I'm still here.'

I embraced her. She carried a different smell, the smell of a different place. I asked her, 'Where have you been?'

'At work.'

'What sort of work do you do?'

'Seasonal work in a hotel. I make up the rooms.'

The smell she was carrying was the smell of a bus, of a crowd.

At dusk, we went out. We walked hand in hand, almost without speaking, through that ghostly suburb. We listened to the sound of our footsteps in the silence, entrusting our thoughts to the nocturnal world. I never loosened my grip on her hand, and she never loosened hers. It seemed strange to me to be by the side of this woman whom I didn't know very well, and yet with whom I felt so intimate. Before we went out, she'd put on some make-up. I'd watched as she bent over a bit of mirror and hurriedly traced the outlines of those features that must have seemed too delicate to her. Her battery of cosmetics, the platform-soled shoes she climbed on to, her bleached hair – there wasn't a single thing in her appearance that corresponded to my tastes. And yet she was herself, Italia, and I liked everything about her. Without knowing the reason why. That night, she was all that I desired.

'Let's run!' she cried out.

And so we ran, and we tripped over each other, and we laughed, and we embraced against a wall. We did all the senseless things that lovers do. The next day, when we said goodbye, Italia started trembling again. She'd made me an omelette with eggs laid by her hens, she'd washed and ironed my shirt, and now she was trembling as I kissed her, as I turned away from her. New lovers are full of fears, Angela; they have no place in the world; they're travelling to no destination.

My mobile phone's vibrating. I've got it on the window sill, because that's where the reception is best. I don't answer right away; I need air, and so I open the window before I press the green button. Your mother's voice is incredibly present. There's no airport bustle around her, no announcements of flights landing and taking off. 'Timo, is that you?'

'Yes.'

'They told me . . .'

'What did they tell you?'

'That someone in my family's been in an accident – that I have to return at once.'

'Yes.'

'It's Angela?'

'Yes.'

'What's wrong?'

'She had a crash on her scooter. They're operating on her.'

'Operating on what?'

'Her brain.'

She doesn't burst into tears; she makes a harsh braying sound, as though someone's tearing her to pieces. Suddenly, her gasping stops and her voice returns, toneless and subdued. 'Are you at the hospital?'

'Yes.'

'What have they said? What are they saying?'

'Well, they're confident . . .'

'And you? What do you say?'

'I say that . . .' A tearful sob closes my throat and slips into my mouth, but I don't want to cry. 'We can only hope, Elsa. We can only hope.'

I hunch my shoulders and lean out of the window. Why don't I fall? Why don't I fall to the ground down there, where two patients with coats on over their pyjamas are taking a walk? 'When is your flight?' I ask.

'In ten minutes. British Airways.'

'I'll be waiting for you.'

'What about her helmet? Wasn't she wearing her helmet?'

'She didn't fasten the strap.'

'What? What do you mean, she didn't fasten it?'

Why didn't you keep your promise, Angela? Why are young people always so absent-minded? Just a smile in the wind and fuck you, Mum. You've cut off her legs; you've cut off her head. How will you apologise to her now?

'Timo?'

'Yes?'

'Swear to me on Angela that Angela's not dead.'

'I swear to you. On Angela.'

The patients downstairs have interrupted their walk. They're sitting on a bench, smoking. A middle-aged woman with a brick-coloured overcoat is strolling among the flower beds. It's humanity, my child, humanity swarming and scrabbling. Humanity going on. What will become of us, of your mother and me? What will become of your guitar?

We've made love, and now we're lying there, unmoving, listening to the sounds of the cars and lorries on the viaduct, so close they seem to be rolling on the roof. I should get dressed and go home, but it's hard for me to get free. I'm caught in the pitch that's holding us prisoner. *Where are my socks, my pants, my car keys?* And meanwhile, I stay where I am. I'm leaving tomorrow for a surgical oncologists' conference, where I'm supposed to give a talk. I have no desire whatsoever to attend this thing. Italia's slowly stroking one of my arms and measuring the weight of her imminent solitude. I visualise the conference hall, my glasses, my face above my printed name, my colleagues with their laminated photographs pinned to their jackets, the hotel bathrobe, the minibar in the night. I say, 'Come with me.'

She turns over on the pillow, her eyes wide and incredulous.

'Come on.'

She shakes her head. 'No, no.'

'Why not?'

'I don't have anything to wear.'

'Come in your knickers. You look great in knickers.'

And later, in the heart of the night, I'm reading through the paper I'm going to give. I go over every line with a red pencil, make corrections, scratch out words, add words, call her up.

'Were you asleep?'

'It's better if I don't come, right?'

'I'll pick you up at six. Is that too early?'

'If you change your mind, don't worry about it.'

★

96

And at six o'clock the next morning, she's already on the street; she's already put on her make-up. A clown in the grey light of dawn. I kiss her; her skin is icy.

'Have you been waiting long?'

'I just got here.'

But she's frozen. The shoulders of the short-sleeved black jacket she's wearing have too much padding; they're climbing up her neck. The skin of her arms is mottled, like marble. She rubs her hands together between her thighs. I turn on the heat full blast – I want her to get warm right away. She's got a look of shock on her face; even her eyes are cold. Stiff and immobile, she sits on her side of the car and makes no move to adjust her position. Her upper body leans slightly forward, away from the back of the seat. The car speeds along a deserted stretch of the autostrada, and eventually the heat makes her relax. I touch the tip of her nose. 'You feel better?'

She smiles and nods.

'Hi,' I say.

'Hi,' she replies.

'How are you doing?' I ask, slipping my hand between her legs.

It's a country town of tuffaceous stone, one-way streets and direction signs with arrows that keep bringing you back to the same circular piazza. I leave the car in a car park. I've reserved a room for her in her name. We've discussed this, and she knows I can't take the chance of booking us into the same room. Many of my colleagues will be attending this conference, including Manlio. On the street, we walk a little apart. Italia's more worried than I am. She doesn't know where she's going, but she squares her shoulders and walks straight ahead. The wheeled suitcase she's brought is too large for a stay of just a few days; it bounces along behind her, half empty and listing to one side. Unlike her, I'm accustomed to short trips, and I've got a small, functional, elegant leather bag, a gift from Elsa. This morning, I've tightened my belt a notch, and my pot belly is gone. I step forward lightly, in an extremely good mood. I feel like a schoolboy on a school trip. From behind, I reach out and touch her backside. 'Excuse me, miss,' I say. She's serious, she doesn't turn round to look at me, she knows she's an interloper. In an effort to be less conspicuous, she's wearing that wretched jacket and a longer skirt than usual.

I get my room key quickly; Italia's still talking with one of the staff at the reception desk. Two colleagues come up to me, and we exchange greetings.

I want an excuse to remain at the desk, close to her, so I ask a question of the girl in the blue waistcoat who has just signed me in: 'Is the sauna warm already, or do you have to wait?' The man taking care of Italia is holding a pencil and going over the reservations list. She turns towards me with a look of desperation. I step over to her.

'Is there a problem with my colleague here?'

The receptionist raises his eyes and looks at me, then casts an exaggerated glance in Italia's direction. 'The lady doesn't have authorisation,' he says. 'We're trying to accommodate her.'

She's wearing too much lipstick. Bleach has stripped and flayed her hair. She hunches her shoulders inside her little synthetic-fibre jacket and pulls her overlarge suitcase closer to her. She senses that the hotel receptionist is judging her. She looks at his bowed head as he works behind the desk; maybe she already regrets coming here with me.

She crosses the lobby with a brazen, almost hostile expression on her face. Her features seem coarser because of the gloom in her soul. She's doing the best she can. We take the lift together. Although we're alone, I don't put a finger on her. Now I feel sorry for her; she's walking down the hotel corridor with her shabby high-heeled shoes, and I feel sorry for her. Our rooms are on the same floor. There's no one around. Italia comes into my room. She remains standing, not even looking around, and gnaws her hands.

The conference goes on for four days: lectures, meetings, refresher courses. Italia doesn't want to leave the hotel; she stays in bed and watches television. I order her something to eat and have it delivered to her room. I eat dinner in the hotel restaurant with my colleagues. I'm not in a hurry; I savour the food, talk, make jokes. A subtle pleasure mounts inside me. She's upstairs, hidden, ready to slip into my arms. The door is locked, and she's waiting for me. Every time I knock, I hear her bare feet hurrying across the wall-to-wall carpet. She speaks softly – she's always afraid that someone can hear us. She feels bad about that other room, the one that's empty and unused. When she read the price on the door, she turned red. She takes nothing from the minibar, not even mineral water; she drinks from the tap. I get irritated, but she persists. And she doesn't even leave the room when the maids come to tidy it up; she sits in a corner and watches them. At night, we make love for hours on end; we never fall asleep. Italia twists her neck over the edge of the pillow, her throat trembles, her hair brushes the floor. It's as if she's looking for something beyond me, a place where she can be reunited with a lost part of herself. She takes flight; pieces of her flee from my hands. Her eyes watch the window, which reflects the lights in the interior courtyard of the hotel. Down below, there's a fountain that gets turned off every night at a certain hour. Italia gets out of bed to watch the spouts shut down; she likes to see that final spurt. She doesn't talk much, she doesn't lay claim to any position; she knows she's not a bride on her honeymoon. *I'll never know how many men have loved her before me, but I know that each of them, whether he was good to her or did her wrong, did his part in shaping her, in making her what she is.*

The second evening, we leave my room in the middle of the night, drop off the key at the desk and slip out of the lobby. Italia's wearing a pair of white shoes I saw in a shop window and bought for her. They're too big for her feet, so she's padded them with a bit of toilet paper. The little town, built on a steep hillside, is a warren of narrow streets with rough stone houses. Italia's new shoes are too wide; her heels come out of them with every step. We hike up past the town hall, all the way to the fortress, where we stand on the lookout platform and gaze out over the plain, a sea of darkness studded with points of light. We go down a few steps and find ourselves in an open area paved with cobblestones. In the centre of this space, there are a few pieces of children's playground equipment. A swing, jostled by the breeze sweeping this high ground, grates and squeaks. In the darkness, only the illuminated bell tower with its Romanesque spires stands out among the black roofs. We sit on a stone bench and look at the wooden horse a few feet away – it's got a giant spring where its legs should be – and a tinge of melancholy seeps into our secret tryst. This playground without any children makes us sad. The swing squeaks incessantly, spoiling the mood. Italia gets up, walks over to the swing and sits down on its iron seat. She gives herself a push, then another. Her legs thrust up into the air; her back comes and goes. She allows her shoes, white as a bride's, to fall from her feet.

The next day, I find her in the corridor. She's struck up a friendship with the hotel chambermaids; as they move from one room to another, she follows their cart, helping them out by stooping to the pile of clean sheets and handing them as many as they need. She doesn't see me right away, and so I have time to watch her. She's talking fast, in her southern accent, more herself among those young women in their smocks. She has sneaked away from her prison and joined up with some of her own kind. Clowning around, she puts a shower cap on her dry hair and imitates a demanding hotel guest whose water ran out while she was taking a shower. The plump girl by her side laughs heartily. I didn't know Italia was such a joker. I call her; she turns towards me, and so do the maids. Italia snatches the cap from her head and comes towards me. Her face is blushing red, and she's trembling like a little girl. She whispers, 'You're back already?'

The last night we're there, she has dinner in the hotel restaurant. It was my idea; I pleaded with her to come downstairs. I felt like seeing her in the midst of all those people who don't know about us and would think us strangers to each other. Arriving late, she hurries over to a table at the back, near a glass door that opens on to another large room. The people I'm dining with are exhaling wine fumes and professional malice. Manlio arrived only that morning, and already he's fed up. He's firing potshots at an American researcher, a guru in the field of alternative pharmacology, whose distaste for Manlio extends to his cigarette smoke. My friend's gold lighter lies on the table next to his napkin. I wonder what Italia's ordered; I'd like to serve her a glass of wine. They haven't brought her anything yet – maybe they've forgotten her – and I look around the room, searching for the waiter. She doesn't seem very calm. She's come into the restaurant as a favour to me, and now, with her elbows on the table and one hand picking at her chin, she can't wait to leave. Even at this distance, I can sense her embarrassment. The waiter arrives, leaning towards her and taking the lid off whatever he's carrying. Maybe it's soup, because Italia eats it with her spoon. I turn to Manlio; he's staring at her. Before long, she notices, stops eating and starts playing with a corner of her napkin. She raises her eyes and lets them wander, without any attempt at caution, as far as I can see, into Manlio's line of sight. Once again, she has that brazen expression on her face. Manlio pokes me with an elbow and hisses, 'She's looking at me.' His smile is so wide, it distends his lower jaw. 'She's alone. Let's invite her for a drink, shall we?'

And before I can stop him – assuming, of course, that I even want to – he's on his feet. He keeps that chimpanzee smile on his face all the way to her table. Our other dinner companions, by now a little tipsy, burst out laughing. I watch Italia shake her head, rise to her feet, take a few steps backwards, collide with the dessert trolley and leave the restaurant. Manlio returns to his seat beside me and reaches for his gold cigarette lighter. 'From a distance, she just looked trashy,' he says. 'But up close, she's ugly.'

She's on the bed, paging through the hotel brochure. 'Who was that clod?' she asks without looking up.

I say, 'He's a cloddish gynaecological surgeon.'

I've eaten well, I've drunk well and I feel like making love. But Italia takes too long in the bathroom, and when she comes out, she doesn't get in bed. She puts a chair close to the window and looks down at the hotel courtyard. The light rising from below turns her face yellow; she's waiting for the fountain to die away.

Italia has made some sandwiches for our return trip. She went out and bought bread, cheese and salami, then came back and broke up the bread on the bed. When I woke up, she was picking crumbs off the spread. On the way to the lift, she said goodbye to the maids. They exchanged addresses and embraced one another like sisters. In the car, during the drive back, we don't talk much. Somewhere along the way, Italia says, 'You're ashamed of me, right?' She says it without looking at me, huddled against the door on her side and staring at the road. Her patchwork bag is filled with the little jars of honey and preserves she got with breakfast at the hotel; she saved them every morning. I smile, stretch out my hand and adjust the rear-view mirror. My head is a muddle of confused thoughts, mingling with one another, despite their lack of any definite connection. Elsa called my room this morning. When the phone rang, our bags were already packed. I thought it was the hotel desk, and I answered carelessly. Italia said something, something about her ID card – she'd forgotten to get it back from the desk – and your mother heard her voice. 'Who's there with you?' she asked.

I said it was the maid – that the door was open and I was about to leave. Towards the end, I raised my voice. She asked me, 'Why are you getting angry?'

'Because I'm in a hurry.'

Then I apologised. She talked for a little while longer, but her voice was slightly different. And as I drive, I'm thinking that I no longer know exactly what I'm doing. I drop Italia off in front of the unfinished block of flats, the one with the squatters. Before she gets out, I catch up her hand and kiss it. I'm in a hurry to get away from her; maybe she realises that. I'm nice and polite – I get her case out of the boot for her – but when she disappears into the entrance, sucked inside that bad smell, I breathe a sigh of relief. I don't stay a minute longer. This morning, the whole place strikes me as appalling.

I go directly to the hospital and plunge single-mindedly into my work. The scrub nurse is a bit uncertain – she must be new – and passes me the instruments without any force. I get angry. She drops the forceps. With a kick, I send those forceps spinning to the other side of the operating theatre.

The summer's almost over. In the beach house, your mother's starting to gather her things together. I'm sitting in the garden, looking at the Big Dipper, the Little Dipper and the North Star. She comes out and joins me. She's got a sweater over her shoulders and a glass in her hand. 'Do you want something to drink?' she asks.

I shake my head.

'What's wrong?'

'Nothing.'

'Are you sure?'

The autumn will come, the sea will turn grey, the sand will be dirty, the wind will blow it around and the house will already be shut up. Elsa can feel that little twinge of melancholy in her shoulders.

In bed, she snuggles close to me; she wants to make love. She asks, 'Do you want to go to sleep?'

I lie quietly, keeping to my side of the bed, facing away from her. I ask her, 'Do you mind if I do?'

She minds. She stops kissing me, but she deliberately keeps breathing on me. The heavy sound of her breath penetrates my drowsiness. 'I'm sorry,' I say. 'I'm really tired . . .'

I turn towards her. Her face is like iron in the dark. Her body rustles the sheets and moves away from mine. Now she turns her back on me. I wait. I don't want her to be sad. I reach out to her, but she shakes off my hand with a slight movement of her shoulder. 'Let's go to sleep,' she says.

★

The next morning, I get up late and find Elsa in the kitchen, wearing her raw-silk dressing gown. 'Hi,' I say. 'Hi,' she says. I put water and ground coffee in the little espresso maker, set it on the stove and sit down to wait. My wife is tall; her shoulders form a perfect trapezoid, wide across the top, with two oblique lines running down to her narrow waist. She's putting some long-stemmed flowers in a vase.

'Where did you get them?' I ask.

'Raffaella gave them to me.'

She's still angry. I can tell from her hands, which are making short, sharp movements, whose sole purpose is to ignore me. I think, How long has it been since I gave her flowers? And perhaps she's having the very same thought. She's tucked her hair behind her ears. She's standing in front of the window, silhouetted against a vivid light barely softened by the cotton curtain. I look at her profile. Her pale lips are two pads of grouchy flesh. Those lips reflect many thoughts about me, not all of them favourable. I get to my feet, fill my little cup and sip my coffee. I say, 'Do you want some?'

'No.'

I pour another cup and drink that one, too. Elsa cuts herself, drops the scissors on to the table and raises the wounded finger to her mouth. I go to her. 'It's nothing,' she says. But I take her hand and hold it under running water. Her blood turns the water pink before it disappears down the black hole in the middle of the sink. I dry her finger on my T-shirt, then go to the medicine cabinet for the disinfectant and the plasters. Your mother doesn't object; she likes it when I take care of her as her doctor. Then I kiss the back of her neck. I find that it's right next to me, her neck, and so I kiss it, there at the line where her nape disappears under the mass of her hair. And we embrace in the kitchen, leaning against the flower-strewn table.

When I get out of the shower, she's in a sheltered corner of the living room, typing. She has to work fast, she says, because her deadline's approaching and she's behind schedule. She's no longer interested in swimming and sunbathing; her deep tan will start to fade now and continue to fade all winter long. She hasn't got dressed – she's still in her dressing gown. The silk cloth spreads out on the floor at her feet, revealing her legs. I've put Tchaikovsky's *Pathétique* Symphony on the turntable, and the notes invade the sunny living room like a crystal shower. I sit there barefoot, reading. Your mother's eyes scan the keyboard. Every now and then, she stops typing, rips the sheet of paper out of the machine, crumples it up and drops it into the wicker wastebasket beside her. She's naturally haughty; there's a prideful intentionality in everything about her, including the lines of her body. She doesn't belong to me; she's never belonged to me. Now I'm sure of it. *We're not meant to belong to each other; we're meant to live together, to share the same bidet.*

She looks up, abandons her typewriter and comes towards me. She sits down on the sofa, facing me, with one leg folded under her buttocks and one bare foot brushing the floor. She starts talking, and her words are a planned manoeuvre, an encirclement. She starts with generic chit-chat about her work, about one of her colleagues at the newspaper who's behaved badly, but then she asks me point-blank, 'What did you do at the conference?' And next she wants to know who was there and who wasn't, and I feel the circle closing around me when she says, 'So how was the room?'

'Anonymous.'

I smile. I'm not the one who's having trouble; she is. I'm letting her stew in her thoughts, but I couldn't be calmer. If she has something to ask me, let her ask away. *Be strong, dear wife; don't stop. If you really need total clarity this time, you're going to have to reach it by yourself, without any help from me.* Try as I may, I don't feel guilty. Tchaikovsky plays on, but this morning I don't find anything all that dramatic in his music. Elsa is pitilessly torturing a hank of her hair, which looks white because of the sun behind it. She's struggling, trapped between her curiosity and her fear of suffering. If she asks me to, I'm ready to blow the lid off of everything, right now; but truth has sweaty armpits and is therefore unsuitable for my regal wife. She looks at me in a familiar way, a way I recognise, and yet there's something different. For the first time, I feel capable of figuring out what lies imprisoned inside those opaque eyes: there's a deficiency, a stop sign, a wall. Her eyes are the eyes of a stupid woman. This is an explosive discovery: behind so much apparent intelligence, there's a part of her that is resolutely blind. It's almost an absence of conscience; it gives her an escape hatch, a refuge from pain. Those are the eyes she puts on when she's having trouble, the ones she uses to pretend she understands me, when, in fact, she's leaving me on my own.

Now she gets up and heads for the kitchen, her straight back and her magnificent hair bouncing with every step. When she's almost at the door, I take aim at the middle of her body and hurl my knife: 'You want to know if I'm screwing somebody else?'

She turns round. 'Did you say something?'

Tchaikovsky's fortissimi have covered my words. She hasn't heard me. Or maybe she has, and that's why she staggers a little.

That night, we make love. And it's your mother who ravishes me; I've never seen her so audacious. 'Easy,' I murmur through giggles. 'Take it easy.' But she's stronger than I am, and she has a project. She's discharging on to me a mighty load of pent-up energy; tonight, I'm her ground wire. Inspired, no doubt, by some movie or something she's read, she's putting on an erotic farce. The effect she's decided to go for tonight is burning passion. And I'm caught in the midst of it, a spavined nag flung into a race at full gallop. Now she slips under me and pants against my stomach. I'm not used to seeing her so submissive. It makes me feel guilty, as though I'm the cause of her choosing to abase herself. I want to go away, to escape from the bed, but instead, I stay where I am. By now, I'm excited, too, for I've looked at your mother's head and I've thought . . . a thought that excites me. I fall upon her body; I mistreat her. I push her to the foot of the bed and take her like a goat, and while I'm doing it, I'm wondering what I'm doing.

Afterwards, she lies under me like a broken egg. Then she turns over in her shattered shell and looks at me with new intention. She seems happy and cruel, like a witch who's cast a successful spell. For the first time since we met, I think about leaving her.

My lover's little body lay curled up on the edge of the bed. I was looking at the point where her thin back broadened into her buttocks. I'd licked her all over; my tongue had travelled from her hairline to her feet, slipping into every cleft, into the spaces between her toes. She liked it, but it made her shiver, and my passage left goose pimples on her skin. I realised that was how I wanted to love her: stroke by stroke, in stillness, in silence. It was no longer the way it had been; our embraces weren't so blind and furious as they used to be. I'd taken up the habit of holding her down on the bed and just kissing her. I wanted my ministrations to be a means by which she might perceive herself. I'd plough her skin with my tongue; towards the end, it would begin to ache, and I'd run out of saliva. When having sex, she was immodest, almost shameless; but she felt embarrassed by the tough calluses on the soles of her feet, and she felt embarrassed by love. I took her only at the end, when I was already tired. I slipped inside her like a dog – a dog that has run for days, through brambles and briers and rocks, finally finds its way home and creeps exhausted into its bed.

She whispered, 'Leave me.' Her voice was thin and cold, like a strip of metal.

'What are you saying?' I drew close to her and stroked her lonely back.

'I can't, I just can't any more . . .' she said. She shook her head. 'It's better to do it now, don't you see? Now.' She was holding her face in her hands. 'If you love me at all, leave me.'

I held her close; her elbows dug into my skin. 'I'll never leave you.'

And I was so sure of what I was saying that my body hardened, every fibre in me hardened, as if I'd grown a mighty carapace. And we stayed like that, our chins on each other's shoulders, each of us staring into a separate void.

What does *love* mean, Angela? Do you know? For me, love meant holding Italia's breathing in my arms and realising that every other sound had fallen silent. I'm a doctor; I can always recognise the pulsations of my heart, even when I don't want to. I swear to you, Angela, the heart that was beating inside me was Italia's.

She has a recurring dream. She dreams that her train leaves without her. She gets to the station early. She's wearing a nice dress. She buys a magazine and steps out on to the sheltered platform, perfectly calm. The train's there, waiting for her; an elegant train, she says, red and grey and gleaming. She's about to board it, but then she starts wasting time, digging around in her bag, looking for her ticket. After she finds it, she loses more time trying to read the destination. The train leaves the platform, and she's still there; but now her bag is gone, and so are her shoes. Then the station behind her is empty and she's naked, 'like in a painting,' she says.

She told me that dream had tormented her for a long time, from when she was a young girl, and then it had vanished; but it came back after she met me.

I believe we punish ourselves with our dreams, Angela. They don't seem much like rewards.

'Give me your hand,' she said. 'The left one.'

She spread it out, passing her palm over mine as though she wanted to clean it, to disencumber it of other things: dusty things, of no concern to us. 'You've got a long lifeline, with a break in the middle.'

I don't believe in such nonsense, so I shrugged my shoulders. 'What does it mean?' I asked.

'It means you'll survive.'

But now I wonder if that break was you, Angela. If Italia encountered you in my hand.

'Now make a fist, tight, and we'll see about your children.' She scrutinised the creases around my little finger. 'There's one – no, two. Bravo!' she said. She started to laugh.

'How about you?' I said. 'Show me your hand. What's your lifeline like?'

She stood up, but she didn't stop laughing. 'Don't worry. It's really, really long – weeds are hard to kill. My mother used to call me "Crabgrass".'

After we said goodbye, she ran after me and threw her arms around me. 'Don't ever take me seriously when I tell you to leave me,' she said. 'Keep me, please, keep me. Come when you want, once a month, once a year, but keep me.'

'Of course I'll keep you. I love you, Crabgrass.'

She burst into tears, an eruption of tears, tears that burned me like lava. 'Why?' I asked.

She stepped away from me. Her face was red; her eyes were red. She stared into mine, and then she started punching me on the arm. 'I've been screwing since I was twelve, and no one ever said to me "I love you". If you're fooling me, I'll kill you.'

'With these little fists?'

'Yes!'

And you, Angela, have you ever made love? I remember the day you became a woman, three years ago. You were at school, an English lesson; the teacher took you to the principal's office. You called your mother at the newspaper, and she picked you up and drove you home. When she joked with you in the car, you smiled weakly, like a sick person. You were confused and a little angry. You'd been waiting for that moment, but now growing up didn't seem so great. You were always a tough, independent child, accustomed to handling things on your own. Now you were twelve, sprouting up like a mushroom, but you still had a child's body – your girlfriends were way ahead of you – and your thoughts and your games were those of a child. But in spite of all that, something had moved inside of you. Your first egg had matured and fallen away, and the end of your childhood was sealed with your blood.

Your mother met me at the door and told me what had happened. There was a light in her face. She wasn't the same person who'd left the house that morning; now she had the face of a midwife. You women are so changeable, so ready to grab hold of life, to capture all the butterflies. We males are like earthworms, lined up at the foot of your walls. I smiled, dawdling as I took off my overcoat. You were lying on your bed. With those big black eyes of yours and that long face, you looked like a skinny cat.

I walked over to you, leaned down and said your name: 'Angela . . .'

You barely smiled, crinkling your pale skin a little. 'Hi, Daddy.'

I had no idea what I wanted to tell you, and nothing came out. At that moment, you and your mother were alone together, and I was an awkward guest, the kind that knocks over glasses. You were lying with your hands on your stomach; your legs were bent, unmoving. You were my little asparagus, my favourite perfume. How many times had I pushed you on a swing? How many times had you swung away and then back into my hands? And yet I didn't try to hold that moment, I let it go – maybe I didn't even feel like pushing you; maybe I wanted to read the paper. I brushed your forehead with my fingers. 'Good girl,' I said. 'Good girl.'

Later, in my study, bent under the art nouveau fixture that sheds a warm light on my desk and my bald head, I'm still thinking about you, Angela. I've beaten a retreat to my lair, leaving the rest of the house to you two women, along with the white cloths, the pads, the virgin blood. Your mother has brewed some tea and carried it into your room on the tray she bought in London, the one with the cats. You'll sit on the rug with your legs crossed like two young girls and dunk *biscotti* into your tea. Today's a special day. We'll stay home, where it's nice and warm. And we won't have dinner. Later, I'll go to the kitchen and eat a little cheese, by myself. I think about the day that's coming, when you'll make love for the first time. A man will approach you with his hands, with his patter. He'll approach my long, lean girl, whose trousers are always too short for her, and he won't want to swap picture cards or claim his turn on the swing; he'll want to stick his dick in you. I squash my eyes with my hands, violently, because the image that rises up before my sight is too strong. I'm your father; for me, your sex is that sandwich of hairless flesh that gets filled up with sand on the beach. But I'm a man, too, and once I was a livid, barbarous man who raped a woman, a girl grown old before her time. I did it because I loved her right away and I didn't want to love her; I did it to kill her and I wanted to save her. While I knead my eyes to drive away that image of myself, I see a person, a male with a lustful back, approaching you. And now I snatch him by the scruff of the neck and I tell him, *Be careful. That's Angela, the joy of my life.* Then I let him go. And I let these offensive thoughts go, too; I have no right to think about you making love. It will be the way you want it to be. It will be sweet. It will be with a better man than I am.

My birthday. It's not an anniversary that I particularly welcome, as you know; despite the passage of time, I still feel the same bitterness I felt when I was a little boy. The schools weren't open yet, my friends had absconded to parts unknown, and so I never had a real party. When I was growing up, I started ignoring the date myself. Later, I begged your mother not to waste time organising surprise parties, which I've never found at all surprising. She took me at my word, and without ever confessing it, I felt a certain amount of resentment towards her for having agreed so readily to disregard me.

It wasn't one of my best days. The sun remained smothered behind a great mass of chalky, amorphous clouds. Your grandparents, my in-laws, who had just come back from a cruise in the Red Sea, were visiting us. In the afternoon, we went and sat under the beach umbrellas. Grandma Nora's suntan was spotted with abrasions inflicted upon her by her beautician in an effort to erase her age spots. The visor of a master mariner's cap shaded Grandpa Duilio's forehead. This was his standard summer outfit: shorts, long socks snug around his still-robust calves, rope-soled shoes. He sat in a low beach chair and drummed on his knees with his fingers, beating time to his mighty silence. I didn't feel comfortable with my father-in-law. You know him as he is today – vague, gentle, and always very affectionate with you. But sixteen years ago, he still retained the arrogant manner and the disinclination to pardon that had carried him so high in his profession. He was one of the most powerful architects in the city; when he dies, he'll definitely get a street named after him. Back then, he was just starting to be an old man, and he had a lot of trouble staying in the discreet corner indicated by his age. He behaved horribly towards his wife, who was too flighty to notice. Elsa felt an authentic veneration for her father; in the first years of our marriage, I used to get offended by the inordinate amount of attention she lavished on him. When he was present, I didn't exist. Then, with the passage of time, things improved. He grew unequivocally old, and, unfortunately, I began to age, too. Now that he spends his days in front of the television set with the little Philippine woman who assists him, we're good friends, as you know. If I don't drop by at least twice a week and take his blood pressure, his feelings are hurt.

Elsa was lying on her side with her face in her arms, talking to her mother. I would say theirs was a moderately close relationship; Elsa couldn't completely forgive poor Nora for being so frivolous. Like her father, Elsa has never been indulgent – that's her real weakness. 'My mother is so good-hearted,' she'd say, 'and such a nitwit.' After Nora died, she miraculously stopped being a nitwit. Driven by a furtive impulse from her unconscious, Elsa began to mould her mother into a different woman, vulnerable but strong-willed, and a shining example to herself. This process is now complete; a few days ago, I heard her tell you, 'Your grandmother didn't have a lot of education, but she was the most intelligent woman I've ever known.' I looked at her, and she returned my look quite calmly. Your mother knows how to forget; she knows how to move things around so that they're available to her in the proper form and at the exact moment when she wants to make use of them. On the one hand, this is unconscionable; on the other, it's as if she gives everyone and everything around her the power to be continually born again. I must have been reborn under her hands many times without noticing it.

So there I was, buried in the silence of the familiar life. In this setting, I was a free man; I didn't need to hide. The people here knew me; my wife, my father-in-law, everybody knew me.

And yet it seemed to me that *this* was the parallel life, not the other one. That one, the one with Italia – with its whispers, its segregation – that was the real life. Secret, enclosed, frightened, but real.

A woman was swimming in the sea, her head disappearing and reappearing in the foam. She emerged from the waist up and wrung out her hair, twisting it in her hands, then shook her head. As she waded ashore through the increasingly shallow water, her figure was gradually revealed. She was wearing a turquoise two-piece swimsuit. She didn't have a suntan. Her white belly protruded slightly, the way children's stomachs do when they've just eaten. She headed in my direction, swinging her bony hips. I thought I could hear the rush of her breath and the sound the sea water made when it dripped from her moving body and fell on to the sand. I thought I wanted to raise an arm and stop her, but none of my limbs budged. Everything was at a standstill; everything was frozen. She alone was in motion, in slow motion. Fixed in my block of stone, I waited for the end. She passed us, and I couldn't even find the courage to turn my head and follow her with my eyes. The shock had stiffened my neck. But the mirage of her – that wan shape, kicking up sand as it approached – stayed locked in my irises.

Then the soundtrack came back up around me: first, the whistling of the wind, which had started to blow again; next, my mother-in-law's chattering, which gradually grew more and more audible; and finally, my father-in-law's laboured breathing. It was like what happens when you're out in a boat and you approach the shore and you begin to hear the murmur of the beach, closer and closer. At last, I turned my head, but behind me I saw only the sandy wall formed by the dunes. Italia had vanished.

I passed the remains of the day in a trance. Everything seemed excessive; voices were too piercing, gestures too aggressive. Who were these dull people? Who parked them in my house? And to think, there was a time when I believed marrying into this family of respectable imbeciles meant a big step up on the social ladder! At dinner, I could barely lift my fork to my lips;

the distance between the plate and my mouth had increased enormously. I left the table and went to the bathroom. My mother-in-law's Yorkshire terrier lunged at me with bared teeth out of a dark corner in the hall. I replied to the attentions of this little parlour mutt with a solid kick. He ran limping to his mistress, who was already rushing to his side. 'I'm sorry, Nora,' I said. 'I accidentally stepped on him.'

I went upstairs and lay down on a rug. I felt like one of those limp worms that hang on dried-up shrubs in the summer – one of those stupefied, tremulous worms that fall to the earth without a sound.

Elsa's parents left after dinner, and I was right behind them. Elsa had asked me to follow them back to the outskirts of the city, where the first street lights were. My father-in-law was driving slowly along dark country roads that he didn't know very well. I looked through the window at those two mute, immobile heads. What were they thinking about? Death? It's easy to think about death on a Sunday evening. Or maybe they were thinking about life – that is, about buying something or eating something. In the end, life becomes unadulterated greediness. You take, and you just don't feel like giving anything in return. So there they were, en route to the same silence that Elsa and I were heading for. In a few years, the solitude my headlights were shining on would be ours as well. I had two puppets in front of me, cruising into the night. But I still had time to stop, to change direction and consign myself to life again. To a different life, one in which I probably wouldn't live long enough to reach the same state as those ancient figures in front of me.

I yanked the wheel to the right and stopped on the edge of the asphalt. My in-laws' car disappeared round a pitch-black curve in the road. That evening, I felt I would die young, and I knew that Italia was a gift I wouldn't turn down.

I said, 'How did you find the house?'

'I walked along the beach.'

'But why?'

'I wanted to give you a birthday present. I wanted you to see me in my bikini.'

She was in her bathrobe, half asleep and holding her dog.

'I'll let you go back to bed.'

'No, let's go out.'

In the street, she took my arm and walked along slowly. We went into the usual bar. 'What will you have?' I asked her.

She didn't answer. She was leaning on the counter with all her weight. I saw her hand sliding over the metal surface towards the paper napkins. With a jerk, she ripped them from their container and rushed back out the door, bent forward and limping. When I caught up with her, she was leaning on the wall with her head down.

'What's wrong?'

She was squeezing her hands between her thighs, and her hands were squeezing the wad of napkins. 'I don't feel good,' she whispered. 'Take me home.'

There wasn't very much light, but I could see that the white napkins had turned dark between her fingers. 'You're losing blood,' I said.

'Please, take me home.'

But she fainted on the way. I picked her up, carried her to my car and put her in the passenger seat. I'd decided to run the risk of taking her to the hospital. As I drove, I tried to work out whether one of my friends was on duty that night. She came to;

her face was ashen, and she gazed sad-eyed at the city lights. 'Where are we going?'

'To a hospital.'

'No, I want to go home. I feel better.'

She slid off the seat and squatted on the floor under the dashboard. 'What are you doing?'

'This way, I won't soil the seat.'

I took one hand off the wheel, leaned towards her, and grabbed a handful of her T-shirt. 'Get up out of there!'

But she managed to hold her ground. 'I'm fine down here,' she said. 'I'm watching you.'

The casualty department was practically empty. The only patient was an old man, sitting in a corner with a blanket draped across his shoulders. I knew one of the nurses on duty, a portly young man with whom I occasionally talked about football. I'd found a terry-cloth beach towel on the back seat of the car and given it to Italia, who wrapped it round her hips. The nurse made her lie down on a stretcher in the first-aid area. She lay there with her neck twisted round, looking at me. The physician on duty, a young woman, arrived almost at once. I didn't remember ever having seen her before. She said, 'Come, we'll go upstairs and do an ultrasound.'

The three of us got into the lift. The doctor's face looked as though she'd been asleep – her hair was pressed flat on one side – but she smiled at me obsequiously, plainly well aware of who I was. Italia had walked into the lift on her own two legs, and her colour was somewhat improved.

While the physician was examining her, I went over to my wing of the hospital. I wanted to check on a patient I'd operated on the previous day. I stood beside his bed; he was asleep, breathing normally. The nurse who'd followed me into the room asked, 'Can we remove his drain tube tomorrow, Doctor?'

When I returned, Italia was coming out of the ultrasound room. 'Everything's all right,' the physician said. 'The placenta has partially detached, but the embryo is in good shape.'

For a fraction of a second, I stared at the physician's face: square jaw, shiny nose, eyes too close together. I took a step backwards and instinctively looked over her shoulder, as if I was afraid someone had overheard her. 'Fine,' I think I said. 'Fine.'

The woman had no doubt detected my agitation. Now she was giving me a look of strange complicity. 'Nevertheless, Doctor, I think the lady should stay in the hospital. The best thing for her would be complete rest, at least for a while.'

The lady in question, dazed, confused and visibly agitated, was hovering a few steps away. She wasn't a lady; she was an unmarried woman, and also my lover. For just an instant, we exchanged surreptitious looks. I moved slightly, shifting my weight to my other leg and effectively removing her from my line of sight. I mustn't have any sort of contact with her, at least for now. I was there in my hospital, face to face with a woman who knew me by my professional reputation and now, in addition, had surely guessed a few things about my private life. I thought, I must get Italia out of here; she has to disappear first, and then I can think about what to do next. We were walking towards the lift; the doctor's buttocks undulated under her smock. What guarantee did I have that this woman was discreet? There was something careless about the way she walked. Maybe by tomorrow, the news would be making the rounds in the hospital. Sly glances would be aimed my way like arrows, piercing my back. There would be gossip I'd be helpless to stop. Italia was behind me, and now I was furious with her. She hadn't told me a thing; she'd kept me in the dark. She'd hidden this news from me, this news of all news, and left me to find it out from a stranger, right here in my hospital. She'd enjoyed the look of astonishment on my face. I almost felt like hitting her, like giving her a good smack, five fingers printed red across her lying mug.

We went downstairs to Admissions. I turned to Italia, and with a look that must have seemed terrible to her, I said, 'Well, madam, what do you want to do?'

She stammered, 'I want to go home.'

I turned to the nurse. 'The lady will sign a discharge form,' I said. 'Give me one.'

I took a pen from the inside pocket of my jacket and filled out the form myself, then shoved it under Italia's gnawed hands and held out my pen. When I looked at her face, I saw that she'd become quite pale again. I lost all certainty about what I was doing and held on to the pen. I was a doctor; I couldn't put her at risk. Suppose she should have a haemorrhage – what would I do then? I couldn't let her go like that. I'd get my chance to abuse her later on, but now it was important for her to stay in the hospital, where she'd be safe. I tore up the form. 'Let's admit her.'

She made an effort to resist, but it wasn't very forceful: 'No – I want to leave here – I'm fine.'

The physician was still with us, and she took a step towards Italia. 'Madam, the doctor's right. It would be better for you to stay here tonight.'

We dispatched the admissions process in a hurry and went back upstairs to Gynaecology. The lift doors opened on to the nocturnal silence of the corridor and the usual smells of medicine and soup. I love the hospital at night, Angela. For me, there's something furtive about it, like a woman without make-up, like the whiff of an armpit in the dark. Italia, however, seemed terrified, practically clinging to the wall as she walked. She still had the beach towel with the starfish wrapped around her bum, like a survivor from a shipwreck. We were left alone for a few seconds, so I asked her, 'Why didn't you tell me you were pregnant?'

'I didn't know.'

She pulled the towel tighter around her waist. Her voice trembled as she said, 'I don't want to stay here; I'm all dirty.'

'I'll have one of the staff give you something.'

A nurse came up to us. 'This way, miss. I'll take you to your room.'

'Go on,' I whispered. 'Go on.'

And I watched her move away down the half-lit corridor, never once turning round.

★

Back home, I took off my shoes without undoing the laces and flung them across the room, then lay down on the bed with my clothes on. I sank into a black hole and woke up at dawn, perplexed and still tired. I turned on the shower. Italia was expecting a baby. The water ran along my skin and down my body in channels, and Italia was expecting a baby. What were we going to do now? Naked in the bathroom of the home I shared with my wife, I lathered up the clump of hair in my crotch. I had to slow down and reflect, but instead I was speeding ahead. My thoughts kept overlapping one another, like backdrops in the wings of a theatre.

I got to the hospital very early. I was anxious, because I had a feeling she wouldn't be there. And in fact, she wasn't; she'd signed a discharge form and left.

'When?' I asked the nurse.

'A few minutes ago.'

I got back in my car and started driving along the avenue that borders the hospital grounds. I found her at the bus stop. She was wearing a nurse's smock, and I almost didn't recognise her. She was leaning against the wall, and my beach towel showed through the top of the plastic bag dangling from her fingers.

I pulled up to the kerb not far from her, but she didn't see me. The streets were just beginning to revive. I recalled the time I'd waited for her in my car, spying on her. It was hot; she had make-up on; she swung her hips. I'd liked her high heels, liked her vulgarity. And how much time had passed since then? At the moment, her face bore no trace of make-up, she was dressed in an oversized nurse's smock – she was still losing weight, as she'd done all summer – and, only now, I realised something had changed. Her colour was gone; maybe it was my fault that she was so pale. An unpainted clown. And yet, to me she seemed even more beautiful, even more desirable. I could see nothing else: just her, lined up in my sights with her back against a wall. An insane thought assailed me. *What if someone is indeed taking aim at her? What if a bullet strikes her in the chest and I watch her slide to the ground, leaving only a streak of blood on the wall behind her?* I wanted to shout to her to move away from there, because someone was squeezing the trigger, someone lurking somewhere I couldn't see, maybe on the roof of the hospital. Her face was like that; it was the face of one about to be struck by a blow she hasn't got the strength to avoid. But nothing happened, and she moved away from the wall. The bus arrived, shielding her, and before I had time to stop her, she climbed on. I started to tail the bus, keeping my bumper close to its black exhaust pipe, which belched out clouds of reeking smoke. At the next stop, I left my car double-parked and jumped on the bus, looking for Italia. I wanted to make her get off with me, but I found her too late; the driver had already closed the doors. She was collapsed in a seat, with her head against the window. They're going to tow my car, I thought. Too bad. I said, 'Hi, Crabgrass.'

She jumped, turned her head, caught her breath. 'Hi.'

'Where are you going?'

'To the station.'

'You're taking a trip?'

'No. I want to look at the timetable.'

We remained silent for a while, staring at the streets, which were beginning to fill up with the first traffic of the day. Italia watched a mother and two children cross at a traffic light. I put a hand on her belly, a big steady hand. Her stomach growled. I said, 'How do you feel?'

'Fine,' she said, removing my hand. She was ashamed to be making that rumbling noise.

'How far along are you?'

'Not far. Not even two months.'

'When did it happen?'

'I don't know.'

Her eyes were huge and serene. 'You don't have to worry about anything,' she said. 'You don't have to say anything. I've already made up my mind.'

I shook my head, but I kept quiet. Maybe she was expecting me to say something. She looked out of the window again as the bus jounced along. 'I've got only one favour to ask: Let's not talk about it any more. It's too horrible.'

We got off the bus and walked down the street side by side, not touching each other. Italia was dressed like a nurse, and we were a sorry couple. Inside a shop window, a girl took down the SALE sign and started to arrange the autumn display, walking barefoot on a carpet of plastic leaves and chestnuts. Italia stopped and watched the shop girl slip a dress on a mannequin with ruffled hair. 'Green's in fashion this year,' Italia observed.

We walked towards a taxi rank, where three cabs were waiting. The traffic light was about to change, and we had to run across the street. I opened the door of the first cab for Italia and helped her in, then leaned in myself and put the fare in her hand. 'Thanks,' she whispered.

'Don't worry,' I said in a low voice, not wanting the driver to hear me. 'I'll arrange everything. You just take it easy.'

She tensed her lips in what was supposed to be a smile, but the result was only an exhausted grimace. She wanted to be alone, and maybe she didn't trust me any more. I reached into the cab and passed a hand over her face; I wanted to mollify her wounded, wide-eyed expression. Then I closed the door and the taxi pulled away.

Left to my own devices, I took a few steps. And where was I going? I needed to gather my thoughts; I needed to get my car out of the middle of the street. I was late for the operating theatre, but that couldn't be helped. Right up to the last moment, she'd hoped I'd say something different. I'd seen hope leaning in the depths of her eyes, like a broom forgotten in a corner, and I'd pretended not to notice. I didn't even have the courage to be pitiless, to browbeat her into making her decision. I let her choose for herself, I let her shoulder all the blame, and in exchange I gave her the cab fare.

Your mother has returned to our flat in town, and my solitary bivouac has vanished without a trace. The table I used to rest my feet on while I read has returned to its place in the centre of the carpet, surrounded by sofas and far from my reading chair. And now the inlaid wooden surface of that same little table bears a festive load – glasses with long pink stems, a dish of crudités, a bowl of prunes wrapped in bacon – because Elsa has invited some friends to dinner. I've come home late from the hospital, where I performed an operation that went on for ever. Several members of the operating theatre staff were absent because of the strikes, which started up again in September, and I was slowed down by many errors. When I tossed my keys into the ebony bowl in the hall, I heard the voices coming from the living room. I slipped into the small lavatory off the hall and splashed water on my face before I made my entrance. Hello, hello, hello. Shoulder pats, kisses. Clouds of perfume, shocks of hair, fumes of cigarettes and wine.

I'm leaning on some bookshelves, and Manlio's in front of me. He's speaking on a range of subjects: boats; Martine, who's in the detox centre again; an abdominal suture that came out smooth as a baby's behind and then got infected and hyper-granulated and now has to be done over. Manlio has a cigar in his hand, and that hand's too close to my face.

He says, 'And how are you doing?'

'Manlio, that cigar . . .'

'Oh, right. Sorry.' He moves his arm a little to one side.

'I have to talk to you.'

He looks at me and expels a large puff of malodorous smoke. 'You look like a zombie. What have you done?'

'We're serving the pasta.'

I don't take part in any of the conversation at the table. I eat, stare at my plate, wield my fork, drink a glass of wine, then reach for the tureen and take a second helping. I'm boorishly hungry. The table is a clamour of sounds and voices. I spy on the tablecloth a fallen *rigatone,* which I pick up with my fingers. Your mother looks at me. She's wearing a green watered-silk top with transparent openwork stripes, and a small emerald adorns each of her ears. Her hair is pulled back, except for one loose lock falling across her forehead; she's very beautiful. I think about that barefoot girl in the shop window, and Italia remarking that green's in fashion this year. I get up from the table.

'You don't want dessert?'

'Excuse me, I have to make a phone call.'

I go to the bedroom and dial the number, which rings away. I lie down on the bed. Elsa comes into the room and asks, 'Who are you talking to?'

'No one. The line's busy.'

She goes into our bathroom and pees. I can see her reflection in the armoire mirror, her skirt hitched up over her behind. She says, 'A patient?'

'Right.'

She pulls the chain, turns out the light, and leaves the bathroom. 'A "noteworthy" cancer?' she asks, smiling. It's not easy to live with a man who has such a sad profession. Sometimes she uses my jargon, but only to make fun of it.

I smile in response.

'At least take your shoes off the bed,' she says as she leaves the room.

'Hello?'

'Where were you?'

'Here.'

'I called and called.'

'Maybe I couldn't hear you.' She's breathing hard, surrounded by a great roaring.

'What is that?'

'The vacuum cleaner. Wait – I'll turn it off.'

She goes away, the roaring stops and she comes back.

'What are you doing cleaning the house at this hour?'

'It's therapy.'

'I wanted to send you a kiss.'

Manlio's outside with me – I've dragged him on to the terrace. I tell him, 'I operated on this patient's breast two years ago. Now she's pregnant, but it's too risky. She needs to terminate the pregnancy.'

'She's in the first trimester?'

'Yes.'

'So why doesn't she go to hospital?'

Down in the street, one of the municipal dustcarts is lifting a rubbish container. Manlio turns up his collar and starts whistling softly. Maybe he understands.

The party ends on the sofas; eventually, their occupants depart, and all that's left are the deep imprints left by their bodies, the crushed sofa pillows, the glasses everywhere and the overflowing ashtrays. Elsa already has her shoes off. 'Good party,' she says.

'Yes.'

I rise and pick up an ashtray.

'Don't touch anything. Gianna will see to it tomorrow.'

'I just want to toss the cigarette butts so they don't stink up the room.'

She goes into the bedroom, removes her make-up and puts on her nightshirt. I stay in the living room for a while, looking at television in the midst of that cemetery of dirty glasses. Eventually, I join her; I lie on the edge of the bed, make a few adjustments and settle down, stretched out on one side. Your mother throws a leg across me, and then her warm mouth grazes my ear. I freeze; I can't do it, not tonight, I really can't. She searches for my mouth and finds it, but I don't open my lips. With a sigh, she falls back on the sheet, face down. 'You know,' she says, 'maybe we could try making love in a different way.'

I turn towards her. She's staring at the ceiling now, a strange look on her face. She goes on: 'We could try looking into each other's eyes.' There's an undertone of spite in her voice that hums proudly around every word.

'Are you drunk?' I ask.

'A little.'

It seems to me that her eyes are shining and her chin is trembling. I say, 'We look at each other; you know we do. You're so beautiful, why wouldn't I want to look at you?'

I lie on my back and adjust the pillow, but I'm not sleepy. I think, Let the night of conjugal attrition begin; let us dance the retaliation waltz. But what I get is a kick in the stomach, followed at once by another and another after that. Then your mother is slapping me in the face with both hands. I try to ward her off, but her attack has caught me completely unprepared.

'You! You! Who do you think you are? Who the hell do you think you are?'

Her face is contorted; her voice is hoarse. I've never seen her like this. I let her hit me. I pity myself and her, too, as she gropes for sufficiently insulting words. 'You're . . . you're . . . you're a shit! A selfish shit!'

I manage to capture one of her hands and then the other. I embrace her. She weeps. I stroke her head while she pants between sobs. *You're right, Elsa, I'm a selfish shit. I'm ruining everyone's life, all the people who are close to me, but believe me, I have no idea what I want. I'm simply marking time. I desire a woman, but it may be that I'm ashamed of her, I'm ashamed of desiring her. I'm afraid of losing you, but it may be that I'm doing my best to make you leave me. Yes, I'd like to see you pack a bag and disappear into the heart of the night. I'd run to Italia, and maybe then I'd discover that I miss you. But no, you're not going anywhere. You're staying here, clinging to me, to our bed. You won't go away in the night, you won't do it, you won't take the chance, because it could be that I wouldn't miss you, and you're a prudent woman.*

The windscreen wipers are turned off. There's a film of dirt on the windscreen, a blurry curtain that separates us from the world. The car smells like a car, with its floor mats and its leather seats. (These seem stiffer than usual this morning; they creak every time we move.) There's also a trace of fragrance emanating from the old tree-shaped, sun-faded air freshener, a little of my own smell, my aftershave lotion, and the smell of my raincoat, which hung on a coatrack all summer long but is with me once again, rolled up on the back seat like an old cat. And above all, there's Italia's smell: her ears, her hair, the clothes she's wearing. Today, she's got on a flowered skirt with a broad black elastic waistband and a stiff cotton cardigan. There's a cross on her chest, a silver-plated cross hanging from the tiny links of a thin, thin chain. While she stares through the windscreen at the hazy world, which seems so far away, she puts the cross in her mouth. Her hair bristles with enamelled metal hairpins, many of which are cracked and chipped. She's a little clodhopper who buys her clothes in market stalls, or in those doorless shops with the benumbed, gum-chewing salesgirls. It's the first Saturday in October, and I'm taking her to have an abortion.

She's come into town on the bus. When she saw me waiting at the stop, she smiled. I don't know if she's suffering. We haven't talked about that. Maybe she's already had several abortions; I've never asked her. She seems calm. We didn't kiss when she got into the car. We don't take such risks in the centre of town. She's a prudent traveller, a creature in transit, far from its familiar pen. This morning, she seems austere and stiff, like the cardigan she's wearing. She sucks her silver cross, and I have the sense that she's missing something, something she's forgotten back in her little lair. She's so reserved that I feel somewhat lonely. Perhaps it would be easier for me if she were weepy and depressed, as I expected her to be. Instead, she seems strong this morning, and her eyes are lively and combative. Maybe she's less delicate than I thought, or maybe she's just trying to keep up her courage. I ask her, 'Do you want some breakfast?'

'No.'

The private clinic where Manlio works is a villa built at the beginning of the twentieth century, situated on a piece of woodland and surrounded by trees. We turn into the drive, which climbs amid the dark trunks, and reach an open area where other cars are parked. Italia takes in the building with its pale red terracotta façade. She says, 'It looks like a hotel.'

I've explained everything to her; she knows what she has to do. She'll go to the reception desk, where they're expecting her, and state her name. They'll admit her to the clinic and show her to her reserved room. Naturally, I can't stay with her − it's already a mistake to have accompanied her this far. I'll call her in the afternoon. As we were driving up and she was distracted by the view, I stared at her belly. For a moment, I thought I could see something under her clothes, some swelling. I don't know what I was looking for − something I wouldn't see again? − and then one of my wheels slammed into a huge pothole. I quickly veered and accelerated, but I've remembered that jolt to this day. Time doesn't always move in a straight line; sometimes it operates differently, and a whole life can appear in a flash. In that fraction of a second, when I was trying to steer my car out of that depression in the road, I believe I saw the torment awaiting me, and I saw you, too, Angela; I saw your haematoma on the light scanner. I made a leap into the circular room of time, the leap one makes when the unreal appears and becomes permissible. The room has a multitude of doors, all there in the circle, to be entered in no particular order.

I stop the car in the open area in front of the clinic. Italia looks at the polished glass of the sliding doors; I take her hand and kiss it. 'Don't be worried,' I say. 'It's nothing; it'll be over before you know it.'

'I'm going,' she says, gets out of the car and walks to the entrance. I start to reverse so I can get out of there, and I see her in the rear-view mirror. She's walking even more unsteadily than usual, maybe because of the gravel. However, I know she won't fall; she's used to those excessively high heels, to that bag with the excessively long strap knocking against the insides of her legs. And yet, she *does* fall. She takes one more step and goes down like a sack. She hauls in her bag, but she doesn't get up; she stays huddled up on the ground. And she doesn't turn round, because she's sure I'm already gone. *Don't move,* I say, without knowing what I'm saying. Maybe she knows I'm there. *Don't move.* Because now it seems to me that what she was missing has returned to her. It's covering her back like ragged wings.

I open the car door and sprint across the gravel. 'What's the matter?'

'Breakfast. Maybe I ought to have breakfast.'

I help her to her feet, and as I embrace her, I look up over her head. On the second floor, standing at a big dark window, a man in a white coat is watching us.

So what? What if this is the beginning of the end, if this is the way we enter the darkness? Those eyes of hers are on me; those sticky hands are holding me back. No one has ever loved me like this, no one. I won't carry you in there; I won't let any curette scrape you clean. I want you, and now I'm strong. I'll find a way; I won't ever offend you again.

'Think of yourself,' she whispers. 'I mean it. Think of yourself.'

I've already decided. I love you. And if you want my head, give me a hatchet, and I'll give you the head of a man who loves you.

'Let's get out of here,' I say.

And I was saying that to our child, Angela. Without a sound, a little red leaf fell on my windscreen and slid under the wiper. It was a finely veined leaf, perhaps the first of the season, a gift to us.

I got back behind the wheel and started driving again, further and further away from the clinic. We headed north and stopped in one of the first little towns beyond the city limits, where the landscape changes and gets wilder. It was still an urban setting, but we could smell the woods, and we could feel the breath coming down from the flat-topped mountains that loomed up on the horizon like sleeping buffalo.

We went to a film in one of those cinemas in the provinces that open only on Saturday and Sunday. It was the first showing, and the place was nearly empty. We sat on wooden chairs in the middle of the auditorium, which didn't seem to be heated. Italia laid her head on my shoulder.

'Are you tired?' I asked.

'A little.'

'Go to sleep.'

She stayed like that, dozing on my shoulder in the darkness. The light from the screen barely illuminated her cheek. The film was a comedy, a little trivial, perhaps, but very enjoyable. In fact, I was enjoying everything. Perhaps for the first time, we were a couple. A couple on a holiday trip, taking in a movie, stopping in a bar for a sandwich and then heading out again. Yes, I would have liked to take a trip with Italia, to sleep in hotels, make love and be on our way. Perhaps never to return. We could have gone abroad. I had some friends in Mogadishu. One of them was a cardiologist who worked in a psychiatric hospital. He had a little house by the sea, and there, in the evenings, he smoked marijuana with his lady companion, a woman with legs as thin as arms. Yes, a new life. A poor hospital, and little dark-skinned children with no shoes on their feet and eyes as shiny as beetles. To go where I'd be needed, perform operations in tents, care for the poor and the wretched.

'Would you like to take a trip somewhere?'

'Yes.'

'And where would you like to go?'

'Wherever you want.'

Your mother's leaving on a trip. Her job will take her away for a few days, which means a nice stretch of free time for me. She puts the last items in her suitcase, the same spotted suede bag she took on our honeymoon. Her arm brushes me as she searches for a foulard scarf in the cupboard with the multiple doors that cover an entire wall. She's wearing a soft nutmeg-brown trouser suit with a shawl collar and a very simple necklace made of big amber beads strung on a thin strip of black satin. I take out a shirt. All my shirts are white, and to keep from making mistakes, I keep an appropriate tie wrapped around each of the hangers that hold my suits. Occasionally, Elsa urges me to be daring and wear something different, perhaps a hat. She's got a friend, a writer from Berlin, who affects ostentatious headgear: berets, panamas, cocked hats, felt hats. On him, they look good; he's eccentric, bisexual, extremely intelligent. I'm sure she'd be happier with the writer from Berlin. Maybe they have assignations in literary cafés. He places his sombrero or busby on the chair and reads her some things he's written; she gets excited. Yes, she's reached the right moment; she's ripe enough, and bourgeois enough, for a bisexual lover.

Having so elegant a woman at my side has always filled me with pride; today, however, her elegance depresses me. The umpteenth disguise. This morning, she's the comfortingly feminine journalist, travelling on an assignment. Even her gestures annoy me; she's abrupt, perhaps a bit rude. She's already slipped into the role that she's going to play out in the world, among her riff-raff colleagues. I pull my trousers on, the ones with the belt already passed through the loops to make things easier. I'm going to tell her now. Yes, this is probably a good time to tell her. This way, she can go on her trip and think over what I said. By the time she gets home, she'll have given it a lot of thought. So now I'll tell her: *I love another woman, and that woman is going to have a baby; you and I, therefore, must part.* I don't intend to tell any face-saving lies, to say I want to live alone or some such palliative nonsense. I don't want to live alone; I want to live with Italia, and if I hadn't met her, I probably would never have found a single good reason for leaving Elsa. I have nothing to reproach her for – or perhaps too much. I don't love her any more, and maybe I've never loved her; I've merely been seduced by her. I've submitted to her tyranny, sometimes enraptured, sometimes intimidated, and at the last quietly exhausted. Now, if I watch her closely – and I can, for she'll never notice – if I watch her closely now, while she's making an inventory of the cosmetics in her beauty case, and I see her fixed stare, her dull eyes, her slack jaw . . . *What's this woman doing here? What does she have to do with me? Why doesn't she live with our neighbour across the way? I see him pass a window in his pants now and then, a paunchy but muscular fellow. Why doesn't she cross the street, enter his building, get on his bed and rummage around in her beauty case there? Yes, it would be better if she were over there now, with that narcoleptic look on her face. Maybe I'll take the little redhead who lives with the paunchy, muscular fellow. Maybe she's nice. Maybe we'll talk a little. Maybe she'd like to hear the thoughts of a man who spends his days disembowelling people. I look at my wife, and there's not a single thing I like about her, nothing that interests me. She's got very beautiful hair, it's true, but there's too much of it for my taste. Her breasts are perfect, full but not excessively large, and yet I have no desire to touch them. She's putting on her earrings; the taxi's on the way. I'll let her keep everything; I'll haggle about nothing. I won't even try to divide up the books. I'll throw some things in a suitcase and leave. Goodbye.*

'Goodbye, I'm leaving.'

'Where are you going?'

'I told you: Lyons.'

'Send me a postcard.'

'A postcard?'

'Yes, I'd like that. Goodbye.'

Elsa smiles, picks up her spotted suede bag and leaves the room. *I wonder about the writer from Berlin. Is his dick limp, like a skullcap, or stiff, like a kepi?*

I was kissing Italia's navel. She had a wrinkled navel that sucked me in deeper and deeper, like a whirlpool. That little knot of flesh had been her link to life. Now I felt I could penetrate it, could open that soft passage with my lips and slip inside, one part at a time, first my head, then my shoulders, then the rest of me. Yes, I wanted to be inside her belly, all curled up and grey as a rabbit. I closed my eyes, wet with my own saliva, and I was an unborn infant, afloat in the warm sea. *Help me, my love. I want to be born. I want to be born again. I'll take better care of myself, and I'll love you without mistreating you.*

I opened my eyes and looked at the few things around me – the lacquered chest of drawers, the bedside carpet with its faded stripes and, outside the window, the grey pier of the viaduct. And across the room, leaning against the mirror, the photograph of the unknown man. 'Who's that?'

'My father.'

'Is he still alive?'

'I haven't seen him for many years.'

'Why not?'

'He was never a family man.'

'How about your mother?'

'She's dead.'

'And you don't have sisters and brothers?'

'They're all older than me, and they all live in Australia.'

'I'd like to see your village.'

'There's nothing there. There used to be a pretty church, but the earthquake knocked it down.'

'That's not important. I want to see where you grew up, the streets where you lived.'

'Why?'

'So I can picture where you were before I knew you.'

'I was in here,' she said, touching my belly. Her hand was burning hot.

That afternoon, I took her to see the place where I grew up, Angela. It used to be a respectable working-class neighbourhood, mostly labourers and low-level office workers, and when I was a kid, it seemed far from the city centre. But now the city has expanded so much that my old neighbourhood's practically the hub; there are cinemas, restaurants, a theatre, and an infinite number of offices. We went into the park that seemed so immense to me when I was little. It turned out to have quite modest dimensions and was, moreover, badly maintained and smothered on all sides by large buildings. It looked like a remnant of green wool lost amid rolls of cheap synthetic fabrics. I looked for the exact spot where my mother used to sit and wait for me while I played in the park. She always brought a blanket to sit on, and she'd spread it out under a certain tree. I thought I recognised the tree, so Italia and I sat down under it. She was staring straight ahead when a man passed, walking a dog. She asked me, 'What were you like when you were a kid?'

'Nothing special. I was always a little irritated.'

'Why?'

'I was fat, I was afraid, and I sweated a lot . . . Maybe I was irritated because I was sweating, and I was sweating because I was fat and afraid of getting hurt.'

'And then?'

'Then I grew up, I became thin, and I stopped sweating. But I'm still always a little irritated – it's my character.'

'You don't seem like that to me.'

'Well, I am. And I'm also a great liar.'

Later, we stopped to look at my old school. Thirty years had passed, but it was still there; it hadn't changed. I recognised the strip of playground, surrounded by the same iron fence with the same black bars. Even the colour of the terracotta façade was unchanged: the very same, pale yellow. The day was ending, and the light was starting to fade. We'd been outdoors for a long time. We could still see each other, though; there was enough light for that. The colours of our clothes seemed more sombre, and our clasped hands were hard to distinguish in the gathering gloom. I wanted to speak, and yet I remained silent, holed up in my memories. We were sitting at the top of the marble steps with our backs against the iron bars of the fence. It was from this very vantage point that my school companions and I had observed the progress of many a morning, but I'd never sat there and watched night fall. And while the darkness was erasing everything, I had the sense that life is sweet, however fleeting. The school was still there. That's the important thing, Angela. You can still lean against the gate; you can still visit it by chance, on a random weekday, and relive a part of your childhood. That was when I knew that I hadn't changed, that I was still the same. Maybe one never changes, I thought; maybe one just adapts.

'Did you do well in school?'

'Yes, unfortunately.'

'Why unfortunately?'

Unfortunately because I raped you, unfortunately because I didn't weep when my father died, unfortunately because I've never loved anyone. Unfortunately, Italia, Timoteo is afraid to live.

As we walked along, my mind was in a strange limbo, where memories overlapped with one another and mingled with the present. I held Italia close and we wandered the streets, stumbling a little, like two lovers in a strange city. That night, this part of town, which I knew when I was a boy, seemed unfamiliar to me.

People passed us, brushed against us. They didn't know how much in love we were. By accident, we found ourselves in front of the building where I used to live. We'd just come to the bottom of a narrow, descending street. There was a bakery on the corner, and a delicious smell of pizza filled the air. I was thinking that we could go in and eat a slice or two, and then I realised I was outside my old house.

'I lived there until I was sixteen. We had a flat on the third floor, facing the courtyard, so you can't see the windows from here. But wait a minute . . .'

We climbed over a low brick wall, and we were in the courtyard. 'There it is. That window was mine.'

'Let's go up there,' Italia said.

'No . . .'

'The porter's in his booth — let's ask him. They'll let you in. You think they won't let you in?'

She dragged me upstairs, all the way to the flat. A young woman opened the door. I didn't look at her; I looked past her shoulder as she invited us in. Even the walls were gone. Now there was a single large room with dark parquet floors. Looking over at the far side of the room, I saw a large metal bookcase, a white sofa and a television set on the floor. The young woman was pretty and, like her home, modern. She and Italia looked at each other like dogs of two different breeds. I didn't recognise a thing, and I smiled at our hostess, who said, 'Would you like something to drink? Some tea, perhaps?'

I shook my head. Italia shook hers as well, although with less conviction. If she could have, she probably would have stayed for a while, looking at that sophisticated young lady with her straight black hair, the colour of petroleum. The handles on the windows, I thought, are they still the ones . . .?

'You're right. I kept the fixtures.' She'd lived here for less than a year, she said. 'The couple who lived here before me split up. I got the flat at a good price.'

I went over to one of the windows and touched the handle. Behind my back, in the big room, there was nothing I remembered, nothing at all. So now I knew that my memories dwelled in a place that didn't exist, a place that had been swept from the face of the earth, and those four rooms, that bathroom and that kitchen lived only in me. All the things that had once seemed irremovable were gone. The toilet was dust; the plates were dust; the beds were dust. There was not a trace of my family's passage; our smell had disappeared for ever. I thought, What am I doing here? I held on to the window handle, the only thing left, a little brass leg. I used to pull up a chair so I could reach it. I peered through the window now, and the view, the whole perspective, had changed as well. New buildings crowded out the horizon. The courtyard looked the same, except it was full of parked cars. 'Thanks,' I said.

'Don't mention it.'

Soon we were in the street again, and again there was the aroma of the bakery. Italia said, 'How did that make you feel?'

I said, 'You want a pizza?'

We ate it on the way home. Since I was driving, I took big bites. Italia stroked my ear, part of my face, my head. She knew I was suffering, and she didn't like it. She herself didn't turn away from pain, but rather went to meet it. Her hand comforted me.

Later, in bed, I was kissing her belly again, when she said, 'I'll give it up, you know. If you want me to, I'll give it up, but tell me now, tell me while we're making love.'

Loving wasn't easy for me, Angela, believe me. It wasn't easy; I had to learn. I had to learn how to caress a woman, how to move my hands the right way. Plaster hands; in lovemaking, I've always had plaster hands.

The cars are passing over the viaduct and shaking the walls of the house. The sound comes in through the window and reverberates in the room. The windowpanes vibrate. They can't last; the sun is destroying the adhesive tape that holds them together.

'I was almost twelve. There was a dress on one of the market stalls, a voile dress with red roses on it. It was Saturday. I roamed all over the market, but I kept coming back to that stall to look at the dress. It was lunchtime, and the market was emptying out. The merchants were putting their stuff away. A man folding T-shirts says to me, "Do you want to try it on?" I tell him I have no money. "Trying on is free," he says. He helps me up into his van. I try on the dress inside a kind of tent. The man comes inside the tent and starts touching me. "Do you like the dress?" he asks. I can't move, so I stay still when he touches me.

Afterwards, he's all sweaty. "Don't say anything about this to anyone," he says, and he gives me the dress. When I walk, my legs are like rubber. I've got my old clothes in my hand, and I'm wearing the new dress with the flowers on it. After I get home, I take it off and put it under the bed. But that night, I wake up and pee on the dress, because I think the only thing it's going to bring me is bad luck, and the next day, I burn it. Nobody knows about any of this, but in my mind everyone knows everything. It seems to me that anybody can take me inside the back of a van and do dirty things to me.'

It's the first time she's ever talked to me about herself.

Elsa's back from her trip. Her bag is on the table in the hall, next to her sunglasses. There's a scent of curry and some music I don't recognise. It sounds like rain on windows and wind in trees. Your mother, it seems, has bought a new record. The table in the living room is laid for dinner. The usual piles of books and newspapers are gone from the slate-and-cherry surface, replaced by a bottle of wine, a blue candle and the glasses with the long stems.

Your mother looks through the door of the kitchen. 'Hi, darling,' she says.

'Hi.'

She smiles at me. She's put on make-up, she's brushed her hair, and she's wearing a short-sleeved ivory-coloured sweater and black trousers. A cook's apron is tied around her waist.

I pour the wine into the glasses and go into the kitchen. She's in front of the stove, stirring a pot with a wooden spoon.

'How was your trip?'

'Boring. Cheers.' Our glasses touch.

'How come?'

'Everyone's become so mediocre.' She arches an eyebrow and sips her wine. Then she stops stirring and takes a step towards me. 'Kiss,' she says.

I bend to her lips; she holds me close. It's as if her body is searching for a new place in my arms. Maybe it's the exact opposite of what I think; maybe her trip was a real disappointment to her. I ask, 'Have they fired you?'

'No, why? Do I seem like an unemployed person?'

I start cutting the bread. She's behind me, sumptuous as

143

always, filling the place with herself. But she seems more withdrawn; there's an unusual reserve about her as she stands there, curved over her cooking pot, giving her lamb stew close attention. I must talk to her; I must tell her that I'm leaving. I'm not going to be the man of the house any more.

We sit at the table. The food, too, seems more complicated and refined than usual.

'It's too spicy, isn't it?'

'No, it's delicious.'

My mouth's on fire, and I take a sip of wine. I want to eat in a hurry, lead her to the sofa and tell her how things stand, but I haven't expected to find her so defenceless. Now she seems positively mortified, just because she's put too much spice in this ridiculous foreign concoction. She's displaying a side of herself she generally keeps well hidden. Maybe she realises she's lost me. Too bad, she should have thought about it sooner. Now it's too late; all these unexpected attentions embarrass and annoy me. French wine and a blue candle aren't enough to turn back the clock. Or is there a surprise in store for me, something nestled under that ivory-coloured cashmere sweater? Maybe it's she who wants to leave me. She's holding a glass against her cheek. The wine sways a little in the light, colouring her nose and part of one eye.

I pick up my napkin. There's a postcard underneath it. It shows an image of old Lyons, a woman and a man in regional costume sitting in front of a blue door. 'You didn't post it to me,' I say.

'I didn't have time.'

I turn over the postcard and read it. Two words, nothing more. Two words written with a ballpoint pen.

I say under my breath, 'What is this?'

Elsa's eyes are the colour of wine, and the wine sways in her glass, throwing its red reflections on her smile. 'It's the truth.'

I don't say anything. I sigh, I sigh deeply, and I sit still, because if I get up, I'll fall, I'll stumble and fall backwards, pushed over by that smile.

'Are you happy?'

'Of course.'

But I don't know where I am or what I'm thinking. Her eyes remind me of a road at night, vanishing in the distance among trees, among branches. She says, 'I'll go and get the crème caramel.'

Two words written with a ballpoint pen on the back of a blue postcard: *I'm pregnant*. Now she's rummaging around in the fridge, and here I am, sitting in the wind in front of this steady candle. It's come up suddenly, the wind, and the dust it blows around blinds my eyes. I close them and let the storm buffet me. I can't think about anything; it's too soon. I swallow the crème caramel in tiny bites, then stick my finger in the plate, scoop up some brown sugar and put it in my mouth. I say, 'When did you find out?'

'My period was a little late, and I forgot my earplugs. So when I got to Lyons, I went to a chemist to buy some more and picked up a pregnancy test as well. Then I forgot about that, too, until this morning. I gave myself the test in the hotel room before I left. When the little ball came out, I sat and stared at it for I don't know how long. The taxi was downstairs, waiting for me, and I couldn't leave the room. I wanted to tell you right away. I tried calling you at the hospital, but you were already in the operating theatre. I've been walking with one hand on my stomach. I was afraid someone would run into me.'

Her eyes are shining. A tear runs down her cheek, next to the glass, and the candlelight dances on her excited face. This is the first news of you, Angela, the first whisper, and I hear it joylessly, with a burning throat.

'Put your arms around me.'

I embrace her, bury my face in her hair and try to find peace. *What am I going to do with her? The wind's carrying off everything I thought I wanted. I'm a miserable wretch, ricocheting through life.*

I drink some whisky. The wind abates, allowing me to reach the sofa and sit down. Elsa curls up on the other end, puts a pillow under her back, and takes off her shoes. A moment ago, the record ended, but she started it again, and the watery music is back. She's chosen it because she's pregnant. She twirls her hair in her fingers and says something every now and then, but mostly I listen to the long pauses between her words. She doesn't take her eyes off me. I look horrible – I haven't even washed my hair – but she's gaping at me like I'm some kind of miracle. I have impregnated her, I have demonstrated an ability to change the course of all her projects, and to her that must seem like a miracle. She's weighing our future, considering the mother and father we'll be. Behind those dreamy eyes, bowing down from the heaven of her fullness, she's adjusting my position in the earthly life that she's decided will be mine. And you're already in the midst of us, Angela. If you'd been able to read my mind when I heard the news of your existence, would you have chosen me as your father? I don't think so. I don't think I deserved you. You were already there, a little bug in your mother's belly, and I didn't deign to give you a single kind thought. Don't think I've forgotten that. You entered our house the same evening I planned to leave her, and you swallowed up my destiny. I didn't even have a thought for you, my innocent little bug. Nothing for you, stuck in a powder keg with adults who weren't certain about anything. They didn't know who they were or what they wanted, and they didn't know where they were going.

Ada comes out of the operating theatre, with two nurses running behind her. They open the instrument cabinet; I can hear the rattle of its glass door. I stand up like a robot. 'What's going on?'

Ada, very pale, is coming towards me. 'We have to give her adrenalin. There's a problem with her pulmonary ventilation, and her blood pressure's going down.'

'How low is it?'

'It's at forty.'

'She's haemorrhaging.'

Ada's face is a mute plea. I look through the round window into the operating theatre. I know what these moments of extremity are like, when silence falls, when people become shadows, moving together in waves. They work frantically, then step back from the operating table. They look at the monitors, waiting for a sign, waiting for a graph to start moving again. Trapped in that no man's land, where life has stopped and death is still on the way, they stand aside, as if they can feel the chill of its passage. It's the moment when hands become impotent, when helpless looks are exchanged, when you know you can't pull it off, when that shroud of green cloths evokes the raw truth: under it, there's a person passing away from here, passing away. I hear the alarmed beeping of the monitors. Your blood pressure's still going down. Alfredo shouts, 'Quick! She's in arrest!' His surgical mask has slipped down to his chin.

I rush over to you, to your heart. My hands, a father's hands, pounce on your thorax like talons; I press down hard once, and then again and again. *Listen to the fury in my hands, Angela. Tell me they're still worth something. Help me, my brave little girl, and excuse me if I leave a bruise on your breast.* There's silence all around us. It's as though we're inside an aquarium: fish without gills, mute and gasping. There's nothing but the sound of my hands thumping your chest and my groaning hope. Where are you? You're floating somewhere above me. You're looking down on me from a height, from beyond this group of masked shadows, and maybe you feel sorry for me. No, I won't let you go. Don't even think about it. With every blow I'm getting you back, piece by piece. Your feet sticking out of the bed, your back curved over your school books, you eating a sandwich, you singing, your teacup, your hand on the handle. I won't let you go. I promised your mother. She's on her way back. Before she boarded the plane, she called me again, sobbing into the telephone: 'Please, Timo, save her . . .' She doesn't know that love is contraindicated for surgeons. She doesn't know anything about my profession. It frightens her to think that I caress her with the same hands I use to carve people up. But I'm like a sanguinary watchmaker: I've got precise hands, and I've seen amazing things happen under them. I've felt stirrings that didn't originate in the flesh. I've watched lives struggling to hold on with unexpected tenacity, as if they were receiving some assistance that came neither from me nor from my battery of machines, lives that asked and kept asking and finally received, right before my incredulous eyes. Now you're face to face with that mystery, which, they say, is Light. *Please, Angela, ask God to leave you here on the benighted earth, in the little shadows where your mother and I live.*

I hear Ada's voice: 'It's coming back . . . It's back.'

What's come back is your heartbeat, showing up at last on that miserable fucking monitor.

And now the intracardiac needle is sticking straight up in your chest, and Ada's pressing down the plunger. My hands are trembling; they can't make themselves stop. I'm drenched with sweat. I breathe deeply, gulping in air, while the others around me start breathing again, too.

'Inject dopamine.'

'She's stabilising.'

Welcome back, sweetheart, you're in the world again.

Alfredo looks at me, tries to smile and says softly, 'She was joking. She played a little joke on us.'

'It was her spleen; that's what was bleeding . . .'

I didn't look at the hole in your head. I saw a pale flap of something that must have been your skin, but I didn't look inside. Alfredo quickly goes back to work. I don't stay. I'm sweaty and trembling; I sense a great darkness; I'm about to faint.

I looked into the patients' rooms as I went down the corridor, searching for an empty bed. Yes, I would have liked to slip into one of those white slots and get comfortable and wait for someone to come and take care of me. I would have liked to have a thermometer in my armpit, a baked apple, a pair of pyjamas to detach me from the world.

I wanted to tell Italia the truth, but instead I held her tight and closed my eyes. She already had a face like a pregnant cat, and frequent spells of nausea distorted her features; I couldn't frighten her. We made love, and only afterwards did I realise that I loved her then as if I had already lost her. I didn't want to pull away from her; I stayed inside of her until I got small, until we both got cold. Those days, her house was always chilly. She'd put an old plaid blanket over the chenille bedspread, but that wasn't enough to keep us warm. The dog curled himself up at the foot of the bed, close to our feet. Crushed under the weight of my body, she asked, 'Why do you love me?'

'Because you're you.'

She took one of my hands and laid it on her belly. I was lost in a maze of tragic thoughts, and my hand was deadweight. Italia was too focused on me not to notice. She said, 'What's wrong?'

'I've got a slight temperature.'

She put effervescent aspirins in water and brought me the fizzing glass.

And maybe a presentiment crossed her mind, but she dismissed the thought at once. Pregnancy endowed her with a timid trustfulness. For the first time, she turned her eyes away from the present and dared to gaze beyond it. I was the reason why she contemplated a benevolent future, a happy horizon she was ashamed of desiring.

Your mother's in the hospital. She got here about eleven o'clock, and we're having a bite in the snack bar. Manlio and some of my other medical colleagues are standing around her. They know she's pregnant, and they shower her with compliments, which she accepts with a series of smiles that dimple her cheeks and fill her face with light. She's my wife, here for her first ultrasound. Tall and elegant in her anthracite-grey suit, she walks up the stairs by my side. Manlio follows us, joking, envying me. In those sad, monochrome surroundings, among patients walking around in their pyjamas, Elsa is so beautiful that she could be an actress on a charity visit. Pallid and exhausted – so like the place where I spend most of my existence – I hide behind her, like a boy clinging to his mother.

She lifts her top, lowers her skirt and bares her stomach. Manlio spreads the gel on her. 'Is it cold?'

'A little.'

She laughs. Maybe she's more nervous than she feels like admitting as ultrasound waves scan her abdomen. I stand aside and wait. Manlio moves the probe below her navel, looking for the region of the uterus where the embryo is attached. I don't know what it is I'm thinking, Angela – I don't remember now – but maybe I'm hoping that nothing's there. Your mother's face is stiff as she stretches to study the monitor, fearful that her dream won't make itself visible. And then you appear, Angela, a tiny sea horse with a white spot that comes and goes. It's your heart.

That's how I saw you for the first time. When the monitor was turned off, she relaxed her neck muscles and laid her head back, breathing hard. I kept staring at that black screen, but you were gone. I thought about Italia. She, too, had a tiny sea horse in her belly. But it wouldn't be appearing on any monitor screen; it was destined to remain in the dark.

That evening, I walked over to the place where they had the rice balls I liked, the *arancini*. As I ate, I looked at the television set mounted on the wall. I couldn't hear the audio, which was drowned out by the people in the bar, solitary people who ate their dinners standing up, with their feet in sawdust and greasy paper napkins in their hands. I went back out on to the street, feeling scatterbrained and powerless as I collided with the dark. The shops were empty, and the city was settling down for a rest. I went into a telephone booth, but the receiver had been torn off its cable, which was hanging down dead. I said to myself, I'll call from the next telephone booth. But I didn't stop again; I went straight home.

Elsa and Raffaella are chatting on the sofa. I hear their voices while I'm putting up my bag. Raffaella gets up and drowns me in her flesh; I respond with my usual reticence. She's barefoot, and out of the corner of my eye, I see her shoes on the rug. 'I'm so happy,' she says. 'At last I can be somebody's aunt!' Carried away, vibrating with joy, she wraps me in another ardent embrace. Her shoes lie there, worn and stretched by her feet.

I say, 'Good night.'

'You're going to bed already?'

'I have to get up very early tomorrow morning.'

Elsa leans over the back of the sofa, presenting a lukewarm cheek, to which I give a brief peck. Raffaella looks at me with her round, infantile eyes. 'Do you mind if we sit and talk a little while longer?'

Talk all you want, Raffaella. Breathe on your heart until it comes alive. We're all out for a ride together, passengers in a wagon without wheels.

The next day, I'm on an aeroplane, about to leave for a conference. This will be a quick trip: there and back in the same day. Manlio's by my side, taking up more than his share of the armrest between us. I can smell his aftershave lotion. I'm in the window seat, looking at the white wing against the grey background of the runway. We're still on the ground. Down here, it's not much of a day – the air is thick and dirty – but maybe we'll get above the clouds and into the sunlight. The flight attendant is moving down the aisle, pushing a trolley with newspapers and magazines. Manlio looks at her behind. After we take off, I'll have a coffee, a cup of what Manlio calls 'septic coffee'. *I have to get off. This plane is going to crash. I have to get off. I don't want to croak next to Manlio with a cup of septic coffee in my hand.* I feel bad. I'm perspiring, my heart is hurting my chest, and I can't feel my arms. *No, I'm going to die of a heart attack, standing on my feet inside that little lavatory, that box of quivering metal, where some plastic wrappers from the refresher towels are afloat in the washbasin.* I rise from my seat.

'Where are you going?'

'I'm getting off.'

'What the fuck are you talking about?'

They've already closed the cabin doors, and the aeroplane is moving. The flight attendant stops me. 'Excuse me, sir. Where are you going?'

'I'm ill; I have to get off.'

'I'll get you a doctor.'

'I am a doctor. I'm ill. Let me get off.'

I must look pretty impressive, because the young woman starts to back off. She's in her uniform, of course, and her blonde hair is pulled back. She has an innocuous little nose. I follow her into the cockpit. Two men in short-sleeved white shirts turn round and look at me. I say, 'I'm a doctor. I'm having a heart attack. Please open the cabin door.'

The mobile staircase moves back into place. The door opens. Air, finally, air; I run down the steps. Manlio follows me. The attendant calls to him, 'Sir, are you getting off, too?'

The wind's about to blow Manlio's jacket off. He raises an arm and shouts, 'He's my colleague!'

So here we are again, back on the asphalt. An airport worker picks us up in his tiny vehicle and drives us to the exit. I don't speak. My arms are crossed; my lips are pressed together. My heart has returned to its proper place. Manlio puts on his sunglasses, even though there's no sun. We get out of the airport car. Manlio says, 'May I ask what came over you?'

I force myself to smile. 'I saved your life.'

'You mean the plane's going to crash?'

'Not now it won't. You can't get off a plane that's going to crash.'

'Were you scared shitless?'

'Yes.'

'Me, too.'

We laugh and go to the bar and drink some real coffee, and we miss the conference. 'With all those wankers,' says Manlio. He likes to deviate from the programme. And it's while we're standing there that I tell him everything. I keep my head down, bent over my empty espresso cup, pushing the sugary black dregs around with my spoon, and my cheeks sag as I give him the whole story. There at the airport bar, among people eating their sandwiches with one eye on their luggage, I spill all the beans, confessing my feelings and my desires like an old, love-struck adolescent. And it doesn't matter that Manlio is the last person I should tell about this. I need to tell someone about it, and here he is at my side, looking at me with his boar's eyes. We're friends – the wrong friends, as we both know – but we share this intimate moment, leaning together on the metal counter long after we've drunk our coffee.

'But who is this woman?'

'You've seen her.'

'I've seen her?'

'It was during that oncologists' conference. One evening, she was sitting at a table near us . . .'

He shakes his head. 'I don't remember her.'

People pass by. Even though there's no smoking, Manlio lights a cigarette. I look straight ahead and make my declaration to him, to myself and to the flood of unknown people rushing around us: 'I'm in love.'

Manlio crushes out his cigarette with the toe of his moccasin. 'Shall we take the next plane?'

I park the car, grab my bag off the passenger seat, and walk towards the hospital. Suddenly, Italia comes out of nowhere. And suddenly she's very close to me. She puts a hand on my arm, feeling for the flesh under the material of my jacket. Not only does she surprise me, she frightens me too. She's not wearing any make-up, and she looks wan and thin. She hasn't even bothered to cover her forehead with her hair. Her forehead is broad and oppressive; it weighs down her eyes. I look around, consciously protecting myself from her, from the burden she's bearing this morning. I say, 'Come.'

I cross the street without touching her. She walks behind me, head down, wrapped in her shabby little cotton jacket. A car slows down for her, but she pays no attention; her stare is fixed on my hurrying feet. I walk away from the hospital like a thief with a bundle of indecent swag. We turn into a narrow street where there's a little café I know.

She follows me up the spiral staircase to the first floor, an empty room that stinks of old smoke. She sits next to me, very close. She looks at me, looks away, then looks at me again. 'I waited for you,' she says.

'I'm sorry.'

'I waited so long. Why didn't you call me?'

I don't answer. I wouldn't know what to say. She puts her hand to her face, and now her face is red, her eyes are grey with tears. There's an aquarium against the wall. From this distance, the fish look like confetti.

'You've changed your mind, right?'

155

I don't want to talk, not this morning, not at this hour. 'It's not what you think,' I say.

'It's not? What is it, then? Tell me what it is.'

There's defiance in her eyes, in those tears that won't fall. Her lips are inside her mouth, and she's insistently picking at the wrists of her jacket. Those nervous hands of hers irritate me, and so does that face, which leaves me no room for escape. I should tell her about Elsa, but I'm not in the mood for emotional upheaval today. It's tiring enough just being here with her, stuck at this little table. There isn't much light, the place stinks of smoke, and then there are those little fish back there, forgotten like confetti after the carnival is over. All at once, she bursts into high-volume tears. She throws her arms around my neck; her nose and her lips are wet. 'Don't leave me . . .'

I stroke her cheek, but my hands are hard as claws. She breathes on me, kisses me. Her breath smells odd, a mixture of sawdust and upset stomach. I hold her close, but her breath makes me nauseous. She says, 'Tell me you love me.'

'Stop it.'

But she's lost all her self-control. 'No,' she cries. 'No, I won't stop . . .'

She shakes and sobs in her chair. Footsteps come up the stairs. A boy disappears into the toilet, a schoolboy with his knapsack on his back. With an effort, Italia pulls away from me and sits up. She's calmer now, and I take her hand. 'There's something I have to tell you.'

She looks at me. Now her forehead looks as though it's made of plaster. I say. 'My wife . . . isn't well.'

'What's wrong with her?'

Tell her, Timoteo. Tell her now. Tell her to her face, to her dirty mouth, stagnant with her misery. Tell her you're expecting a legitimate child, the heir to your sterile, cautious life. Tell her she has to have an abortion, because now's the right time, now when she's scaring you and you're thinking, What kind of mother would so desperate a woman make?

'I don't know,' I say, leaning back into my cowardice.

'You're a doctor, and you don't know what's wrong with your wife?'

The boy leaves the toilet. We look at him as he comes out, and he looks at us. He's got black eyes and a wispy beard. He walks past the aquarium and disappears down the spiral staircase. Italia says, 'I'm going to the toilet.'

She wobbles a little, backs up a few steps, and runs headfirst into the wall, so hard that the sound echoes around the room. I get up and go to her. I say, 'What on earth are you doing?'

She laughs and shakes my hand from her shoulders. That laugh scares me more than any amount of weeping. She says, 'Every now and then, I need a blow to the head.'

We go outside and walk slowly down the street. I ask, 'Does your head hurt?'

She's distracted, looking at the people coming towards her. I ask, 'Shall I get you a cab?'

But instead, we walk to a bus stop, and she climbs into the first bus that comes along.

I turn round and walk back to the hospital, thinking exclusively about myself. Today, not loving her was the easiest thing in the world. And during the operation, while I've got somebody's liver in my hands, she stays with me like an unpleasant memory. I see her knocking at the door of my flat, pretending to be a sales rep or something, one of those shadowy figures that slip past the porter and roam around buildings. As she rings the bell, she's shaking and gloomy-eyed, but her eyes light up when she sees Elsa and asks for permission to enter. Elsa's half asleep, wearing her ecru nightshirt, her body naked and warm under the silk. Italia's little; her armpits are stained with perspiration, because she's been sweating. She sweated on the bus; she sweated all night long, tossing and turning. She looks at the flat, the books, the photographs, and Elsa's firm breasts, still dark from the sun. She thinks about her own breasts, stuck to her ribcage like hollowed-out onions, and she thinks about the heart beating in her womb. She's wearing that ridiculous skirt with the elastic waistband that slides down on to her hips. Elsa smiles at her. She feels solidarity with all members of her sex, even the lowliest; as an emancipated woman, she thinks it's her duty to show some indulgence. Not Italia; she's got a child in her belly under that flea-market skirt, and she's not indulgent. Elsa turns to her and says, 'Tell me what you want.' She speaks familiarly, as she usually does to working-class girls. Italia doesn't feel well; she's dizzy, and she's gone a long time without eating or sleeping. 'Nothing,' she says, retreating towards the door. Then her eyes fall on the white envelope with the ultrasound results, lying on the table in the hall . . .

Between operations, I call Elsa. 'How are you feeling?'

'Terrific.'

'You're not going out?'

'In a little while. I'm transcribing an interview.'

'Don't open the door to anyone.'

'Why? Who's coming over?'

'I don't know. Ask who it is, make sure you know them.'

There's a pause, then her laughter erupts out of the receiver. I imagine her cheeks, the little dimples in her flesh when she laughs. She says, 'Paternity is having a strange effect on you. You're turning into my grandmother.'

I laugh, too, because I feel ridiculous. My house is in order, and my wife is strong, tall and strong.

In the evening, I look out of the bedroom window. I part the curtains and examine the street below, the branches of the trees, the traffic light signalling a few blocks away. The street's empty except for one passing car, an anonymous vehicle taking someone home. I'm looking for her. I don't know if I'm looking for her because I need her, or because I'm afraid she's got the place staked out and is spying on us from down there. I look out at the roofs, the aerials and the cupolas in the direction where she lives, out past the road lined with nocturnal shapes lit up by car headlights, out near that bar I know all too well; I wonder if it's still open at this hour. There's such a mass between us, all these walls, all these existences curled up in sleep. So much separates us, and good thing it does, too; I need to catch my breath. *Don't be distressed, Italia. That's life for you: wonderful, intimate moments, followed by blasts of cold wind. And though you may be suffering out there, out beyond the last concrete outpost, at this distance your torment is unknown to me, and alien. What does it matter if one of my obscene spurts got you pregnant? Tonight, you're alone with your baggage on a railway platform, and the train is leaving the station; you've missed it.*

'Aren't you coming to bed?'

I lie down next to your mother. She's reading. Her hair, still wet from the shower, surrounds her face in damp clumps. I'm turned away, well on my side of the bed, but I feel her hand pulling on my pyjama top. 'I wonder what it'll be like,' she says.

I roll over, not too far, just giving her my profile.

'The baby, I mean. I can't seem to imagine it.'

'He'll be like you, utterly beautiful.'

'And maybe it'll be a girl,' she says, lowering her book. 'Ugly, like you.' She moves close to me; her wet hair brushes against my skin. 'Last night, I dreamed that it didn't have any feet, it was born and it didn't have any feet . . .'

'Keep calm. Its feet will show up in the next ultrasound.'

She moves back to her side and starts reading again. She asks, 'Will the light bother you?'

'Not at all. It'll keep me company.'

I lie there in the yellowish half light with the sheet over my eyes. I don't really sleep, but I doze off, reassured by the light and the sound of Elsa's breathing, which suggests that life will go on this way – easy, uncomplicated, shampoo-scented. I dream and drowse, my thoughts moving along benignly, until I see a maimed child coming towards me. Now the light's off and I'm asleep, but not soundly enough. I hear your mother cry out, 'Damn you, give me back his feet! Give them back to me!' And then, drowned in the blue waters of the night, I have a terrible vision: I get up, go to my bag on the hall table, take out the scalpel and cut my member off. I open the window and toss the thing down on to the pavement for the cats, or for Italia, if she's around. *There you go, Crabgrass. There's your child's father.* And now I'm pressing my thighs together as tightly as I can. What a horror it is, Angela, when life starts taking bites out of you at night, too. It bites you when you're awake; it bites you in your dreams.

The recurring drone in the receiver I was holding to my ear echoed the telephone in that hovel, ringing away. Far from me, far from my hand, far from my ear. She wasn't there at ten. She wasn't there at noon. She wasn't there at six in the evening. Where was she? Cleaning up some office, probably, having her way with a WC. I could picture her walking along the city streets, grazing the walls, wearing the wasted look I'd seen on her the last time, in that café, when I'd found her general unpleasantness intolerable, humiliating for both of us. Whenever a romance is bound for dissolution, humiliation's a part of the tale. Sometimes lovers emerge from their confining silhouette and see an objective image of the beloved, a bright, focused image no longer camouflaged by their own desires. Afterwards, they pretend that nothing has changed, but by then – at least to some extent – they've already passed from love to ferocity. For we become ferocious with those who have disillusioned us, Angela.

And so, while we were in that café, I looked at her as though she were just another anonymous pedestrian, one of those useless bodies that crowd the streets, the buses and the world. Bodies like the ones I split open and root around in every day, without joy and without compassion. I passed my surgeon's eyes over her, from her forehead down to the hand supporting her head; I examined her, peering at her ugly little flaws: the fuzz on her chin, the crooked finger, the two deep rings around her neck. She had crawled back into her wretched shell, and I could look at her like that, without interest or sympathy, cataloguing the details of her unsuitability. I caught another whiff of her dismal breath. It was like breath from a decaying body, like the breath of patients when they wake up from the anaesthetic.

The telephone wasn't disconnected. It was a working line, an operator with a metallic voice had assured me of that; but she didn't answer. Maybe she was home after all, curled up into a ball, lying on her bed, letting the sound of the telephone hover above her body before entering it and jolting her with its monotonous alternation of rest and alarm, making her shiver. It was the only way I had of telling her that I hadn't abandoned her. So I continued to call her into the evening, telling myself a lie about how this mournful sound was a way of communicating with her.

I left the hospital exhausted and drove home, running through quite a few not-yet-green traffic signals along the way. Occasional shafts of light revealed that my eyes were dilated and my expression grim . . . I would never be free of her; wherever I might go, I'd be haunted by the thought of her. Italia dominated me. She foiled all my intentions. Her voice hammered at my temples, so present that I turned and looked for her. Had she been sitting there in the passenger seat, with her frayed little jacket, her white, blue-veined hands, and her faded eyes, maybe then it would have been easier to forget her.

Nora puts her arms around me, and I feel her pasty lipstick sliding along my cheek. She and Duilio have stayed for dinner, which is already on the table.

'Congratulations, Dad!'

'Thanks.'

'It's great news.'

'Let me go wash my hands.'

From the other end of the table, Nora tosses a package wrapped in white tissue paper. Elsa, distracted, fails to catch the package, which lands in the tuna sauce. She picks it up and cleans it off with her napkin. 'Mama,' she says, 'I told you not to.'

'Just a little thought, something for good luck. Remember,

the first baby dress has to be new, and it has to be made of silk.'

Elsa unwraps it and passes it to me. 'Here, isn't it wonderful? We've got a new baby dress.' She laughs, but I know she's annoyed. She doesn't want baby presents; it's still too early for that. The baby dress is a handkerchief with a pair of holes I can stick four fingers into. The water jug on the table is empty, and I stand up to fill it. When I turn on the tap, the sound cancels out the voices of the others. They're having a family conversation; I watch the movements of their faces and their hands. As far as I'm concerned, they're already behind a glass panel, the three of them, the usual smudged glass panel I put up around the world when I want none of it and it wants none of me.

Elsa is talking to her father, touching his arm. I see her in isolation, as if she were emerging from a cloud of steam; I see her very well. She has returned to the centre of the world. Gone is the fragility she displayed that evening not so many days earlier; gone is her sudden, touching uncertainty. She's herself again, steady and tireless, only more mysterious. She casts her eyes upon me, and they, too, are the same as always: attuned to surface stimuli, but intimately distracted. She doesn't need me any more.

I return with the jug and pour everyone some water. Then I say, 'Excuse me,' and leave the room. I don't even bother to close the bedroom door, so eager am I to dial her number.

She wasn't there; even at night, she wasn't there. I put down the receiver, put down the solitude that I felt everywhere – in my heavy hand, in my ear, in the silence of my study. I was sitting in the dark, and Nora's shape appeared in the mirror on the door. She looked like a crow. The light from the hall barely illuminated her as she looked at me in the darkness of the room. It didn't last long, but in that brief space of time, I had the feeling that she'd grasped something. It wasn't so much the fact that I was sitting in the dark alone with the telephone in my hand that gave her the intuition about my double life. No, it was my body, so different from what she'd seen at the table. My shoulders were slumped, collapsed; my eyes were shiny and wet. I was too far from my usual self. And so an unexpected intimacy, precipitated by coincidence (she'd been on her way to get her cigarettes, which she'd left in her bag on the hall table), was established between my mother-in-law and me. It's remarkable, Angela, that sometimes the least likely people are the ones who manage to see through us. She took a step towards me in the dark and said, 'Timo?'

'Yes?'

'I've got a mole on my back that's a lot bigger than it used to be. Would you mind looking at it?'

It's three o'clock in the morning. Once again, your mother is asleep. Her body is a mountain at sunset, a dark, impenetrable shape. Maybe leaving her is less difficult than I think; it's just a question of getting dressed and going away. All of them – Elsa, her family, our friends – will form a united front against me, like a wall. And eventually, everyone will be resigned to the wall. In my place she wouldn't hesitate, she wouldn't be afraid; she'd leave me out on the rear balcony, just as I did a little while ago with the rubbish bag.

A rain as fine as face powder was falling. Damp but not drenched, I wrapped myself more tightly in my overcoat as I walked. I had no destination – I just wanted to keep the night from turning on me. I wasn't tired. My legs felt light. I'd eaten very little, and that little had already been digested. The streets were deserted and silent. It took a little while for me to notice that the silence wasn't total; the asphalt was emitting its own peculiar groan. At night, the city is like an empty world, abandoned by people, yet imbued with their presence. Someone is being loved, someone else is being left, a dog is barking on somebody's terrace, a priest is getting to his feet. An ambulance takes a sick person to my hospital, far from his warm bed. A whore with legs as black as the darkness makes her way home; a man who isn't waiting for her sleeps like a mountain, secure and appalling. Exactly like Elsa. When you can't sleep and you know sleep won't come, all sleeping people are the same. They all look alike.

As I walked, every form I saw seemed to be Italia: the trees, which were giving off an odd phosphorescence; the metallic shapes of the parked cars; the street lamps, bending down into their own light; and even the terraces and the cornices of tall buildings. It was as if her body were everywhere, dominating the city.

I put my arms around a tree. That's right; I suddenly found myself pressing my body against a large wet trunk. And as I hugged it, I realised that I'd wanted to do that many times before. This was news to me. *Maybe she's killed herself and that's why she's not answering the phone. Her grey hand is hanging down from her grey arm, which is dangling over the edge of her rusty bathtub. With her last gasp, she ripped down the plastic shower curtain. She died thinking about me, trying one last time to embrace me in her thoughts or drive my image from her mind. It's the middle of the night – the water must be cold by now. When she filled the tub, she made the water scalding hot so that the blood would flow more easily from her slashed wrists. Did she use her little penknife, or perhaps a razor blade I left there? The instrument one chooses for suicide is important; it's already a kind of testament.*

A cry comes out of the darkness. I've tripped and fallen on to a mound of rags, under which a man was sleeping on the ground. He sticks his head out of his filthy nest and cries, 'I don't have anything!'

He clamours, he bawls, he thinks I want to rob him. Of what? His toxic bedclothes? His teeth, perhaps? But no, I see he doesn't have any when he opens his mouth to utter his hoarse lamentations. I say, 'Excuse me, I fell.'

What have I touched? What emanations have entered my lungs? The man's stench is loathsome; he smells like a disembowelled dog on the shoulder of the road. *Italia stank, too, when her tragedy came round again, when she understood that I was leaving her, that I wasn't going to keep her or her baby, and that, once again, I was going to offer her money.* I want to run away, but instead I hold on to the man with all my strength. I lay my head against his filthy neck, my nose in his congealed hair, stiff as fur, and I breathe. I breathe in his odour of unburied dog.

Angela, I was looking for the contagion that would push me irretrievably to the other side, to that swamp between the city and the sea, where the only person I ever truly loved made her home. The plague-bearer, my new nocturnal companion, did not recoil from me. Rather, he put an arm around me and turned his face (deeply creased, with dirt in the creases) towards me, searching for me in the cavern where I was hiding. He found me and stroked my head, as merciful as a priest absolving a murderer. Did I deserve so much compassion, daughter of mine? In that dark corner of the world, a miserable wretch welcomed me, guided me. On the wet street where he lay dreaming, now I was dreaming too, embracing the stinking accoutrements of a life of total destitution, far from my home, far from my parquet floors and my whisky. For me, this was love: love orphaned and shrivelled, love in extremity, when fate takes pity on us and gives us a comfort blanket.

'You want a drink?'

From under some cardboard, he pulled a bottle of wine and offered it to me. I drank without thinking about the mouth that had touched the chipped rim of that bottle before mine; I drank because I was thinking about my father. My father, who died on the street, who fell against the rolling shutter of a closed shop and then slid to the ground with one hand around his throat, where life was leaving his body.

Before I went away, I gave the man some money, all I had on me, in fact. I thrust my fingers into the recesses of my wallet and pulled out everything that was there. He accepted the money like any ordinary down-and-out, hiding it in his rags, obviously terrified at the possibility that I might change my mind. Then he watched me with incredulous eyes as I made my way to the intersection, where I disappeared from his view.

The darkness was beginning to fade, washed by the rain that had not ceased to fall, gently but relentlessly. I drove through the hesitant light; every now and then the headlights of an oncoming car struck me in the eyes. Two Philippine nuns, standing under two little umbrellas, were waiting at a bus stop. A bar was opening. A soaking bundle of newspapers lay beside a news-stand that was still locked up. I was weary when I stopped the car, done in by my dense, sleepless night. Now I could go to sleep in her arms, and only later would we gather our future together. I had already fought my battle over the course of that long night. There was nothing to say; all that remained for me to do was to embrace her in silence. When I got out of the car, my cheeks were flushed from the heated air inside. The streets were dry in the growing grey light, and now I could distinguish every object; maybe it hadn't rained here. The absence of that rain, which had hounded me all night long, seemed a sign that the struggle was indeed over. Italia had waited for me, safe and dry.

I was halfway up the second flight of stairs when I heard the thud of the lift arriving below me, followed by the clicking of a woman's high-heeled shoes, the echo fading as she crossed the lobby. I ran down the stairs and saw her back as she left the building.

'Italia!'

I caught up with her just as she was turning round. I didn't look at her; I simply embraced her. She went limp, allowing herself to be squeezed, not even raising an arm; she remained exactly as she was. Holding her head against my shoulder, I saw her hand dangling loosely at her side. *Now she's going to raise her hands and put them on me. She's going to respond to my embrace. Then she'll collapse, and I'll hold her up.* But in fact, she didn't move. She remained motionless until my breath stabilised and I could feel the beating of her heart, calm and deep. She was warm; she was alive. Nothing else mattered. A few caresses would have sufficed to restore her to me. I knew her; she'd let herself be loved without useless displays of pride. I let her go and backed away to get a look at her. I asked, 'Where are you going?'

'To the flower market.'

'Where?'

'I work there.'

'Since when?'

'Not long.'

In the half-shadow, her grey eyes seemed set, like stones, and there was something more adult about the expression on her face. I, on the other hand, had come armed only with my need for her. I said, 'How are you?'

'Fine.'

I put a hand on her stomach. 'How about him? How's he doing?'

She didn't reply, Angela. I caught up her hands and held them against her stomach. I felt her breathing. The weather was already cool, and she was dressed too lightly for the season, for that sunless dawn. I felt the weight of that empty lobby behind us, and the cold penetrating my body through my damp clothes. She let me move her hands about without opposition, without will, like two leaves in the mud. I remembered the red leaf, the first of the autumn, that fell on my windscreen when I was parked outside the clinic.

'I had an abortion.'

I looked into her light, impassive eyes and shook my head. With my heart in my throat, I said, 'That can't be true.' I was holding her by the arms, jerking her around, ready to do her harm. I asked, 'When did you do it?'

'I did it, that's all.'

She didn't seem sad, but I thought I saw pity for me in her stony eyes. I said, 'Why didn't you tell me? Why didn't you try to reach me? I wanted it, really. I wanted it . . .'

'Tomorrow you would have changed your mind.'

Now she was going to leave me. Now that my multiplied life was no longer growing inside of her, I'd lost her. Desperate, I started to cover her with little kisses that fell like hail on her rigid face. *It doesn't matter – we'll have other children. Let's start tomorrow; let's start now. Let's go make love, now, on that chenille bedspread. I'll hold you close, and you'll be pregnant again. We'll go to Somalia, and our house will be filled with children: children in cribs, children in hammocks, children in shawls . . .*

But we were already an old photograph, Angela, one of those

photographs ripped down the middle, where two lovers lost to each other for ever are separated at the shoulder. Now she would go and clip stems and sell flowers to anyone who came along: to a lover, to someone on his way to the cemetery, to someone who's just had a child.

'Where did you have the abortion?'

'I went to the Gypsies.'

'You're crazy! You have to go to hospital for a check-up.'

'I don't like hospitals.'

You don't like surgeons, I thought, and I grabbed one of her wrists. 'You have to come with me!'

'I'm all right. Leave me alone!'

She threw off my hand. I wasn't her man any more. My hand was the hand of no one in particular. Her face had returned to immobility and emptiness; I caught no glimpse of any of the countless expressions I knew so well. The ashes of dawn entered her ears and slid down her cheeks, which were painted to simulate good health. She was standing in front of me, but she'd already disappeared into her own life, distracted and anonymous, like one of those wet hands that passes you your change in the market. 'I have to go,' she said.

'I'll give you a lift.'

'It's no use.'

I sat down on the kerb while she walked away. I didn't look at her; I had my head in my hands. And I stayed like that until the sound of her footsteps faded to nothing, and even afterwards, when nothing remained but silence. The telephone in her house had rung and rung while she was inside a flimsy caravan just a few yards away, letting some hag, perhaps the same person who taught her fortune-telling, thrust a hook inside her. That was how it had ended, that was what she had come to, with her teeth clamped on a rag to keep from screaming.

Why am I telling you all this? I don't have an answer to that question. I can't give you one of my brief, precise 'surgical responses', as you call them. I think it's because life is haemorrhaging and pounding in my temples like the haematoma in your skull. I see it now, Angela: you're operating on me.

I'm not asking your forgiveness, and I'm not taking advantage of your absence. Believe me, I passed judgement on myself many years ago, sitting on that kerb. The verdict was irreversible, fixed for all time, like a tombstone. I'm guilty; my hands know it.

But if you only knew how many times I've tried to imagine that lost child. I watched it grow up at your side like an unfortunate twin. I tried to bury it, but in vain. It came back whenever it wanted to, fell in with my steps, slipped into my ageing bones. It came back in every defenceless creature I saw, in the hairless children in Paediatric Oncology; it came back in a porcupine I ran over on a country road. It came back in the damage I did to you.

Do you remember judo classes? You didn't want to go, but I forced you to in my own way – with silence, with those mute reproaches that made you feel bad before you caved in. I drove around that old gym, which featured old equipment, old teachers, a punch bag and unglued linoleum. I got out of the car and went in. The air was dank with perspiration as I considered the faces of the combatants. I took a flyer with the class times. What can I tell you, Angela? It's a familiar tale. When I was a boy, I would have liked to be a martial arts champion and visit a gym at night, a gym like that one, filled with sleeveless workout shirts and real muscles and tough faces, and there arm myself with an invisible, unfailing strength, which I would dissemble under my well-mannered jacket and glasses. Two moves and your opponent is down; a colleague, perhaps – say that nurse who's so heavyset it's scary to look at him. The dreams of a cowardly man, of a feeble little boy. That's what I could tell you, and it would be true; there *was* that little boy, that little clump of feelings, some praiseworthy, some contemptible. But there was also something else, something unconfessed: the desire to subdue you, to play a crooked trick on you, because my crooked life was falling on your shoulders. The conditions necessary for getting away with it were in place. It was a good sport, for one thing. Your mother was unable to find any contraindications in my paternal face. Of course, you wanted to take dancing lessons, and you bounced around the house on the tips of your toes, with one of your mother's scarves tied around your waist. You wanted to be a dancer, Angela, but you were too tall for ballet. By contrast, you were just right for judo. It's a good sport, as I said; it disciplines the spirit. You have to be fair; you have to have respect for the movements and for your comrades, male and female alike. I took you by your little hand, bought you a pair of judo slippers and took you to that basement gym.

And there you were, with your judogi on and the belt wound around your waist. You fought joylessly, doggedly, resisting only because you hated being thrown. You fought for my sake, because I was watching you. You fought so you wouldn't land on the mat, so you wouldn't get kicked in the behind, so you wouldn't hear the instructor's heavy voice shouting at you to get up. You fought with tears in your eyes. You didn't like the judogi – it was stiff; it was a sack. You wanted a nice filmy tutu and some little shoes with plaster tips. You wanted to feel light. And instead, there you were, matched against that classmate they were always saddling you with, the big strong one with the ponytail that snapped like a whip. Big, strong and agile, whereas you were thin and wooden. I gave you advice: 'You have to be smoother in the exchange of techniques.' But you couldn't be smooth. You were fighting too many battles.

I sat down on one of those little chairs they had – they looked as though they belonged in a kindergarten – and watched the belt promotion ceremony with the other parents. You were sitting huddled in a corner of the blue rubber mat with your legs crossed and your feet bare, waiting your turn. You flashed me a lame smile. You were afraid: of the instructor, of those movements that you didn't have under control, of the little girls who were more nimble and less damaged than you. When your turn came, you got up and bowed in salute. The instructor called out the movements, and you executed them nervously and uncertainly. Your cheeks were blotchy; you kept biting your lip. When you were the holder, you looked at your opponent and seemed to implore her not to resist, to just let herself go. When you were the receiver, you let yourself go completely, like an empty sack. You took a lot of hard knocks. Sweaty, defeated, with your judogi askew, you made your bow and got your promotion.

'Are you happy?' I asked you in the car. You weren't happy; you were exhausted. I tried again. 'When you fall on a tatami, it doesn't hurt you, right?' Wrong; it hurt you a lot. You looked at me. Your face was flushed, you were close to tears, and you asked me with your eyes, Why?

Good question. We were at peace – why start a useless war? To make you stronger, to teach you some discipline. But I didn't make you stronger. I did you harm; I robbed you of strength. I took your gaiety and built a wall around it. Forgive me.

And then one day, you stopped. It was in September, we had just come back from the seaside, and your belt rank was orange-green. You said, 'I don't want to do it any more. Full stop.' I didn't insist; I let you alone. I was tired, too. I frequently passed that gym, but it no longer interested me. The thrill, the obsession, my unborn son – all that was dead and buried. And all of it fucked-up nonsense, Angelina, the madness of fathers and rapists who don't know how to grow up. Full stop.

It was just a matter of time. Time would perform its corrosive task and eat away at my remorse until it was reduced to powder. All things considered, Italia had done me a favour, removing a messy complication from my life. She hadn't wanted to go to the clinic a second time; as far as she was concerned, it was a sham hotel, and its elegance filled her with scorn. I was only partly to blame, having limited myself to leaving her on her own. That abandonment was the beginning of the process whereby I became inured to my own vileness.

One evening, Manlio called me up and we went out for a pizza like two old classmates getting together again. After we sit down, he asks me, 'How did things turn out with that girl?'

'She's all right.'

'And how about you?'

At a table some distance away, a blonde woman with her back to me is smoking a cigarette. All I can see is the whitish cloud of smoke around her hair, and the face of the man sitting across from her. From his expression, I try to guess what she looks like. 'I don't know,' I say. 'I'm waiting.'

'For what?'

'I don't know.'

I'm waiting for that woman to turn round. There's a chance she looks like her.

Sometimes I go and pick her up at the market. I arrive when the vendors are taking down the stalls, and she's standing in the midst of a flood of damaged flowers. She greets me with a movement of her head. She stacks the boxes and carries the pots of unsold plants to a small pickup truck that is covered with a green oilcloth, parked behind the stall. I wait for her to finish her work, posted there in my elegant clothes like a stalk among the dewy petals. Italia takes off her rubber boots and slips into her normal shoes. When she's in the car, we treat each other kindly but joylessly, like two friends whipped with the same stick. Or maybe like parents who've lost a child. In any case, we're a pair of survivors. We're both walking next to an open wound, and we have to be careful about choosing our words.

'How are you?'

'Fine. And you?'

'Are you tired?'

'No, not at all.'

She's never tired, but she rubs her cold, chapped hands. She's grown; in the car, her forehead seems broader, but her shoulders are more hunched. She never sits back completely in her seat. Her necklines are always too low. She's trying to put up some kind of a fight. She looks through the car windows at the world, which has done nothing to protect us.

We're like two convalescents, waiting for the time to pass, and meanwhile the traffic is rolling along and the days are growing shorter. The bright lights from the shop windows reflect in Italia's eyes, apparently without bothering her, for she pays no attention to them. I haven't touched her again. When a woman's recently had an abortion, you don't have sex with her; you leave her alone. Besides, I'm terrified even at the thought of her nakedness, terrified of finding my arms around her again, of clasping that pain she carries inside her, inert under her wet clothes. It's too cold for her at the market – her nose is red and peeling. She pulls a thoroughly soaked handkerchief out of her pocket and blows that nose. Not long ago, I brought her some vitamins, but I'm not certain she takes them. It's unhealthy for us to let time pass this way. We're not friends now, nor will we ever be. We were lovers even before we knew each other. We exchanged flesh in a wild fury. And now such an odd courtesy has sprung up between us. I look at her and wonder what she and I are doing here, becalmed in these still waters. It can't end like this, without a cry, without anything at all. If a demon is required, let him fall upon us; let him burn us. As long as we don't have to stay in this limbo.

Maybe a change of scene would do the trick, I think. Her house gives me the creeps. That tobacco-coloured coverlet, the naked chimney, her blind dog and that monkey on the wall, holding the baby's bottle like a tasteless joke. One afternoon, therefore, I ask her if she'd like to go to a hotel. 'So we won't spend all our time sitting in traffic,' I say.

And so here we are, in a room completely new to us, a lovely room in the centre of the city, with heavy damask curtains and damask walls. She doesn't even look around; she throws her bag on the bed and goes straight to the window, raising a hand to push the curtain aside. I ask if she wants something to eat or drink, and she says no. I go into the bathroom to wash my hands, and when I return, she's still there at the window, holding back the curtain and looking out. When she hears my footsteps coming towards her, she says, 'It's really high. What floor is this?'

'The ninth.'

She has her hair pinned up. I draw close to her and kiss the nape of her neck with my lips open and my eyes closed. How much time has passed since I've kissed her like this? Already, I'm wondering how I could have given her up for so long. Once again, her warm body is next to mine, and that virgin room will help us to forget.

Now she'll feel the wetness of my lips on her neck. She'll baulk at first, but then she'll be mine again, just as she's always been. She can't give me up; she told me so herself. When she lowers her arm, the curtain shuts out the daylight and the view of the city. I start to undress her right there, leaning against that stiff, heavy fabric. I take off her jacket, which she's kept on until now; it's an ugly faded jacket made of some kind of fluffy wool. It weighs nothing and appears to be held together by mucilage. My fingers brush her breasts, those small, droopy breasts that please me so much. She lets me have my way. 'Darling,' she says, 'my darling,' and holds me close. I take her by the hand and lead her to the bed.

I want her to relax and be comfortable. I take off her shoes. She's wearing cheap nylon tights. I rub her legs and her feet, which are like a mannequin's. She slips off her skirt herself, folds it carefully and drapes it over the foot of the brass bed. Then she does the same with her shirt. Her movements are slow; she's trying to take her time, to postpone the moment of intimacy.

I get undressed in a hurry and throw my clothes on the floor, taking advantage of her averted eyes, because now I feel ashamed. She undoes her side of the bed, lies down and pulls up the covers. I get in next to her. The bed's cold. She's lying there stiffly, hands at her sides. I throw a leg over her, but it slides off, because she's left her tights on. I say, 'We don't have to do this if you don't want to.'

'I know.'

What a considerate lover I've become all of a sudden! How ridiculous I must seem! She didn't feel the slightest desire to take off her clothes. She would have gladly stayed where she was, looking down through the parted curtains at the world below, wondering if there was a place for her somewhere. When I enter her, she gives a little start, then nothing; she lets me move back and forth in absolute silence. I keep my face buried in her hair. I don't dare look at her; I'm afraid of meeting her impassive eyes. I let out a loud groan, hoping she'll take pity on me and respond. But nothing happens. We don't take off – we don't even leave the ground. I've got blood in my eyes and her hair in my mouth. Despite my efforts, I don't exactly get carried away, either. I see and hear everything: the soft hum of the minibar; the bathroom fan, which I've left on with the bathroom light; the sound of my flesh sliding in and out of hers. This last is the sound that's truly terrible. Italia's not here; her flesh is empty, and now I'm a weight inside her, the deadweight of dead love. This embrace is our funeral. I feel my sweaty bulk pressing down on her skeleton. She doesn't want me any more; she doesn't want anything any more. Her body is a passage that's closing itself off. At this moment, I understand that I've lost everything, Angela, because everything I want is here in my arms, lifeless. I push my chest off of hers, looking for her face.

Her eyes move around under her tears like two fish in a very narrow sea. She's crying; it's the only thing she's felt like doing since we entered this hotel room. My shrunken member withdraws, swift as a rat crossing a street at night.

I lie next to her in silence until her weeping becomes gentler, less anguished. There's a fixture on the ceiling, an oval of whitewashed glass, a blind eye looking down on us with total indifference. I say, 'You can't not think about it, can you?'

A gust of wind blows the window open, and icy air assaults our naked bodies. We stay as we are, unmoving, letting the cold wound us. Then Italia gets up, closes the window and goes to the bathroom.

I watch her nude figure cross the room, one hand covering her breasts. I stretch out my arm on the sheet where she's been lying. The lukewarm outline of her body is still there, and I think that it's all over, that it has come to an end like this, in a hotel. My thoughts slide into the folds of the sheet. I think about a friend of mine who used to go to a prostitute – always the same one – when he was a young man. By his request, when they made love, she pretended to be dying. I think about all the men I've known, men who made love, like all men, and now are dead. I think about my father. He went with all sorts of women, always using extreme discretion, not that it was necessary; after he separated from my mother, he lived alone. Still, he liked to keep certain matters as abstract as possible. He'd choose strange, solitary figures, middle-aged women with few attractions. They all seemed like dullards, but perhaps each of them had her secret ways. One worked as a cashier at a second-class cinema. She had dyed hair, aquiline features and large breasts tightly bound inside a rigid brassiere. I saw her only once, when my father took me to a bar that connected with the cinema lobby through a glass door. As I observed the woman through the glass, I noticed that my father was watching her, too, but furtively, with a look in his eyes I didn't recognise. They were a child's eyes, overhung by his bushy old satyr's brows. He seemed happy with his location, his son on one side of him and his lover on the other.

Maybe she'd told him she wanted to meet me. I pretended I didn't know what was going on. Later, I learned this woman's name was Maria Teresa, she was married to an invalid and she had no children. She and my father often went to eat in a little restaurant at the back of a delicatessen; her favourite dish was beef tongue in green sauce. I never found out anything more about her. But now the sheet my hand's resting on becomes a movie screen, and I watch that woman undress. She slips off her little watch and places it on the marble top of an old bedside table. My father's by her side, taking off his trousers and hanging them on the wooden clothes rack. The perfume on the back of her neck is bitter. In a little *pensione* in a side street near the delicatessen, where she has just eaten beef tongue in green sauce, my father and the ageing cashier with the stricken face make love.

Whatever happened to those two? Like us, they left behind a rumpled, lukewarm bed in a *pensione* with narrow staircases, where a closing door sends a rush of wind through the crack under the other doors on the same floor. My father smokes while the cashier's in the bathroom, splashing water into her armpits, puckering her lips and applying her lipstick. Then she turns off the light, just as she does in her own home. Later, after they've gone, a maid comes in, carrying a bucketful of cleaning products in one hand and clean sheets rolled up under her other arm. She opens the windows and throws the dirty sheets on to the floor. Then comes another woman, with her own particular smell and her own particular undergarments, and she undresses by the side of another man. She, too, makes love; she, too, submits to the probing of her insides.

I wonder if my father's cock was bigger than mine. I never saw it, but deep in my heart, I think it must have been. Meanwhile, he's still in the coffin, where I left him a few months ago, dark-faced, cotton wool in his nostrils, a flower in his hand. Who put that flower there? The cashier, maybe. No, she wasn't at the funeral; that was an old affair, years and years ago. They probably broke up, but she continued to eat beef tongue in green sauce with somebody else. Maybe she's dead, too. Italia's in the bathroom, and I'm stroking the sheet where she lay. It's still a little warm. The movie's over; the screen is blank and wrinkled again. I know I'm going to cry soon, for all the dead lovers, for myself and for her, in there looking at herself in the mirror, like my father's cashier. When she gives me my turn in the bathroom, I'll cry. Because she and I are like all those who have been here before. We'll keep on going, and we'll die far apart. No one will ever know anything about how close we were, how deeply each of us entered into the other, nor anything of our life together up to now, when I'm lying here with my arm flung out across the sheet where she was lying a little while ago. It's not warm any more. We're needy flesh, Angela, self-duplicating flesh projected on to an empty screen. Or perhaps our energy nourishes another world, a perfect world that lives very near ours, where there's no need to be afraid or to suffer. Maybe we're like those black sailors who shovelled coal in the bellies of steamships so that a pair of lovers could have a romantic dance up on the bridge, above the twinkling carpet of the sea. Someone will gather up our dreams, someone less imperfect than we are. We're doing the dirty work.

I'm in the bathtub with the taps running. My member, abandoned to its own devices, bobs in the moving water. Later, bent over the bidet with my hands on my head, I weep. Soon a maid will come in and throw our sheets on to the floor. On one of them, there's a little spot of wetness that trickled out of Italia's intimate parts. I have kissed that spot.

When we leave the room, I raise my arm to turn out the light, but then I hesitate. Italia turns and looks for the last time at that pool of darkness before it disappears behind us. We're both having the same thought: *What a shame! What a missed opportunity!*

They must be almost there. Your haematoma's been aspirated and removed from your head; the tube filled up with red blood. They're irrigating you with saline solution.

Manlio got here a little while ago, and now he's sitting across from me. He embraced me, tried unsuccessfully to cry and glued himself to his mobile phone. Your mother's flight will be a little late, and he insisted on knowing the exact minute when the landing would take place. A discussion began, and he raised his voice. Getting pissed off at an airline information agent – that is, at nothing at all – is his way of showing his solidarity with me. The mobile phone is still hot in his hand; he can't put it down. He wants to call someone else, but he doesn't know who. He's afraid of being alone with me in the midst of this silence. You know how he is: he's accustomed to lighting up life the way he lights up his cigars. He fidgets around, exhaling loudly. His mouth has fallen down, and so have his eyes; he's in a cage. Closed up in a cage with me, his best friend, on the worst day of my life. I watch him unconcernedly, thinking about the question I saw on a mural: *How can you see the bottom if you keep splashing around on the surface?*

'Excuse me, I have to telephone Bambi.'

He goes to the window, hunching his shoulders to isolate himself, and mutters. He doesn't want me to hear him. I consider his backside. He made fifty-seven last month, and he is unequivocally fat.

He clears his throat and changes his tone. He's talking to his extremely blonde, extremely beautiful, extremely obnoxious twin girls: the 'Pukies', as you call them, Angela. Manlio's dark, stocky, immediately likeable; they don't resemble him at all. They look like their mother, Bambi, that north-easterner with the fashion model's slender figure and the peasant's hard heart. She made him leave the city and move to that big estate they live on with the horses, the deer and the olive groves, where she has herself photographed for magazines dedicated to country living. She poses in front of the stables, dressed as a cowgirl from the Maremma, together with her daughters, wearing checked skirts and embroidered blouses. They cold-press the olive oil, put it into fancy bottles and ship it to America; they're making pots of money. Bambi's a stickler for organic agricultural products. Manlio, on the other hand, gorges himself on fried foods in noisy restaurants in the city. Then, in the evening, he zooms down the autostrada at 190 kilometres per hour, rushing to get home to the decorative ears of corn and the bunches of dried lavender. He detests nature, particularly its silence. Of course, he's got the swimming pool, with a vanishing-edge spillway and a spectacular rock arrangement designed by his architect; but he's pissed off about the pool, too, because it's got that robot cleaner swishing around the bottom. It's implacable, like his young wife. He misses Martine, the jack-in-the-box. He attends a growing number of conferences, and every time he can, whenever he has to fly somewhere, he makes a stop in Geneva and goes to visit her in her antique shop with the little statues that all look alike. She's alone, decrepit and happy. He writes out cheques and tries to buy everything she has. 'I like helping you,' he says. She smiles and tears up the cheques under his nose. 'Thanks, but no thanks, Manlió.' That accent on the last vowel in his name drives him wild with joy. And who knows? Maybe – when he's in the aeroplane, way up in the intercontinental sky with the sleeping mask over his eyes – maybe it drives him to tears.

He puts his mobile back in his pocket and touches his balls. His lips are dark, and the cigar between them has gone out. He adores you. He's always considered you the ideal daughter.

'I'm going to the airport to pick up Elsa. See you later.'

I didn't knock. I pulled the key off the chewing gum and went in. I found her lying on the bed next to the dog. Heartbreaker barely raised his head; she didn't even do that. She had her legs curled up and an absent look on her face, and she said, 'Oh, it's you . . .'

There was nothing left in her kitchen, so I went out and bought a few groceries. I washed out the dog's bowl and dumped a can of dog food into it. Some time before, I'd bought her an electric heater, but every time I went there, it was off, as it was now. I opened the windows so at least a little sun could come in. The air in her house was stale and unhealthy, like the air in a sickroom. I kept going back there without wanting to. With my head bending low, I kept going back there, because I didn't know where to go.

She changed the furniture around. She put the table next to the chimney, and the sofa where the table had been. She even rearranged her knick-knacks, the various little objects she had, organising them according to some new order, which quickly slipped her mind; she spent a great deal of time looking for things without finding them. Her dog clung to her side in bewilderment, as if he, too, couldn't find his place any more. She was subject to sudden bursts of activity. More than once, I found her on a ladder, washing the windows or dusting the light fixture. She did house-cleaning, but she left things lying around: a dripping sponge on the table, the broom leaning against a chair. And she did the same thing with herself. Her eye make-up would be perfect, she'd have her hair neatly pulled back, but she was absent-minded: she'd come out of the bathroom with part of her skirt tucked inside her tights. I'd go to her and pull her skirt straight, as if she were a little girl. And when I did that, I felt her flesh, inhaled the fragrance of her skin. Those were the hardest moments, the times when I would have liked to get a can of petrol and set fire to everything – to her broom, to her bed, to her dog. A cone of black smoke and then nothing at all.

I hoped she'd stage some sort of revolt. I looked at her hands. She'd stopped biting her fingernails, and I hoped she was letting them grow so that she could scratch my face. The thought of leaving behind such a kind, forlorn creature filled me with fear.

There was, on the other hand, Elsa, she of the growing belly. The telephone would ring at unusual hours. Elsa would answer, but the caller didn't say anything. I knew it was her. I'd be hoping she'd speak, make some sound – I didn't care what. An insult, a howl. Your mother would hang up and lie back with her hand on her stomach, calm and serene. Then the telephone would ring again.

'I'll get it.' But even when I answered, she said nothing. I was the one who spoke: 'Is that you? Do you need something?'

I'd sit down beside Elsa again and put my hand on hers, absorbed in her slow waiting. I could have gone on like that for ever. Maybe I'm going insane, I'd think. Maybe this precision without calculation, this constant grace, is madness.

Then one evening, I went to her house. She stank of alcohol, and she didn't even brush her teeth to cover it up. Although her hair was dishevelled and she was wrapped in a bathrobe, she finally seemed like herself again. Her eyes had circles around them, but they'd lost their opaque patina. She asked me to make love to her. She asked me this out of the blue, out of the depths of those black-ringed eyes.

I said, 'You feel like . . .' and made a little gesture with my closed fist. A vulgar gesture.

I'd been to some ceremony, and I was in a dinner suit. I started feeling uncomfortable, so I loosened the clip on my bow tie. Too many tastes were mingling in my mouth, and I was thirsty. She was standing against the wall, under the monkey poster. 'Just like old times,' she said, opening her robe. She didn't have any knickers on, but she was wearing a T-shirt that I recognised at once. I recognised the paste flower dangling down from it, torn askew by my lust on that summer afternoon, so distant now. The thing was there before my eyes, dismally glittering. She leaned on the wall and raised an arm. 'Help . . . help . . .' she muttered, imitating herself. And she laughed like a depraved and desperate little girl. Then she said, in her normal voice, 'Kill me. Please, kill me.'

I looked down at her sparse tuft of pubic hair, grabbed both sides of her robe, and covered her up. 'You'll catch cold.'

I went into the kitchen for some water and drank it straight from the tap. The water was like melted ice. When I returned to the living room, I found her in the fireplace with her hands on her head, as though trying to hold herself still. The alcohol was starting to work on her. 'Turn out the light,' she said. 'My head is spinning.'

'What did you drink?'

'Hydrochloric acid.'

She laughed again, but she didn't vomit. All the while she spoke, she kept holding her head. 'You remember that market vendor I told you about, the one with the dress? He was my father. I did it with him. I screwed my father.'

'Did you report him to the police?'

'For what? He wasn't a monster. He was a poor devil who couldn't tell a rock from an olive.' She shook her head, suppressing a belch that puffed out her cheeks. Her drunkenness had passed like a storm, washing everything clean. Italia was limpid. 'It's better this way, my love. I would never have been a good mother.'

I wanted to pull her out of that chimney, out of that black grotto. She was far away, in a place I had nothing to do with. She was telling me this secret of her life only now, now that we were breaking up. She knew she'd never find anyone else to tell it to. She drank to bolster her courage, because she wanted to help me go away. I went to her and stroked her forehead, but there was a cunning cleft between her flesh and mine. One part of me was already safe, far from her corrupted love. *Was it really you that I loved? Or was it that I expected fate to bring me love, as I still do? I'll go strolling through the world again, and it won't make any difference if nostalgia makes my heart tremble like a tooth in a dead gum. Everyone has a forgotten past dancing along behind him. Now I look at you, and I see what it is you're teaching me. You're teaching me that sin entails retribution. Maybe that's not true for everyone, but it's true for us. Because we've scraped ourselves away, together with that child.*

I don't smoke; therefore, there wasn't even a cigarette butt with the imprint of my lips. There was no visible witness to my passage in that house. The invisible witness was in Italia's body. She cut my toenails once, but she didn't throw the clippings away; she slid them into a little velour bag, the kind used for jewellery. Those clipped toenails were all I left her of myself.

I know the smell of your head, Angela, and all the other smells you brought into the house from outside, year after year. For a while, you smelled like sweaty hands and felt-tip pens and the plastic parts of your dolls. Then you smelled like the narrow halls of your school, like the grass in the park, like smog. These days, on Saturday evenings, you smell like the clubs you go to, like the music you've listened to. You smell like the boy who's found a place in your heart. I've sniffed your contentment, and I've caught a whiff of the clouds passing over you. Because joy has a fragrance all its own, and so does sadness. Italia taught me to be silent and aware; she taught me to smell. To stop and close my eyes and breathe in an aroma. One alone, jumbled together with millions of others – you wait, and it comes; it composes itself for you – a little vaporous wisp, a swarm of gnats. All these years, I've searched for her fragrance. If you knew how many times I've followed a distant scent! I've turned into little side streets; I've climbed up stairs. All that remains of her is in smells. And see, even now, if I sniff my hands in this aseptic room, if I squash my nose against my palms, I know I'll find her smell. Because she's in my blood. Her eyes are floating in my veins, two luminescent holes, like a crocodile's eyes in the night.

The first weeks were the least difficult. To be sure, I was visibly wounded; I kept losing weight and feeling physically exhausted. But, more than anything else, I was catching my breath. I started looking after myself – taking supplements, eating more sensibly. As for the injury to my psyche, I thought that would heal itself with the passage of time. And one day, I let a new exuberance take hold of me. It was exactly like the feeling you have when you're moving house; you carry in the boxes of books, you position the furniture, you fill the drawers and you throw away what you no longer need: out-of-date medicines, half-empty bottles of liqueurs with their corks cemented in place, the old broom. I joined a gym and went there in the evenings, after I left the hospital. I closed myself inside that airless space, in the midst of other men wedged into bodybuilding machines, and I sweated hard. Convinced that strenuous exercise would help me flush out my mind as well, I spewed sweat all over the stationary bike. I shifted gears higher and higher; I was climbing a steep, fictitious grade, and I had to work harder. I lowered my head and closed my eyes, thrusting with every muscle. When I got home, I emptied the wet clothes in my gym bag on to the floor next to the washing machine, and I felt stronger, better prepared to enter the realm of the counterfeit fairy tale. My wife's belly was growing, and outside the window, the tremulous lights of the outdoor Christmas decorations shone through the branches of the trees. One evening, the wave swept over me with great force: the black wave of melancholy, of disaster. Life fell in on me. You can't reach safety by pedalling in the void. My sickness hadn't abandoned me; it had remained where it was, like that wheelless bicycle.

I called her that evening. We had guests in the living room – the usual suspects – playing some party game, sophisticated in structure but vulgar in execution. I bowed out, went quickly to my room and hurriedly dialled her number, but then I had to stop; I'd forgotten the last two digits. Anxiety overcame me. I breathed slowly, holding the receiver on my chest, until the entire number appeared, brightly shining before my mind's eye.

'Hello?'

I didn't speak right away.

'Hello?'

This time, her voice was smaller, a few tones deeper in pitch. Just a few seconds had passed while she was waiting for a reply, but the suspicion that it was me must have crossed her mind already.

'What are you doing?'

I hadn't called her in almost a month. She said, 'I'm going out.'

'With whom?'

I had no right to ask her that. I shook my head in self-reproach. My face was contorted, but I tried to make my voice sound as if I were laughing. 'Do you have a boyfriend?'

She answered in the same tone as before: 'We're going to have a few drinks.'

'We're going'? *You and who else? You've found a way to console yourself already, my little tramp!* And now I wasn't laughing at all; my voice was raspy, strangled, and I obstructed it further with fake-cheerful condescension. 'Well, then, have a good evening . . .'

'Thanks.'

And now there it was, there it was and how, that sadness that I'd hoped to hear, that note of longing, of effort.

'Italia?'

'Yes?'

And now that 'Yes' was different, Angela. I wanted to tell her that I'd already had two ECGs since we broke up – I'd gone up to Cardiology and asked my colleague there to paste the electrodes to my chest. By way of justification, I told him, 'I work out a lot.' And I wanted to tell her that I loved her and that I was afraid of dying far from her.

I said, 'Take care of yourself.'

'You too.'

Maybe she was rebuilding a minuscule existence for herself; maybe she'd gone back to that bar where we met and started over from there. And another man had come up to her and asked her a question. She was used to giving herself in exchange for not much: for a look, say, where she could see an image of herself, any image at all. Yes, she probably wound up in the arms of some random man who let her plunge to her ruin in peace. An idiot who didn't know her, who had no idea how precious she was, who was ignorant of her suffering. She let him screw her so she could have the illusion that she still existed, and she turned away and buried her face in the pillow and wept when he couldn't see her. I saw her.

It was during that period that we determined your sex. Your legs were curled up under you. Manlio gave you a little pat, switched off the ultrasound scanner and turned to Elsa. 'It's a girl . . .'

Your mother turned to me. 'It's a girl . . .'

As we drove back, Elsa was silent, her mouth fixed in a smile. I knew she wanted a girl. While we sped down the street, she was daydreaming about the life that awaited you, Angela, about the torrent of small, momentous events that accompanies a development, a destiny. She was wearing a cape the colour of milk. Next to that majestic swan, I felt like an ugly duck in a dried-up pond. I fixed my attention on the traffic, on the present, and looked for a cushion where I might lay my thoughts. Italia was there, coming and going with the wind-screen wipers. I remembered her words. She never talked very much, and the few things she said issued from her mouth as though they had made a long voyage in her mind, in her soul. She said, 'It's a boy for sure.'

She said it without solemnity, because it was what she felt, and it was true. Now I knew it was true, now that I seemed to be able to perceive a shadow destiny, where the things that never happened were lined up in a row. This thought struck me without wounding me. It would have been easier to make a getaway, to withdraw a bit more every day, until you and your mother were completely alone. Daughters belong with their mothers. They watch them while they're putting on their make-up; they try on their shoes. And I could have faded away unobtrusively and become a background figure in the house, as stealthy as an Indian waiter.

The days passed, one after another, with their collection of things that were always either the same or almost imperceptibly different, such as my face. That's the way time works, Angela, gradually, systematically. An invisible but implacable friction wears us down. Your tightly woven tissue loosens and settles on the loom of your bones, and one day, without a word of warning from anyone, you're wearing your father's face. It's not just because you've got his blood. It's possible that your being is complying with the impulses of a hidden desire, which you know you feel, even though it repels you. This alteration becomes visible in middle age; the years to come won't add anything except a few inevitable final touches. The face you have at forty is already the face of your old age. It's the one that will enter your grave.

I always thought I looked like my mother, but in the car mirror one December morning, while I was stuck in traffic, I became my father. Although I continued to detest him – without any precise reason – my misery had provoked my body to take on an appearance very much like his. I suppose the only reason I detested him was that I was used to detesting him, having done so for as long as I could remember. I took off my glasses and leaned closer to the mirror. My eyes floated gloomily inside two purple circles; my naked nose (grooved by eyewear) appeared much bulkier. Its tip had moved in the direction of my mouth, which for its part had narrowed, like a shoreline invaded by the sea. The face I saw was entirely, or almost entirely, my father's. What was missing was the rampant buffoonery imprinted on his basically gloomy features. That made him unique, and it survived his death. Stone dead and drained of all intention, his countenance still preserved its late owner's insufferable arrogance. I was his bewildered, unlovely copy, a sad gentleman with a rapacious face.

On Christmas Day, I was at your grandparents' house. The *tombola* was going on, and after a while new guests, looking stuffed and sleepy, arrived and joined the game. I couldn't stay indoors any longer. I passed my counters to my neighbour and went outside for some fresh air. After all the frantic activity of recent weeks, the streets were finally empty and the shops were locked up tight. The weather wasn't good; it was very cold, and there was no sun. I took refuge in the neighbourhood church. It was almost deserted at that in-between hour, but you could still feel the presence of the faithful who must have come in droves to the morning services. I walked to one side, under the vaults, until I reached the niche where the Christmas crib had been set up: a few plaster figures, large ones, almost life-size. The Virgin Mary, wrapped in the long, immobile folds of her mantle, gazed with downcast eyes at the small raised pallet of straw where the statue of the baby was lying. My foolish legs buckled before that cluster of ugly statues with expressions of astonishment on their faces. I plunged into a pathetic dialogue with myself, as if some invisible presence were seeing and judging me. Naturally, nothing happened; God's not going to discommode Himself for the sake of a ridiculous man. And anyway, it wasn't long before I became distracted.

No light divine shone upon the rigid baby I was contemplating in the gold-studded darkness of the church. His halo was held up by a thin rod of black iron, which had perhaps been reattached – there was a yellow patch, a stain from old glue, on the nape of his plaster neck. Maybe I can't believe because I see too many things, Angela, too many of the dirty things of this earth, which heaven will never reach. That pathetic statue, for example, which spends most of the year packed in straw and hidden in a wooden box in the sacristy. That's where the newborn with the deep blue eyes spends the winter; that's where he passes spring and summer: lying in a dark wooden box while dust and dampness seep in between the staves. His mother – also shut up in a box, also with straw on her face – rests nearby. Plaster extras, trotted out once a year for the sake of fearful, mendacious hearts like mine.

I contemplated that Nativity sceptically, like one of those tourists in shorts and sandals who enter churches to escape the sultry weather but then become curious and glance around, taking in their surroundings, the domain of incense and litanies, under the furious eyes of a pious old lady half kneeling in the first pew, the one closest to the altar. And indeed there was such a woman, on her knees, partially hidden behind a column. There's always a woman on her knees in a church. I saw the soles of her shoes, and at once I saw my mother. She was a believer, and my father forbade her to practise her faith all her life. To keep from incurring her husband's displeasure, she got used to praying in silence. She'd pretend to read, gazing glassy-eyed at an open book, but she'd forget to turn the page. Only towards the end, when my father's absences grew more and more frequent, did she regain her courage. In the dead hours of the afternoon, she'd slip into the modern church that served the neighbourhood she loathed. She kneeled in one of the side pews, close to the door, the holy-water font and the noise made by whoever else happened to come in. It was as if she felt unworthy of that holy place. The soles of that woman's shoes were like my mother's: the soles of someone on her knees, someone who's detached herself from the earth in prayer. Italia was a believer, too. She had a big cross, draped with a heavy wooden rosary, hanging on the wall of her bedroom, and around her neck she wore a little silver crucifix, which she sucked on when she was sad. I wondered how she'd spent Christmas Day. I saw part of a panettone lying among the crumbs on the oilcloth table covering; I saw her hand cutting a slice; I saw her swallow a mouthful in the semi-darkness, in that unheated house. Maybe she was looking at a Nativity scene too, one of those little plastic all-in-one-piece affairs you can buy in department stores.

Then I forgot. And while I was forgetting, life pressed in on me. In February, I became head of Surgery. This was something that had been in the air for a long time. I deserved it. I'd worked in that hospital for seventeen years. I'd been a surgical registrar, then a consultant surgeon, then a senior consultant surgeon. Now I was the boss. Other people were delighted, particularly your mother, but also my colleagues, who organised a party in my honour. This promotion crowned my career, and at the same time it circumscribed my future. I abandoned for ever the dream of moving to a poor, disadvantaged country, where my profession could finally become what I had imagined it would be when I was a boy: a constant thrill, a mission. Far from the slow, hypnotic routine of this rich, badly administered hospital, where medicines expire and equipment goes out of date while it's still in its containers. Where everything happens under anaesthetic, and the liveliest thing is the mouse that runs across the kitchen from time to time and makes the cooks scream. Each of us, Angela, dreams about something disrupting his everyday world. You dream about it when you're sitting on the sofa with your trousers off, amid the benefits of daily life. Suddenly, driven by an absurd rebellious impulse, you look for the bones of the man you would have liked to be. Fortunately for you, however, you're swathed in a solid, close-fitting wrapper of fat, which protects you against sharp edges and the ridiculous things you tell yourself.

After the director of the hospital congratulated me, I drove home alone, and I found myself reflecting on this change and on how things were arranging themselves. And it seemed to me that this promotion, too, was a precise line on the graph life had traced for me. I thought back on the recent months of amorous stupefaction as a sort of sabbatical year, an intense, passionate holiday that my heart had granted itself in view of the new cycle of responsibility that was awaiting me. I was starting to feel strong again. And if something terrible had happened, now it was drifting into the air behind me, like a scrap of paper blowing in the wind on the beach at summer's end.

Meanwhile, it was getting harder and harder for you to move inside your mother, even though her belly was huge. It protruded from her clothes like a trophy, her navel as prominent as the boss on a shield. Elsa didn't have long to go – less than a month, in fact. She was frequently out of breath. In the evenings, after dinner, I'd put my hand over the oesophageal opening of her stomach and gently massage it. She didn't sleep much, because whenever she lay down you seemed to wake up. At night, I often found her wide awake and silent, immersed in her own thoughts, holding vigil over the cocoon of desires from which you would soon emerge. I could tell that she wanted to be alone, and so I peered at her in the semi-darkness, not daring to disturb her. When we walked anywhere, she leaned heavily on my arm. Her form was imposing and clumsy; it touched me to see her reflection in a shop window. I was also touched by the way she behaved, by the stubbornness that never abandoned her. Such haughty ways, in a physique so transformed, were truly comical. Wishing to show me that she could do quite well all on her own, she conducted a much more active life than her condition might have indicated. She dressed with great care, but never in clothes bought from maternity shops, which she couldn't stand. Her skin had taken on a sheen, her eyes had grown more limpid and she continued undeterred her ongoing competition with other women.

We still made love; her desire seemed unaffected by her toiling breath. She'd lie on her side, and I'd take possession of her large, abundant, welcoming body. I had trouble overcoming my fears – they seemed to be mine alone – when I confronted the vast changes in her, which made me feel puny and inappropriate. The sex we had was gentle, a gift to flesh already heavy with child. I would have gladly done without it. But Elsa demanded attention, and so I gave her what she wanted. I took my place inside her, between the two of you, like a confused guest sitting on a little folding chair at an over-crowded party. I listened in the dark to the sound of the life beating between us, which we had created with the same bodily movements that we were making now, as if we hadn't ever stopped. I was in my own house, between the legs of the woman I'd known for fifteen years, who was pregnant with my child. Little bears romped on the wallpaper in the former guest room, and a crib stood ready and waiting. Maybe I should have been happier than I was. But intimacy is difficult territory, Angela. I didn't think about Italia, but I felt her. I knew she was still in my bones; I could hear the sound of her gloomy footfall, like the steps of an ageing housekeeper who goes round a castle putting out the lights until only darkness remains.

And there we were, entering the chaos at the children's boutique: two floors with giant windows, which exposed the interior to view from the outside. Your mother had asked me to go with her to this shop to help pick out your layette. It was six o'clock in the evening, raining and already dark. Elsa shook the umbrella and left it in the basket by the door. She patted her hair, trying to tell if it was wet, and looked over her shoulder for me. Above our heads hung an army of stuffed animals, stuck on the ceiling with rubber suction cups. In the part of the shop dedicated to children's entertainment, there were plastic toys with blunted edges. The young women at the cash registers wore red peaked caps and red miniskirts and gave every child who left the shop a balloon attached to a little plastic straw.

After going up the escalator, we wandered around in a daze, pushing our trolley past the merchandise displays, unable to make up our minds. In the infants department, the clothes were so tiny, they made us anxious. It was hot in the store. I was carrying Elsa's overcoat but still wearing mine. As I unbuttoned it, she started going over the tiny garments meticulously, reading the prices, checking the fabrics.

'Do you like it?' She pulled out a hanger and held up a regal-looking little gown, all taffeta flounces. She turned it this way and that before deciding that it was too fancy for a newborn. She wanted to buy only practical things, things you could change easily and launder in the washing machine. But after taking a few more turns, we laughed, picked up the taffeta dress and threw it into the shopping trolley. And with the same exuberance, we went around collecting little tops, little skirts, terry-cloth rompers, a pair of fur earmuffs, a blue fish you put in the tub to measure the temperature of the water, a floating book, a windmill of little animals, complete with music box, to be fastened to the pram and a pair of gym shoes size 00, totally useless but too cute to pass up. A smiling shop assistant followed us around, ready to answer questions or give advice. Your mother and I were holding hands. Every so often, she gave me a slight poke, because now I was the one who wanted to buy everything. We had a real party in that shop. Suddenly, we found ourselves wishing you'd be born right away, so we could put that fairy-tale dress on you, and those tiny athletic shoes. Now that we had your clothes, we seemed to see you. When the assistant pushed the trolley into the lift, Elsa, with flushed cheeks and perspiring brow, gave the handle a tap and said, 'Well, I believe we've got everything.'

And now, just for an instant, she looked a little lost, because we were about to go home with all that stuff. You weren't there yet; you were still afloat inside her. And she, always so prudent, who had entered the shop declaring, 'The indispensable minimum' – she, for the first time, had let herself get carried away.

At the cash register, the girl with the red cap smiled and handed me a balloon. Laden with packages, we retrieved Elsa's umbrella from the basket and left the shop. Outside, the street was loud with the sounds of traffic and the falling rain, which splattered on the pavement and drummed on the cars stopped at the red light. I'd asked the assistant to call us a taxi, and then we stood waiting for it under the shop's awning, a bulging canopy where the rainwater collected briefly before it overflowed. There was a small crowd of people around us, also taking shelter from the sharp gusts of what had suddenly become a violent thunderstorm. An umbrella belonging to an inattentive woman was dripping much too close to one of my legs. I squinted to the left, past Elsa's hair, into the blur of the red and green traffic lights and their shimmering reflections in the pools of water covering the street. I was looking for the illuminated sign atop our taxi, which was supposedly on the way. I had the handles of all the shopping bags wrapped around one hand; the other was still holding on to that ridiculous balloon, which I had not yet managed to get rid of.

At last the taxi appears, queued up behind many other cars, and slowly moves towards us. Elsa's at my side. I turn my head, trying to meet her eyes, but she's distracted and looking elsewhere. 'Here it comes,' I say.

And then I freeze. I shift my gaze back a little, back to a point between me and the traffic, where, in the midst of this vexatious downpour, something has caught my eye, has slipped into my field of vision for a fraction of a second, like a shadow. In fact, I've seen nothing, only a shape reflected in the water. But I know for sure, right away. And it's a jolt in my stomach, a clamp on my throat. Italia's there, standing in the rain and looking in our direction. Maybe she saw us as we left the shop. We were laughing at my balloon and the overzealous cashier. 'What a little tramp,' Elsa had whispered in my ear. 'She saw my belly and thought I was out of the running.' I'd laughed at her and slipped on the pavement. Elsa lost her balance trying to hold me up, and we both nearly fell. Then we laughed some more, funny and happy in the pouring rain. Now Italia's looking at Elsa, whose belly swells the front of her overcoat. And I'm still holding that red balloon. I lower it, feeling ashamed, and at the same time I try to hide Elsa's body with my own. I'm protecting her from those eyes fixed on her from a few feet away. I can't make out Italia's expression; she's in front of a lighted shop window, and her face is in shadow. Her hair isn't yellow any more, but I know it's her, and I know she's seen us. And I no longer know where I am. There's nothing but shadows around me, erased by the flashes of light that skim over my face. I'm alone with her in the sound of the rain. She's out in the open, without shelter; her body is stiff and numb, her woollen jacket is soaked through, and her legs are bare. I raise a hand, and the water pouring from the awning runs down the sleeve of my raincoat. I'm telling her to wait for me. I'm telling her, Don't move.

The taxi has stopped in front of the shop. Elsa's getting in, clutching the half-closed umbrella over her head. I hold the door and watch her shoulders, her overcoat slip inside. I turn to look at Italia; she's walking away. I follow her body as she crosses the street, threading her way through the cars as they creep along. The door of the cab is still open. I lean down and poke my head in. Elsa looks up at me, wondering what I'm waiting for. I say, 'I'll see you back at the flat.'

'Why? You're not coming with me?'

'I left my credit card in the shop . . .'

'I'll wait for you.'

Horns begin to sound from the cars lined up behind the taxi.

'No, go on home. I've got a few things to do.'

'Well, at least take the umbrella.'

As the cab pulls away, I see Elsa's face; she's looking at me through the rear window. I cross the street. For some reason, I've still got a plastic bag filled with baby things in one hand and the cashier's balloon in the other, along with Elsa's umbrella, which I haven't opened because I don't have the slightest intention of protecting myself. I look up and down the pavement on the other side of the street, but Italia's not there. I peek into a bar crowded with people on their feet in front of the counter, waiting for the storm to stop. The place smells of wet sawdust and ketchup, and Italia's not there. Now I have no idea where to look for her, but I'm running anyway. I turn into the first street I come to, which ends in a smaller street running off to one side. It's dark and narrow, solitary under the torrents of rain. I see her. She's sitting on some stone steps, leaning back against a large door. She doesn't hear me because the storm drowns out the sound of my splashing feet. She doesn't see me because she has her face buried in her hands. I look at the curve of her neck. Her hair's now dark and very short, no longer the colour of straw; it clings to her scalp like a shiny stocking. That's where I lay my hand, on that incredibly small head, on that wet hair. She jumps; her neck and back recoil, quivering as though she's received a whiplash. She wasn't expecting me. Her face is a sodden mask; her teeth chatter behind her compressed lips. For a few moments, I listen to this wild chattering, which Italia can't seem to stop. I'm standing in front of her, very close to her. My drenched raincoat is heavy on my shoulders, and water is streaming down under my collar, between my clothes and my warm flesh. Out of breath from running, I pant open-mouthed as the rain falls on my face. I've got a red balloon in my hand. How insignificant she is, how soaked, hugging herself, her white legs splayed out on the steps, a pair of glistening-wet calf high boots on her feet. It's awful to see her again, and wonderful. She looks younger. She looks like a sick child. She looks like a saint. The rainwater washes away her features; all she's got left are her eyes, like two bright puddles, staring at me while the black make-up runs down her cheeks like wet soot. She's alone, alone with her bones, with her eyes. It's her, my lost dog.

'Italia . . .'

And her name rolls down that dark, narrow street, between the walls that enclose it. She puts her hands over her ears, shakes her head. She doesn't want to hear me, doesn't want to hear her name. I kneel on the steps in front of her and seize her arms. She jerks away and kicks at me. 'Go away!' she says through her teeth, which haven't stopped chattering. 'Go away, go away!'

'No, I'm not going anywhere!'

And now I'm the dog, and I shove my nose against her, into her wet lap. There's a strong odour in those dripping clothes. The rainwater has revived some old smell that was lurking in the limp fibres of her woollen jacket. It's the smell of a sweaty animal, of childbirth. And I've become a child again, kneeling on the steps and shivering while the downpour drenches us. I put my arms around her thin hips. 'I couldn't tell you – I couldn't bring myself to tell you . . .'

She shifts her back to get away from my embrace. She's breathing hard, but she's not trying to kick me any more.

I raise my head, looking for her eyes. And now she lifts one of her hands from the top step, reaches towards me, and strokes my face. And when that hand, as cold as the stone it was resting on, touches my cheek, I know that I love her. I love her, my child; I love her as I've never loved anyone. I love her like a beggar, like a wolf, like a bunch of nettles. I love her like a scratch on the windowpane. I love her because she's all I love, her bones, her odour of poverty. And I want to howl at all that rain and tell it that it can't win, that it won't sweep me away into one of the gutters running alongside the deserted pavement. I say, 'I want to be with you.'

She looks at me with those eyes, which the water seems to have rusted. Her hand caresses my lips; her thumb slips between my teeth. 'You still love me?' she asks.

'More than ever, Crabgrass, more than ever before.'

And I lick her thumb, sucking it like a newborn baby. I suck away all the time we've spent apart. It's us again, the couple from last summer, leaning against a door under the water cascading down from the terraces, in the fragrance of a wet garden that must be in the back somewhere, us with our tepid, steaming bodies under our soaked clothes, us in the street again like two cats. My tongue follows the crease between her eyebrows. She takes off her knickers and crushes them in her hand. Her legs are spread apart like a doll's legs, her feet encased in little boots, glistening wet. I move my back and squeeze myself into her while the water seeps into our warm huddle as into a gazebo or a greenhouse. Our faces are locked together, and down below there's that viscid pleasure that flings me far away and carries off everything. And I'm no longer afraid that some stranger, outraged by such disgraceful conduct, might come up behind my unguarded back and start kicking me. I'm a fleshy worm, safe inside the body I love. We're here together; it's us again, in the twilight of our breathing, we who will not remain, who will die as everything dies.

And then it's really dark, and there's really a lot of water. Where shall we go? What will be our fate? What room will welcome us now? We shouldn't love each other, shouldn't make love, but we've just done so. Like dogs, in the middle of the street. And the sequel is always opaque, difficult, uncertain: a few awkward gestures of adjustment, a caress, a bit more shame. We've done it, and we shouldn't have done it. I've got a pregnant wife at home, waiting for me. That doesn't matter;

put your knickers back on, Italia, and I'll quickly pull up my trousers, awkward doing that with my raincoat on – at this point, it's more like a wet rag. No one saw us, because there's not a living soul in this street, which has been pulled out of the world for our sake. Italia gets up. I gaze at her spectral body inside her waterlogged woollen jacket. She looks like a lost mountain goat, alone on a high, narrow ledge during a thunderstorm. And everything's terrible again. There's a street light nearby, but it's out. *What if lightning had struck us while we were making love? A snake of electricity, flung down between her and me. A vibrating blue wire, grounded in our pleasure. In that case, yes, it would have all made sense . . .*

But now . . . Now, we try to smooth our rumpled clothing and run a hand over our plastered hair. Though our insides are still in turmoil and our bodies still shaken, we walk back to the busy avenue, which is agleam with reflected lights on the pavement, passing cars, legs flashing swiftly by under umbrellas. It's us again, two poor wretches, two squalid lovers in the middle of the street. On the ground, there's a red balloon, like a forgotten heart. Italia looks at it.

'Why did you cut your hair?'

Instead of answering, she smiles in the darkness; her uneven teeth appear under the thin blades of her lips. This is the way we rejoin the crowd: her little hand in the crook of my folded arm, her fingers digging into my raincoat. We make slow progress. I can feel from the way she hangs on to my arm that she's having difficulty walking. People brush past without noticing us. Now, finally, the rain's abated to a gentle dripping, like the last drops from a wrung-out towel.

'What is it? Show me.'

It's us again, sitting in a bar again, at its most hidden table. The wall behind Italia's back is covered with thin strips of dark wood. The table's small and wet from our wet elbows. Underneath it, our knees are touching, and pieces of old paper napkins are stuck to the soles of our shoes. I made the mistake of putting that plastic bag on the table, without thinking, and now Italia's trying to pull the package away from me. I hang on to it, saying, 'It's nothing.'

'Show me.'

And the little gown with the taffeta flounces slips out, damp and messed up. She says, 'It's a girl?'

I form a funnel with my hands, stare into it and nod. It gives me the creeps to see that white fabric there on the table between the two of us. Less than an hour ago, your mother and I were looking at that baby dress and laughing. We took it off its hanger and tossed it in our shopping trolley. We were happy. And now the thing seems horrible to me. The rainwater ruined it while we were making love. It looks like something worn by a small child that drowned in a lake. Italia's head is bent, and she's moving her hands, moving them too much, smoothing out the material, touching the flounces. 'What a shame,' she says. 'Let's hope it hasn't shrunk.'

She turns it over, looking for the label inside. 'No, it's OK. Fortunately, it can be washed by hand . . .'

What's she doing? What's she saying?

'You just have to iron it a little and it'll be perfect again.'

Now she folds it. She takes the sleeves and folds them inward carefully, as if she can't keep her hands off that fabric. Her eyes don't want to look at me; she gazes past me, at the people moving around in the other part of the bar.

'The morning I had the abortion, I went to your block of flats. You came out of the entrance, but I didn't approach you because your wife was there. The two of you walked to your car. When you opened the door for her, you hit her accidentally, not very hard. She put her hand on her stomach, down low, and that's when I understood. Because all my life has been like that, full of little signs that come looking for me.'

'You'll never forgive me, will you?'

'God won't forgive us.'

That's just what she said, Angela. And now I feel her words returning to me from that bar, from that rain, from that time long ago. *God won't forgive us.*

'God doesn't exist!' I hissed at her, squeezing her icy hands.

She looked at me, and maybe she laughed at me. Then she shrugged her shoulders. 'Let's hope not.'

We didn't talk about seeing each other again; we didn't talk about anything. I said goodbye to her in the middle of the street. She told me that she was moving away, that she had to turn over the house to its new owners.

'So where are you going?'

'I'm going back south for a while. Then we'll see. Maybe I'll go to Australia.'

'You speak English?'

'I'll learn it.'

Your mother had you the following evening. Her contractions began in the early afternoon. I was at the hospital, but I left at once. I found her in the living room, still in her dressing gown, sitting in front of the blank television screen. She gestured towards the empty place beside her. 'Come here,' she said.

I sat down next to her. She put her hands on her sides and set her face against the pain. I looked at my watch; after a few minutes, a new contraction began.

I went into the bedroom, where the bag with your things in it – yours and your mother's – had been waiting for several days. 'Shall I zip it up?' I asked, raising my voice so she could hear me.

But she was already in the room. 'Yes,' she said softly. She took off her dressing gown and threw it on the bed. I picked up her dress from a chair and helped her slip it on. I said, 'Keep calm.'

She wandered around the flat aimlessly for a little while longer. She went to the bookshelf, took down a book, put it back, took another one. She said, 'My sweater . . .'

'I'll get it for you. Which one?'

'The sky-blue one. Whichever one you want.'

I handed her the sweater, which she left on the table.

She went into the bathroom. When she came out, she'd brushed her hair and put on lipstick, but she was trembling. The pains were closing in on her, coming more and more frequently. She stopped in the hall, picked up the telephone and dialled her parents' number. 'Mama, we're leaving now. You don't have to come right away – there's time.'

★

In fact, there isn't very much time at all. Her waters break in the car. The sudden warm stream frightens her, makes her uncomfortable. She really doesn't want to arrive at the clinic in a wet dress. Luckily, she's brought an overcoat, and she's wearing it over her shoulders as we walk into a large entrance faced with dark marble. I'm behind her, carrying her bag. We go upstairs at once. When we get out of the lift, Bianca, her gynaecologist, is waiting for us. She and Elsa are on familiar terms. She says, 'Hi, Elsa. How are you doing?'

'Fairly well . . .'

I've seen Bianca only a couple of times before. She's middle-aged, tall and elegant; she wears her greying hair cut short; she likes sailing. Manlio took it badly when Elsa told him she wanted to continue with a woman doctor. She broke the news to him during one of our dinners, all the while smiling a sweet, pitiless smile. Perhaps she'd intuited the idiotic complicity between him and me. Bianca holds out a hand in my direction. 'Hello.'

Maternity's on the fourth floor. The floor covering – grass-green tiles – gives the department a cheerful ambience, like a nursery school. Cockades made of voile and pink or blue ribbons decorate the closed doors as we walk down the corridor. Elsa's room has an electric bed of gilded metal and a large window, from which you can see the branches of the trees in the garden. Elsa leans on the bed, breathing hard. As I leave the room, Kentu – a black obstetrician from Africa with strong, jovial features – comes in, followed by Bianca, who has to examine Elsa. When I go back in, the machine for measuring the intensity of Elsa's contractions is next to her bed, and she's staring into the blue screen of the monitor with gelatinous eyes. Her lips are dry; I help her drink some water. They've shaved her, given her an enema, subjected her to a great deal of intimate handling and she's been as docile as a newborn. She walks up and down the room with her hands on her sides. Every now and then, she stops, puts a hand on the wall and stays like that for a while, with her head bowed, her legs spread wide and her great belly hanging down. She moans softly. I help her breathe, stroking her back. Bianca looks in from time to time and asks, 'How's it going?' Elsa tries unsuccessfully to smile. She's read in some manual that a woman's character is revealed in childbirth. She wants to seem brave, but maybe not so much as she did before.

'You're paler than your wife,' Bianca says as she shuts the door. Firm and brusque in manner, not without a certain subtle irony, she apparently doesn't think much of men; now I see why Elsa appreciates her. I'm a surgeon, and I should be helping her more than I am, but my knowledge of obstetrics is quite rudimentary. On the other hand, the event that's almost upon us has little to do with science; it belongs to the realm of nature. That's what's causing her body to shake; that's why she's quivering this way. May it all be over quickly, I think, because now, Angela, I'm starting to be afraid that something's going wrong. Your mother's suffering. I support her forehead on my shoulder, and I'm afraid all the while. I'm an impostor. I have a lover, and I can't forget her, because she and I have lost a child, a child who would have come through travail like this into the light. But I let it go without lifting a finger to help it, and it remained in the black screen of a disconnected monitor.

Elsa's lying down again. On the monitor, the red peaks of the contractions are getting higher. She spreads her legs as Bianca examines her. Bianca thrusts one hand deep inside her; Elsa lifts her head and cries out. Her cervix is at ten centimetres, completely dilated.

'We're almost there,' Bianca says, stripping off her latex glove and tossing it into the stainless-steel container. By this time, Elsa's holding on with all her might to the obstetrician's black arms, which look as strong as tree trunks. Bianca says, 'Come and see.'

I draw near and look. Your mother's sex has grown; it's wide and distended, swollen by your head. And there in the middle is a black splotch. It's your hair, Angela. My first sight of you is your hair.

We set out for the delivery room. Elsa gropes for my hand

and squeezes it hard. The nurse pushing the trolley sets a rapid pace; I have trouble maintaining my grip on Elsa's hand. Before we go into the delivery room, she whispers, exhausted, 'Are you sure you want to watch this?'

And in fact, I'm not all that sure. I'm a surgeon, but I'm afraid of falling in a faint. I'm still stunned from the sight of that clump of black hair, spattered with my wife's blood, surrounded by her shaved crotch. I'd gladly wait outside – this business, at once poetic and bloody, frightens me – but I know I can't refuse. My being there is important to Elsa. I feel a mighty force all around me, and I register this mysterious vibration deep inside, like an ultrasound image of my adult self captured in the crystal where life begins.

And so I'm in there, in the delivery room, and the delivery has begun. Bianca moves her hands around between Elsa's thighs. Bianca's face is tensed and serious; her arms are suddenly brash and coarse, like a country midwife's. We have to be quick, and Elsa has to push, which she does, guided by Bianca and Kentu, whose hands are on Elsa's writhing stomach, pressing down purposefully.

'Take a deep breath. Now, push hard. As if you're going to the toilet.'

With the effort, Elsa arches her neck; her head is rigid, her face cyanotic. She stares at her belly, which is still filled with you. She grinds her teeth, closes her eyes, and tries to push, but she has no strength left. 'I can't do it – it hurts too much . . .'

'Breathe! Take a deep breath!'

Now Bianca's voice is loud and authoritative. 'Come on! Like that!'

I stroke your mother's sweaty hair, which sticks to the palms of my hands. Bianca takes a step backwards, away from the bed. Kentu takes her place between Elsa's thighs and peers into her sex. I move closer. Now I want to see. For a moment, Angela, Kentu's hands are inside that bloody opening, one finger on one side, one on the other. There's a sharp sound, like a popping cork, and your head is out. And then, all at once, the rest of your body. You look like a rabbit – a skinned rabbit. Your torso is long, your features squished together. You're covered with dark blood and white slime. The umbilical cord is wrapped around your throat.

'So that's why she wasn't coming out,' Bianca says. She seizes the cord and frees your head. Then she cuts the cord, and a black hand gives you a little blow on the back. Your face is so smirched that I still can't see what you look like. You're blue. You feel the blow, but you don't react; you just hang there inert, like a sausage. There's a neonatologist on the other side of the wall of glazed glass that divides the delivery room. Bianca, with you in her arms, rushes over to him. I can see only the shadows of bodies and heads. I hear the sound of the aspirator at work; your throat is clogged with mucus, and they're getting rid of it. You haven't cried yet. You're not alive yet. Elsa, sweaty and purple-faced, looks at me. Our incredulous eyes do our speaking for us. We're thinking the same thing: *It isn't possible. It isn't possible!* Elsa's hands are cold now, and so is her face. It doesn't last long, Angela, but that brief time is an interstice in hell. I see Italia, and I'm inside her; I see us making love, again and again and again. Punishing myself is all I can do; I stand on the gallows and place my feet on the trapdoor, which is ready to spring. I look at your mother, and I think that perhaps she, too, is making some vow, offering up some sacrifice to save your life. I take hold of my demon, the weight on my back, the invader of my balls, and I say to him, *Let the child live, and I'll give up Italia!*

At last, we hear the cry. Shrill, intense, perfect. We're holding hands, your mother and I; our wet palms are stuck together. A tear slides across Elsa's temple and disappears under her hair. Joy takes its time, placid and slow. The aspirator's turned off, and things return to their proper places. Pacts with the devil are already worthless, and in comes Kentu, carrying you in his arms: a pink monkey, swathed in white. I take you from him and consider you. You're very ugly. You're very beautiful. You've already got strong, well-marked lips, standing out in the middle of your crumpled face. Your eyes are swollen and half closed, because all this sudden brightness is bothering you. The delivery-room light is still on, harsh and violent, and I raise an elbow to shield you from it. It's the first gesture I've ever made to protect you. I bend towards your mother, who looks at you with an expression on her face I'll never forget: gratified, astonished and ever so slightly sad. I understand the feeling mirrored in her face, the sudden realisation of the task that life is handing her. Up until an instant ago, she was just a perspiring woman with her head thrown back, but now she's a mother; maternity has imprinted itself upon her countenance. Isolated in that flood of cold light, her hair dishevelled, her body exhausted by her labour, she has the power and the ungainliness of a prototype.

While your mother stayed on the delivery table for the after-birth, I carried you down the stairs to her room. Although you were as light as a loaf of bread, you seemed to weigh a lot, and I felt somehow unfit for this exceptional transportation duty. A cockade with a pink ribbon was already hanging on the door of your room. At last, we were alone. Gently, I put you down on the bed, leaned over you and stared down at you from the height of my adult eyes. I was your father, and you knew nothing of me, nothing of the life I carried around on my back. I was your father, a man with big trembling hands, a man with a unique smell lodged in the pores of his skin, a man traversed by forty years' worth of days. You didn't move; you remained just as you were when I put you down, like a turtle flipped on to its back. You looked at me with those watery deep grey eyes. Maybe you were wondering what happened to the dark, narrow place you'd been kept in for so long. You didn't cry. You lay there quietly, like a good baby, with your face poking out of clothes too big for you; you put me in mind of a dressed-up mouse. I thought you looked like me. You were minuscule, indecipherable, but you had something I recognised. You took almost all my features, Angela. You passed up your mother's beauty and assumed my not particularly attractive appearance, except that on you, mysteriously enough, it looks good. Yours is not a modern, aggressive beauty. Your face is old-fashioned, broad, placid, infinitely sweet; there are no shadows in it, no twilight. I've always thought you looked special, right from the start. I lay down in a heap beside you, drawing up my legs like a foetus. You were only a few minutes old, and as I looked at you, I felt vague, out of focus, exactly the way you saw me. I wondered if you'd brought me, even me, a little grace from the gleaming world you'd left behind. By now it was dawn – your first dawn.

I left you alone on the big bed and walked over to the window. Down below, past the terrace, a garden was starting to come to life. The air was grainy with fog, the sun absent. I thought about the overcast, sticky day that was beginning among the buildings and the shanties that surrounded Italia's house. What was she doing in that trickling dawn? Reeling in a rag from the clothes line outside her kitchen window, maybe, and pausing with one hand under her chin to contemplate this same gloomy sky, half obscured by the viaduct. I thought about my mother – she would have liked having a granddaughter. For the summer holidays, she'd have taken you with her to stay in one of those big hotels she favoured, room and half board for grandma and grandchild. For lunch, you'd get a sandwich, to be consumed on your sandy bedsheets. Dinners in the dining room would feature bottles of mineral water with rubber stoppers and the previous night's napkins. But I certainly couldn't knock on the door of her tomb. You were born; you weighed exactly six pounds; your eyes were large and sad, like mine.

The day passed, thick with visitors, who filled the room with themselves and their flowers. Elsa's parents trotted back and forth between their daughter's bed and the nursery. Distant relatives and close friends arrived. Grandma Nora rattled on, entertaining the visitors, passing judgements about who you resembled. In the intervals between visits, she tidied up the things that were lying around the room. She collected the fruit jellies and arranged the flowers in vases. As usual, her excessive attentions irritated Elsa, who lay there woozy, her hands crossed on the swelling in her belly, the pink rubber bracelet around her wrist. When she met my eyes, she raised her eyebrows and silently implored me to liberate her from her mother. I took Nora by the arm to lead her down to the little bar in the clinic. But before we left, you were laid on your mother's breast. I leaned over Elsa and helped her position you correctly. You seemed much more of an expert than either of us – you already knew what you had to do. You seized the nipple, sucked and fell asleep. For a moment I stood and watched the two of you. From those very first hours, I felt that the true bond was the one between you and her.

By the time evening comes, I'm dazed and weary. I've moved the chair over to the window. The fog has never completely dispersed, and now it's growing again, gumming up the darkness. In the garden, in the middle of the flower beds, there are lights surrounded by white halos in the thick grey air. A car passes cautiously, slipping between the hedges, and glides away, out of range of my eyes and my nose. *Whatever happens, none of us will live. This circus will come to an end, this whole pervasive meretricious waggle of things, of cars in the darkness, of lights in the fog, of eyes reflected in a windowpane. I'm a sad man now, and so I will remain: a man who stares suspiciously at his eyes in the windowpane, who finds it hard to love himself, who survives despite his indifference to his own life. And what can I give you, my child? You've gone back to the nursery in your wheeled cot; your mother needs to rest. The tray with her dinner lies abandoned at the foot of the bed, and now, sleepy-eyed, she's watching television with the volume turned too low. How will I be able to teach you anything, I of all people? I don't believe in joy; I punish beauty. I love a little woman with a skinny butt. I slash open bodies without flinching. I piss standing up and weep in secret. Maybe I'll talk to you about myself some day; maybe some day you'll stroke my cheek and find it strange to think that what your hand is touching is me.*

Raffaella crosses the garden in her acid-green jacket. She was here earlier this afternoon, taking a lot of pictures. For one of them, she set the timer on the camera and flung herself heavily on to the bed next to Elsa; the bed buckled and swayed under the sudden weight. She said she'd come back later, after work, and now it's a mild, mild evening and she's tripping past the flower beds with a package in her hand: little pastries for her best friend to eat. Raffaella pokes her head round the door, smiling her ineluctable smile. Elsa sits up and they kiss each other again. Raffaella asks, 'Where's Angela?'

'In the nursery.'

'That means I can smoke.' She sticks one of her brown cigarettes in her mouth, opens the package of pastries and places them on Elsa's stomach. It's excessively hot in the room, so I take advantage of this moment to get some fresh air. I take a little walk in the fog, not going very far. Then I enter the clinic cafeteria and join several other men, all brand new fathers like myself. Poor jerks with waterproof jackets, shadows under their eyes and trays in their hands. The place is dark, like its stone floor, its low ceiling and its dismal yellowish glazed light fixtures. Daddies in the dining hall, like grammar-school kids at lunch. The food, naturally, is repulsive. But it's nice to be tucked away like this at the back of the clinic; it's like camping out, or being punished. As it's a little late, the pasta is soft and puffy, and the *scaloppini al limone* has dark edges and a sauce whose principal ingredient seems to be wallpaper paste. But nobody complains. Voices are kept low, as in a sacristy; upended glasses and sets of silverware rest on sheets of paper and tinkle a little as they're transferred to the trays. A few men stop and search among the bottles of mineral water for some of those screw-top bottles of wine. They pause for a bit, but then they take one, because they think, What the hell? Tonight's a night for celebration. Tonight my dick has given the world a gift, and I deserve a little drink.

Then we sit down and eat as men do when there aren't any women around. Quickly and a little crudely, holding a piece of bread always at the ready. We eat the way we masturbate, going faster and faster towards the end. I'm at a corner table, drinking a beer, using my fingers to pull apart a couple of pieces of cheese and eating them without bread. I've got my elbows on the

Formica table top, which bears the marks of a recent sponging. I look into those opaque depths, staring at the backs of men like me.

I spend the whole night in Elsa's room. The imitation-leather couch under the television set turns into a short, narrow bed. But I don't lie on it; I sit in the armchair and put the cool, immaculate pillow behind me, between my head and the wall. I close my eyes and doze. It's not particularly noisy, but it's not silent, either. Around two o'clock, Elsa asks me for a drink of water. I hold the glass to her lips, which are dry and nearly split. She says, 'Come and lie down next to me.'

I stretch out on the big broad articulated bed with all the pillows. Elsa's breasts are large under her nightshirt, and she smells of stale perspiration and medicine. 'I can't sleep,' she says. 'It's as if they threw me into a washing machine.'

After a while, she falls silent, as silent as her hair. Maybe she's sleeping now. I open the door, slip into the darkened corridor and go to the nursery. Its window is covered for the night by a gauze curtain, through which one gets a hint of hulking shapes – the cots and their shadows. I put a hand on the pane of glass; my daughter's asleep there on the other side. Her little hands are blotchy, her closed eyes like seashells on her face.

At dawn, Kentu comes in carrying you. Warm from sleep and red from your recent bath, you're wearing a new little outfit, white, with pink embroidery, and your face seems more relaxed, but your mother's face has faded into a yellowish pallor. She's leaning over you, looking at you, and you look back at her with your misty eyes, staring at her breast like a needy animal.

'I'm going.'

She barely raises her head. I'm standing at her bedside, holding my wrinkled jacket over my shoulder with a tired hand. My unshaven face is the face of a man who hasn't slept. The look she gives me is gentle but anxious, as though a suspicion has crossed her mind. I move towards the door like a moth that's been trapped in a room all night long, and now its wings are heavy as cork.

'When are you coming back?'

I heard a noise, and I felt a sudden blow, a thud inside my chest, as when you fall in your sleep. Maybe it was nothing, a purely internal landslide, the remnants of a thought. But no, something must have fallen in there. Although muffled by a wall, it was a sharp, heavy sound, like metal hurled against a hard surface. It was a trolley – that's what it was – a trolley rolling across the floor at high speed and crashing into a wall. Maybe you're dead, and Alfredo's causing that commotion. Just when he thought he'd pulled you through, you died under his hands, without warning and without a sound, like a flame. Alfredo turned round, saw the trolley they brought you in on and struck it. With an arm, with a foot. The sound was like a scream; I know I heard it. I must have heard it. I can't move; I can only wait for a door to open. I'm waiting for two elegant, merciful legs. I hear the muted steps of Ada's rubber-soled clogs. She's coming to tell me, as I requested. She's walking over to me, and she doesn't realise you've just been born. You're only a few hours old, and you're suckling at your mother's breast. As she walks, Ada's hands are sweaty and chilled from the fear she's been confronting and will continue to confront when she meets my eyes. She takes the last few steps, and I listen to the faint sounds those hands make as she gently smoothes her smock. Now she's here. I see her reflection in the door, but I don't look at her face. I look only at her legs, and I wait. *Don't speak, Ada. Don't say anything. A bit of your skirt is showing under your smock – grey, like the two of us. Thirty years ago, I could have married you. You were the youngest anaesthetist in the hospital, and the best. I sweet-talked you a little, and you remained silent. Until that afternoon – when was it? You* were waiting for the bus. I stopped and gave you a lift, and once you were in the car, all of a sudden you started talking. I'd never seen you without a hospital uniform on. You had a narrow waist and full hips, which spread out on the car seat. The memory of your knee, which you were stroking with one hand, has stayed in my mind. But by then, it was too late; you had passed me by, and I hadn't really noticed. Ah well, let it go, it's better this way. Life is a storeroom filled with boxes, some empty, some misplaced for ever. We're what remains, what we've grabbed hold of. What's your life like now? Do you eat your dinners standing up? Why didn't you get married? Are your breasts very old? Do you smoke? Have men treated you well? Which side do you sleep on? Is my daughter dead?

I come charging up like a bear, like a buffalo with dirty fur. Her front door's ajar. When I push it, it resists; there's something behind it, keeping it from opening all the way. It's dark inside – the shutters are closed – but it's a daytime darkness, the kind with hints of light. I can make out what's blocking the door: two big suitcases and a few boxes. There's a strange disorder in the room, many objects are missing from the shelves, and the place smells of coffee and displaced dust. I take a few silent steps into what looks like an abandoned house. I glance into the deserted kitchen, where a single cup is standing upside down on the worktop next to the sink.

'I'm in here.'

Italia's lying on the bed, propped up on her elbows and peering at me through the plastic strips of the bedroom curtain. 'I woke you,' I say. 'I'm sorry.'

'No, you didn't. I was awake.'

I cross the room and sit down next to her. There are no sheets on the bed, and she's fully clothed. She's wearing a high-necked blue dress that doesn't even seem to be hers – it looks more like one of Elsa's. She hasn't taken off her shoes; they're still on her feet, resting on the bare mattress. Two low-cut wine-coloured shoes. Her uncomfortable position makes her shoulders look tiny. Her neck, taut and muscular, strains between them. She says, 'I was on my way out.'

'Where are you going?'

'To the station. I'm moving away; I told you I was.'

Her neck is as white as light, and around it she's wearing a flowered scarf. One end lies across her chest, while the other trails on the mattress. Her face looks rachitic, held together by make-up, and she has the disoriented air of someone in transit. I say, 'It's a girl.'

'Is she beautiful?'

'Yes.'

'What's her name?'

'Angela.'

'Are you happy?'

I pick up one end of her scarf, then the other, and I hold them in my hands, loosely, gently, and then suddenly I pull the ends tight, clench my fists and yank her head. 'How could I be happy? How could I?'

Without any warning, I start to cry. Big heavy tears, slowly making their way down my unshaven cheeks. 'I can't live without you,' I groan. 'I can't . . .'

'Of course you can.'

And there's a gleam in her eye, like an unspoken challenge, visible against that perpetual backdrop of pity for herself and for whoever's close to her. She says, 'I have to go or I'll miss my train.'

I relax my grip, spring to my feet, dry my eyes with a couple of rough swipes.

'I'll drive you.'

'Why?'

She stands up, thinner than ever, her dark dress clinging to her skinny body. Her breasts seem to have disappeared; all that's left of them is a little ridge below her sternum that shudders as she breathes. She's wearing a hair clip in her extremely short hair, a totally useless hair clip, which gleams in the semi-darkness. The mirror is still in the room. Italia turns round, steps to the mirror and looks at herself. She brushes her eyebrows with a fingertip. That's all she does, just makes this one unfamiliar little gesture: the final, unnecessary adjustment to her appearance, or perhaps just a salute to herself: Good luck in your new life.

I stoop and pick up her luggage. She lets me take the cases, murmurs, 'Thanks,' and walks to the sofa to get her mucilage jacket, which is lying with its sleeves spread out, like a crucifix waiting for her arms.

On the threshold, she turns round and takes a last look at her house, her humble house. I don't sense that she's feeling anything like nostalgia – she's just in a hurry, and at the same time vaguely anxious, as though she's afraid she's forgetting something. Maybe I'm sadder than she is. I've loved her in this house. I've loved her on the sandstone floor, on the sofa, on the tobacco-coloured chenille bedspread, against the wall, in the bathroom, in the kitchen; I've loved her by the dawn's early light and in the depths of moonless nights. And suddenly I realise how much I love this house, which now trembles once again as a car passes over the viaduct.

Italia's shifting eyes come to rest on the bottom of the sofa. The flowered cloth is gone, revealing velvet upholstery, ochre in colour, dirty and torn.

'What are you looking for?'

'Nothing,' she says, but something's narrowing her eyes.

Then I remember the dog, with his nose always sticking out from under that crippled sofa. 'Where's Heartbreaker?'

'I gave him away.'

'To whom?'

'To the Gypsies.'

The poster, by contrast, is still where it always was; the monkey with the baby's bottle has not moved from the wall.

Once we were on the street, I noticed that Italia was lurching more than usual on her high heels. Her weakness seemed to radiate out from her centre. Her back was curved, and she bent forward as she walked; her upper body leaned away from its proper axis, as if she were trying to anticipate something. Some fear, perhaps. I put her cases in the boot and turned to her. She was standing on the other side of the street. I picked up the box she'd insisted on carrying, which was now on the ground at her feet.

She didn't move; she let me do it all and watched me as I closed the boot. When she got into the car, when she crouched to take her seat, I saw her face contort in vexation, as though she'd been dealt some undeserved pain. I asked, 'What's wrong?'

'Nothing.'

A short time later, while I was driving, she put both hands on her stomach and let them slide slowly down into her lap, as though she was trying to be inconspicuous.

I didn't drive to the station; I didn't even pretend I was going to drive across the city. I got on the ring road and headed for the autostrada. She asked, 'Where are we going?'

'South. I'm giving you a lift.'

By this time, we were already on the autostrada. Italia shook her head weakly, then assented and slouched back into her seat without offering further resistance. 'How long will it take?' she asked.

'Less time than the train. Lie back and enjoy it.'

She closed her eyelids, but they continued to quiver, as though the eyes beneath them could find no peace. She opened them again, turned her head towards me, stretched out her hand and stroked my leg. This caress sent a tremor of pleasure and happiness through me, and I had a sudden urge to pull over, park the car next to the crash barrier, and make love to her then and there, to slip inside that scrawny little jewel box of hers. 'Come here. Sit closer to me.'

She obeyed, laying her head on my shoulder – her small, bony, trembling head – and remained still, watching the road with me. As I drove, all I had to do was move my jaw slightly and I could find an ear or some other part of her to kiss. She was breathing softly, and little by little a feeling of great peace took possession of us. It wasn't a particularly pleasant day; the sun, when it shone, gave little warmth, and we even went through some patches of fog. The traffic flowed along in a thick stream. Every now and then, a lorry pulled out into the fast lane, its driver signalling his intentions a few seconds after beginning to carry them out. It was an ordinary day, Angela; there was really nothing very special about it. And yet that was the loveliest trip I ever took. If I think back on my life, if I think about a supreme moment, I relive that drive, the two of us speeding through the landscape outside the car, while inside it everything is still and we're caught up, without injury and without travail, in something like an enchantment – a deep, unhoped-for joy, built out of nothing. It was as if heaven, from behind those anonymous grey clouds, were offering us some compensation.

I don't remember ever having felt so in harmony with myself: my chest under my shirt, my forehead, my eyes, my hands on the steering wheel, the light burden of her head on my shoulder. Italia had fallen asleep. So as not to wake her up, I tried not to move. I changed gears only when I had to, and then softly, gently, because one of her legs was resting on the shift. I had worked hard to love her; I'd rejected her, pushed her away; she'd had an abortion because of me. And now all that was in the past. I was going to keep her by my side for ever, and that flight to the south felt to me like my first real step in her direction. Yes, that trip back into the places of her past was going to give us a chance to start everything over, to begin again. Now I was in a hurry to get there; I longed to see her climbing out of the car in her rumpled dress. I pictured her gesturing to me with one white hand behind her back, behind her wind-blown scarf, asking me not to follow her, to let her take the first few daunting steps into her remembered world alone. Maybe there, I thought, on her native soil, outside some small, crumbling stone church, I'll kneel at her feet and hug her legs and beg her pardon for the last time. Then I won't have to do it any more. From now on, I'll love her without causing her pain.

That's what I was thinking about, Angela. I wasn't thinking about you. You were a healthy baby; your mother was doing fine. I decided to write her a letter, a brief letter, telling her the whole story without attempting to justify myself in any way: the facts, and nothing but the facts, in a few lines. The rest was all mine. There's no explaining love. It stands by itself; it makes mistakes and struggles on its own.

I intended to arrange everything as quickly as possible, without needlessly wasting time. I'd call our lawyer friend, Rodolfo, in the morning and tell him to come to terms with

Elsa. I'd give her carte blanche – she could have everything. The only thing I wanted was the creature whose heart was beating against my side. And now I was carrying her off with me, and we were hurtling down the autostrada. The land had become flatter, and clumps of dusty oleander bushes grew beside the crash barrier. The light had changed. The day was collapsing into night; contrasts were becoming less sharp but perhaps deeper, and Italia's face seemed almost purple. Below the steering wheel, one of her hands fell, half open, between my leg and her seat. I grabbed up that hand and held it tight. It's mine, I thought. Woe to anyone else who touches it, woe to him.

I was thirsty and eager to get to a toilet, so I stopped at a service station. When I slowly withdrew my shoulder from under Italia's head, she gave a little sniff and settled back into her seat. It wasn't cold at all outside. I searched my pockets for some coins to put in the tin saucer the attendant had left on a little table at the entrance to the toilets. Since I had no change and there was nobody around, I took a piss on the house. There was only one other customer in the restaurant, a coatless, solidly built man eating a sandwich. I bought an espresso in a plastic cup, a bottle of mineral water and a box of *biscotti* for Italia and went back outside.

I stood around the service area for a while, drinking my coffee. Two cars pulled up to the petrol pumps. A man got out of one car, spread his legs and rested his elbows on the roof. The air had changed, because the sun, which I hadn't seen all day long, was out in the open, shining as it prepared to set. The slanting light came closer, caressing the earth, and the earth seemed to rejoice in that rose-coloured benevolence, that precious finishing touch. And the unfamiliar, radiant, gleaming quality in the air confirmed that now we had crossed the line into the real south. I looked across the service area at the car wash, whose huge blue brushes hung down unemployed. I turned towards my car. Italia was sitting up, awake, in the passenger seat. She looked at me through the glass and smiled, and I replied to her smile with a wave of my hand.

After that, we were in good spirits. Italia turned on the radio. She knew the words of all the songs, and she started singing along in that hoarse voice of hers, moving her shoulders to the rhythm. Then it got dark, Italia stopped singing, and a voice informed us that there were rough seas.

She was shivering; her legs were shivering, and so were her hands, abandoned between her legs, in the thin white hollow where her flesh became soft.

'Why didn't you put on tights?'

'It's May.'

I turned on the heater. After a while, I was sweating, but Italia never stopped shivering. I said, 'Maybe we'd better stop somewhere for the night.'

'No.'

'We should at least stop and eat.'

'I'm not hungry.'

She trembled as she stared out at the road, at the lights of the vehicles ahead of us, which were beaming through the darkness. We were off the autostrada now, travelling down a two-lane main road immersed in silence. Italia had told me which exit to take, and now she was directing me, but she was hesitant, maybe even a little worried, because it was too dark to recognise anything and she didn't know how much had changed. I asked her, 'How long has it been since you came back here?'

'A long time.'

She'd taken an extended nap, but she was still having trouble holding her head up. I reached out to caress her forehead; it was burning hot.

'You've got a temperature. We have to stop.'

A few kilometres later, as we were passing through an anonymous village – a few ugly houses crammed together beside a badly lit road – we saw a vertical sign that said in fluorescent letters TRATTORIA, and below it a horizontal sign with smaller letters: ROOMS, ZIMMER. I turned into the dirt car park on the shoulder of the road.

'Do you need any of your bags?'

She didn't reply. My words brushed past her neck, which was

bowed inertly in the darkness. I said, 'Come on, let's go.'

I bent over her, putting one arm around her waist, and helped her out of the car. I could feel her bones vibrate as I lifted her, and a deep sigh, an attempt at self-encouragement, shook her chest. The sky above us was bathed in the light of a full moon with a charitable face. Holding tightly to each other, we walked towards the sign, stopping to look at the moon. It looked so close that it seemed to be part of us, no longer part of the sky; so low and heavy that it lost something of its mystery and became humanised.

We entered the trattoria through a glass door covered with sheer curtains. On the right was a long, deserted bar; on the left, a big sad dining room. Several men were sitting at tables here and there. Few of them were eating. Most of them were drinking wine and looking up at a television set that was broadcasting a football match. We sat at a distant table. Someone's eyes moved towards us, uninterested eyes that quickly returned to the TV screen.

A woman came out of the kitchen, wiping her hands on her apron. She had a crude face, surrounded by a cloud of dishevelled grey hair. I asked her, 'Is it possible to get something to eat?'

'The waiter's gone for the night.'

'Some cold cuts, or maybe a little cheese?'

'Would you also like some vegetable soup?'

'Yes, thanks,' I said, quite surprised by the woman's affability.

'I'll heat it up for you.'

'And a room? Could we get a room?'

The woman stared at Italia longer than necessary. 'For how many nights?'

When the soup came, Italia ate nothing but a few spoonfuls. I looked at her short dark hair, which I wasn't yet used to, at her face, which was thinner than ever, made up of hollows and little shadows, and at her blue high-necked dress: She looked like a nun without a veil. I poured her a brimming glass of wine and insisted that we drink a toast. Her response was to push her glass next to mine without lifting it. We toasted on the tablecloth – too low, like the moon in the sky. We could see it through the window, which was set in a metal frame. The moon hung there, displaying its kindly overstuffed face, the air around its sphere diaphanous in the darkness. It seemed curious about us. I was a little tipsy, having gulped down three full glasses of wine, one after the other. Although we were in a roadside inn redolent of stale food and cheap drink, I was happy because I was with her, hundreds of kilometres away from the city where I'd lived like a rat. Happy because our life together was beginning, and every stage of it was going to be splendid; it would have to be. And now I was afraid that Italia was sad, so I gathered myself and tried to cheer her up, fearing that it might not take long for me to become sad, too. I felt that looking for our reflection in that moon might suddenly make us miserable. I didn't want to think about that, Angela, so I drank instead. I was drinking because I was full of confidence, because life had presented me with a way to redeem myself; I was drinking because we'd have another child, Italia and I. I would deny her nothing, never again, and I'd treasure her for the rest of my days. I gazed at her, and my stupid eyes glistened with confident hope. So she isn't hungry, so what, I thought, she's just tired. She needs to fall asleep and dream, while I caress her in spite of that fat-faced moon. And if she gets hungry during the night, I'll walk down the stairs to the darkened kitchen and steal something for her to eat, a little bread, a few slices of sausage. And I'll watch her eat, hovering over her like a Cupid in the night.

She vomited into her plate. The convulsion caught her by surprise, reddening her face while a dark vein in her forehead swelled and pulsed. She picked up her napkin and brought it to her mouth.

'Excuse me.'

I reached across the table and squeezed her hand, which was too hot and sticky with perspiration. 'I should apologise to you,' I said. 'I'm the one who talked you into eating.'

Her face had grown extremely pale, and her eyes were filled

with a strange surrender. She coughed, then looked around, as if afraid someone might notice she was unwell. The place was quiet except for the drone from the television set as the announcer followed the movements of the ball. In the back of the dining room, behind Italia, the kitchen door opened, thrust aside by the woman's body. She approached our table, carrying a tray of cold cuts. The food was well arranged on the tray, with little clusters of vegetables preserved in oil, grilled aubergine slices, and sun-dried tomatoes gleaming among the sliced sausages.

'My friend doesn't feel well. Could you show us to our room?'

The woman gave us a perplexed look; maybe she didn't trust us any more.

'Please excuse us,' I said, placing a note for 100,000 lire on the table, along with my identification. 'I'll come back downstairs and give you the lady's papers.'

The woman picked up the banknote, walked slowly over to the bar, opened a metal box and took out a key, which she placed in my hand.

The room was large and tidy-looking, but it smelled like a place that's been closed up for a while. There was a bed of veneered wood and a matching wardrobe, its feet still wrapped in the plastic it had come in. Two towels, a long blue one and a short brown one, were hanging next to a sink. The curtains were green, and so was the bedspread, which I turned down to the foot of the bed. Italia sat down, bending over herself, clutching her stomach with both hands.

'Are you having your period?'

'No,' she said, and she let herself fall backwards on to the bed.

I took off her shoes and helped her to stretch out her legs. I shoved her pillow under her head. The pillow was half empty – you could press it practically flat – so I took the one that would have been mine and gave her that, too, to lift her up a little more. There really was a strange smell in the room, an unhealthy chemical odour. Maybe it emanated from that nasty furniture, fresh from the factory. I pushed the curtains aside, pulled up the blind, and opened the window to let in the fragrance of the mild night, so mild that it seemed to be summer already.

Italia was shivering on the bed. I closed the window and looked for a blanket. I found one in the wardrobe, a rough brown blanket like the ones they give out in army barracks. I folded it in half and spread it over her. Then I slipped a hand under it and felt for her wrist. Her pulse was weak, but I didn't have my doctor's bag with me, so I was totally unprepared. I hated myself for such negligence.

'Please, let's go to sleep,' she said.

I stretched out next to her without even taking off my shoes. Now we'll go to sleep, I thought. We'll fall asleep as we are, fully dressed, in this ugly room, and tomorrow she'll feel better. We'll get an early start in the cool of the morning. We'll stop for breakfast in a bar; I'll buy newspapers and some razor blades. As I lay there, the wine I'd drunk in such a hurry turned stale in my stomach. I missed Italia's voice; I missed her body. I had a stiffening erection, and I was longing to make love to her, but she was already asleep. I turned off the light. She was breathing heavily, noisily, like an exhausted child or a dreaming dog. The wine really hadn't been very good. It had made me tired for only a little while, and now I was wide awake again. My mouth felt thick and tasted sour. I curled up next to Italia, gently, trying not to wake her. She was mine; she'd be mine for ever.

The moonlight fell upon one side of her face. In profile, she appeared to be frowning, perplexed, as if she'd carried some uncertainty with her across the threshold of sleep. I didn't ask myself what that uncertainty might be. No, I smiled in the darkness, feeling the skin under my cheekbone crinkle against the sheet and thinking about how much I enjoyed watching her while she slept. I was happy — we rarely notice when we're happy, Angela — and I wondered why we're always unprepared for happiness, why it takes us by surprise, unawares, as if we can know such a benign sentiment only by brooding over it when it's past or by longing for it to arrive. Yet at that moment, I was happy, and I said so to myself: I'm happy! The small part of Italia visible to me in the weak light of that simple room, as dreary as a furniture factory, was enough to make me happy.

Her forehead was glistening with perspiration, which I tried to dry with part of the sheet. She was still burning hot, maybe hotter than before, and a trickle of saliva ran from her mouth to the side of her neck she was sleeping on. Soon I realised that each of her exhalations was accompanied by a moan. I listened closely. The moaning began to break up, and eventually it stopped altogether. But then it came back, as piercing as the twittering of a frightened bird. I shook her. 'Italia . . .'

She didn't move.

'Italia!'

She must have been in a deep torpor. Her lips were a little parted, and she seemed to be chewing, although her mouth was empty. Her eyes remained closed. Maybe she was searching for a word, a word she never managed to find.

I got out of bed, bent over her and began to slap her, gently at first, then harder and harder, trying to wake her up. Her head rolled back and forth, offering no resistance to my blows. 'Wake up!' I cried. 'Wake up!'

I didn't have any kind of medicine with me; I didn't have anything. And I didn't know anything, either. I was no diagnostician. I was used to following a clearly outlined plan, used to operating on specified portions of the body, patches of flesh surrounded by cloths. And where were we? In a little inn off a secondary road, in a part of the country I didn't know, far from any city, far from any hospital.

Then she moved and even mumbled a greeting. But she was so groggy and numb that she must have felt my slaps like the soft beating of tiny wings, as if a butterfly were importuning her. I pulled her to a sitting position in the bed, trying to arrange her so that she could lean back against the wall. She abandoned herself to my efforts but slipped a little to one side, her head lolling weakly on her shoulder. I switched on the lights, ran over to the washbasin and turned on the tap all the way. With a cough, the water came rushing out and splashed me. I wet a towel and pressed it on to her face, soaking her hair and her chest in the process. She came to, opened her eyes and kept them open.

'What is it?' she asked.

'You're not well,' I stammered.

But she acted as though she didn't realise that anything was wrong. She seemed not to have noticed the sudden crisis that overwhelmed her in her sleep. With a few violent movements, I stripped her to the waist. 'I have to examine you,' I said, almost screaming.

I palpated her abdomen. It was as hard as a table top. She didn't move. 'I'm cold,' she murmured.

I looked out the window, hoping the moon would set in a hurry and stop shining its light on us. We have to get out of here, I thought. Right away. And then, just at that moment, I saw that she was urinating; a stain was spreading over the sheets. She looked at me without realising what she was doing, as if the body doing it didn't belong to her. I poked her rigid stomach again. 'Can you feel that?' I shouted. 'Can you feel my hand?'

She didn't lie. 'No,' she murmured. 'I don't feel anything.'

Angela, that was when I understood that something very serious was happening. Italia's back slid further down the wall, and she lay twisted on the bed, her grey face between the pillows. 'Let's go,' I said.

'Let me sleep . . .'

I lifted her entirely off the bed. Her body weighed nothing. Colour from her dress had run on to the white sheets, leaving a pale blue blotch. I carried her across the hall and began to kick at the door with the ground-glass windowpane and the little sign that read PRIVATE. The woman opened the door; behind her stood a young man with dazzled eyes.

'A hospital!' I shouted. 'Where's the nearest hospital?'

I was barely finished speaking when Italia – as if to show them the reason for my distress, for my madness – slumped unconscious in my arms. I cried out, and my eyes filled with furious tears, with a refusal so intense that the woman and the boy I took to be her son flattened themselves against the wall while they tried to give me directions to the hospital. I ran to the car and set Italia in the passenger seat. Wearing a nightdress and slippers, the woman followed me outside, for no particular reason. She didn't know what else to do, so she assisted with my fury. I looked at her in the rear-view mirror, standing in the dirt car park in front of the inn, enveloped in the cloud of dust I raised as I drove away.

The directions I'd received were scanty and imprecise, and I was in such a state that I didn't even remember them. But if we must go, life will bear us along, Angela. The road, glimmering in the light of dawn, was the needle of a compass that drew me onward. I trod harder on the accelerator and spoke to Italia. 'Stay calm,' I said. 'We're almost there. Everything's going to be all right. Stay calm.'

Italia was calm. Motionless, burning hot, maybe already in a coma.

Meanwhile, the sea was in the air, in the flat, fractured roads, in the vegetation. The sea of the south, with ghastly buildings lining the beach not far from the road. Finally, in the centre of a little traffic circle, under a jumble of rusty road signs, the bright white sign with the red *H* in the middle. A few hundred feet more, and there we were. A building of modest proportions: not many storeys high, rectangular in outline and surrounded on all sides by cement paving. One of those seaside hospitals that stay practically shut down all winter long. Just a few cars in the car park, and one idle ambulance. The only illumination in the deserted casualty department came from the security lights. I was carrying Italia in my arms; one of her wine-coloured shoes was missing. I looked through the porthole window in a door and pushed it open, only to discover other doors and more silence. I called out, 'Is anyone here?'

A nurse stepped into the corridor, a young woman with black hair pinned up behind her head.

'It's an emergency,' I told her. 'Where's the physician on duty?'

Without waiting for a reply, I kicked open the doors of a

nearby room. Frightened, the girl followed me at a distance, accompanied now by a little chap wearing a white coat that was much too short for him, like a nursery-school smock.

At last, I found an intensive-care room. This, too, was empty of people, its rolling blinds were down, and it was crammed with hospital equipment that had evidently not been used for quite some time. I attached Italia to an oxygen bottle and turned towards the girl. 'I have to do an ultrasound.'

She stood stock-still. I grabbed her by the arms and jerked her towards me. 'Hurry up!'

Soon the ultrasound trolley was rolling in my direction, pushed by the male nurse with the short coat. I opened the medicine cupboard and fumbled with a bunch of useless boxes. When the physician on duty arrived – a middle-aged man with a bristly beard covering his cheeks all the way up to his glasses – I was injecting Italia with an antibiotic.

'Who are you?' he asked. He had the dirty voice of someone abruptly awakened.

Without even turning round, I said, 'I'm a surgeon.' The ultrasound monitor lit up.

'What's wrong with her?' he asked.

I didn't answer him. I pressed the probe against Italia's stomach and kept my eyes fixed on the monitor . . . but I couldn't see anything. Everyone was standing around me in silence. I could hear the physician's breathing, very close behind me, the laboured breathing of a heavy smoker. And now I understood what was wrong, even though I didn't want to believe it, and the others understood it, too. Her abdomen was full of blood, and yet she hadn't had even the smallest discharge. The haemorrhage was wholly internal; it was possible that some of her lower organs were already necrotic.

'Where's the operating theatre?'

The physician on duty glowered at me in great vexation. 'You're not authorised to perform an operation in this building . . .'

I was already pushing Italia's trolley, but without knowing which direction to take. The young female nurse stepped to my side and took hold of the trolley, trying to steer it. The operating theatre, identical to the other rooms, was there on the ground floor, at the end of a corridor lined with pale blue tiles. The lights were off, and the room was stuffy with the odour of evaporated alcohol. The electrocardiograph machine had been shoved into a corner, together with an empty instrument trolley. We entered that dark space. I pushed Italia into the middle of the room, under the theatre lamp that hung from the ceiling. When I switched the lamp on, I saw that many bulbs were burned out.

'Pull the blinds up!' I told the nurse. 'Open up everything!' She carried out my orders robotically. 'Where are the instruments?' I asked.

She slipped into a little room, where the doors of a large metal cabinet were just visible. She opened the cabinet and began to rummage around in it. When I entered the room, she was crouching on the floor, going through a drawer, from which she eventually pulled out a sealed bag filled with scissors – nothing but scissors. She looked at me. She had no clear idea of what I might need. I yanked the drawer off its slides and turned it over, spilling its contents on to the floor. I did the same thing with another one, and then another. In the end, I found what I needed: cold scalpel, forceps, retractor, cautery, clamps, needles. Everything was there, packaged in sterile bags. I threw them all on the instrument trolley.

I cut Italia's dress in two and pulled the two halves apart, revealing her body. The sight of her flesh, surreally white in that cold light, of her bony sternum, of her small pink nipples, criss-crossed by blue veins – this sight struck me like a blow.

'Electrodes,' I said.

They were suction electrodes, and the nurse attached them to Italia's chest for the electrocardiogram. Then I intubated her myself, slowly, so as not to hurt her. I took two green cloths from a stack and gently placed them on her, one across her legs and the other on her upper body, high enough to cover her breasts. I prepared the correct dose of Pentothal, then scrubbed hastily and put on a sterile coat over my street clothes. The physician on duty came over to speak to me. His voice was more metallic than before. He said, 'This hospital is little more than an outpatient clinic. We're not equipped for this kind of operation. If anything happens, you're in trouble, I'm in trouble, we're all in trouble . . .'

'She's septicaemic.'

'Load her in the ambulance and take her to a proper hospital. Please, listen to what I'm telling you. If she dies on the way, it won't be anybody's fault.'

I took him by the face, Angela, by a piece of his beard, an ear, whatever I could get hold of. I grabbed that man and threw him against the wall. He went away. I scrubbed once again.

'Gloves,' I said, spreading my fingers. The dark-haired nurse did her best to put the surgical gloves on me smoothly, but her own hands trembled.

The young male nurse, the one with the ill-fitting coat, was lurking in a corner of the operating theatre. Now he had on a long operating gown and a surgical mask. I glanced in his direction; his face seemed strangely trapezoidal. I asked him, 'Are you sterilised?'

'Yes.'

'Then come and give us a hand.'

He obeyed me and took up a position near Italia's head. 'Don't take your eye off the monitor,' I told him. 'And be ready to defibrillate if we have to.'

Outside the window, a bluish light was making itself visible. Italia's face was serene. I felt strong, unexpectedly strong, Angela. This was a familiar scene – I'd seen it somewhere, who knows where, perhaps in a dream. I'd already lived this moment, and maybe I'd even been waiting for it. We were keeping an appointment, she and I. And it seemed to me that my life finally made sense, that I had penetrated the mystery. The terror at the sight of blood that I'd felt as a boy, the incision, that white moment when the flesh, though cut open, has not yet begun to bleed . . . maybe all that was her. That scalpel sliced into her body. The blood I feared was hers, just as I feared her love. She was already there. One who loves you is always there,

Angela, there before knowing you, there before you. I wasn't afraid now. Warmth suddenly spread through my shoulders, an intense, beneficent sun meant for me alone.

'Scalpel.'

I took hold of the tool, tightened my grip and held the blade over her flesh. I love you, I thought, I love your ears, your throat, your heart. And I made the incision. I heard the sound of her opening, and I waited for her blood.

Then I went to work. Blood from the haemorrhage had damaged the organs; the parts of them that were most exposed had already taken on the dark colour of necrosis. I moved the intestine. Her uterus was grey, her tubes were enlarged and there was pus everywhere. A great mass of it was festering under the pouch of Douglas. I immediately thought about her abortion, Angela. This infection had been caused by a traumatic operation – and yet something didn't make sense: women die of septic abortions pretty quickly. She must have undergone a second curettage, and that one had been faulty. So she had just dragged herself along like that, with the infection inside her. I moved my eyes and took a step backwards. Right, I told myself. Let's add *that* thought to the list. I looked round; the young man with the trapezoidal face was staring at me in terror, and the other nurse wore an equally distressed expression, along with a streak of blood across her forehead. I looked at Italia's little, waxen, sleeping face, slightly tinged with the green reflection of the cloths surrounding her. That was when I asked God to help me. I raised my arms above my head and clenched my bloody gloves into two fists. It was going to be a struggle; I wasn't going to let her go, and I wanted Him to know it.

I put a stop to the haemorrhaging, cleared away the pus, performed a small resection of the intestine. It was only at the end that I turned to her uterus and saw that a hysterectomy was the only choice. Her womb was too compromised – the infection had spread everywhere – and I couldn't risk the consequences of leaving it in place. So I extirpated the grey sheath that should have borne our child. I didn't raise my eyes again, Angela. Sometimes, but only every now and then, when I needed a new instrument, I shifted my gaze to the right, towards the black-haired nurse, who was never certain what she should present.

My hands in Italia's body made the only sound in the room: that slippery, sticky, compressed sound that a surgeon's fingers make when he's performing an operation. But now I was optimistic again, full of confidence once more. I was also soiled and quivering, and I stank. Sunlight was coming through the window, flooding the room, and there was a new light, an abundant light, on me, too. The nurse was perspiring from fatigue and heat, and only then did I realise how close it was in that room. I was sewing up the incision, and I could feel the heat sink into my hair and strike my fingertips. The graph showed a regular heartbeat. I passed the needle through her flesh like a careful tailor giving the final touches to a wedding gown. The night was over. And soon afterwards, at last, I sat down on the chair behind me. I hadn't shaved or bathed for two days, and yet I thought myself angelic, sitting there with my eyes closed and my head leaned back against the wall, like the hero of a television programme.

However, she died. Two hours after the operation, life departed from her. I was by her side, and she was conscious at the end. I'd moved her into another room on the same floor. The bed next to hers was empty. When she woke up, I was standing at the window, which was level with the road. I had seen nothing of my surroundings the previous evening, but now, as I peered out into the daylight, I realised that the landscape was flat and the earth clayey. A large billboard depicted a cowboy straddling a can of beer. This is border territory, I thought, a zone of exchange. The very buildings, the block of structures that constituted the hospital, had the fragile, bureaucratic look of a custom house. Every love story needs its trials, I told myself. A car passed, a little red jalopy; it passed without a sound. The sun shone powerfully, climbing the sky. Soon it'll be summer again, I thought, and I smiled.

She stammered something, and I turned round. The sun was inside her eyes, brightening her grey irises with flecks of silver.

'I'm thirsty,' she murmured. 'Thirsty . . .'

A bottle of mineral water, nearly empty, stood on the Formica bedside table. Earlier, when the nurse had brought me the water, I was so parched – the operation had lasted nearly six hours – that I drank almost all of it down without pausing for breath. Now just a few swallows were left, a little pool on the glass bottle's green bottom. I poured some on to my pocket handkerchief and daubed at Italia's dry, chapped lips. She opened her mouth like a hungry baby bird. 'More,' she said.

I wet the handkerchief again and slipped it between her lips. She sucked at it. And then – this all happened in the course of a few minutes – she suddenly raised her head. Her neck shook, but the voice that came out of her was strong and didn't sound like her own.

'What should I do?'

She seemed to be addressing nothing and no one, or perhaps a detached image of herself, a twin sister dancing before her eyes, on her head, on the ceiling. I planted my hands on the bed forcefully and leaned into her line of sight. *Where do you want to go, all cracked and chapped and out of breath? Where do you think you're going?* I supported myself on my clenched fists, stiff-armed, careful not to fall on top of her, blocking her vision. I was in shadow, and she lay below me in the light. She'd already crossed over. Her pupils were rolling around in the whites of her eyes, searching for something, for some place high above her, and she floundered about, straining to reach it.

'What should I do?' she asked again, this time in a thin, strangled voice. She seemed to be addressing someone up there on the low sun-streaked ceiling, someone who was waiting for her. I stroked her face; her mandible was unnaturally stiff. Blue veins showed through the flesh under her chin, and her tensed neck was as diaphanous as a parchment lantern in the wind. How many times had I seen her slip away like this? When we made love, suddenly she would bend her head back towards the wall, stretching her neck until it became long and thin, searching for a place all her own in the darkness. She'd squeeze her eyelids together and flare her nostrils, almost as if she were following a scent, the heavy fragrance of a happiness she would never enjoy, no matter how desperately she sought it on the sweaty pillow. I tried once again to command her sight, to make her look at me, but her chin slipped out of my perspiring fingers.

'Love . . .'

She took a deep breath. Her chest rose, then sank again, and her whole body sank in that exhalation, surrendered with it. Then she looked at me, but I wasn't sure that she could see me. Her lips moved as she spoke for the last time: 'Carry me.'

And she didn't tell me where. Her head rested, unmoving, on the pillow. She was no longer alive and not yet anywhere else, suspended in the non-place that precedes death. Her face was relaxed, broader; she was looking up, where someone was waiting for her, and her trouble and toil were over. Her last breath was a soft moan, a sigh of relief. That's how she found the road to heaven, Angela.

Don't move.

I saw my saliva dripping on her – my mouth was full of it. I didn't release her, not from my eyes, not from my anguish. I stayed where I was, breathing on her, bending closer and closer to her, maybe hoping I could save her with my breath. Then I lay across her, and my face came undone . . . I felt a gentle force emanating from her, like vapour rising from water. I wasn't thinking about doing anything medical – I'd forgotten I was a doctor. I looked at her the way one looks at a mystery, with attentive, moist eyes; I looked at her the way I'd looked at you a few hours before, when I'd watched you being born. I let her die like that. I let her last breath pass her lips, and the wind from that last breath touched my eyebrows. And she was gone, fled away, absorbed into the ceiling. Instinctively, I raised my head to look for her. And that's when I saw him, Angela. I saw our son. His face appeared to me up there, just for a second. He wasn't handsome; he had a thin, bitter mug, like his mother. The little son of a bitch had come to get her.

After his face was gone from the ceiling, I noticed a crack in the plaster, together with a moisture stain that looked a lot like him. I snuggled beside what he'd left me, that motionless, still-warm body. I took one of her hands and held it against my chest. *All right, Crabgrass, go on, go away where life can't wound you any more. Do that crooked little dog step of yours and go away. And let's hope there's really something up there, some covering, some giant wing, because if the black void is all there is, you got a pretty rotten deal all round.*

There was a lot of stuff lying around that room – chairs, medicines, equipment – and I started kicking everything I could reach. Then I looked at my hands, still chalky white from having been inside surgical gloves for so many hours. I clenched my fists; I clenched my entire uselessness. And I took it out on the wall; I took it out on my hands. I swung my fists with a really exceptional ferocity, pounding the wall until the skin on my knuckles broke and bled and exposed the white bone. I didn't stop until someone came into the room. Many people came into the room, and one of them, a man, overpowered me and twisted my arms behind my back.

Later, they bandaged my hands. I sat on a bed, looking at those wounds without emotion, as if they didn't belong to me. I felt no pain; I was busy thinking about what I was going to do. I'd rinsed my face, stuck my neck under the tap, pissed, stuffed my shirt back into my trousers – I'd done all of that with those aching hands – and now I was just sitting there with the hair on the back of my head wet and plastered to my skull.

They bandaged my hands, or, rather, a nurse did, a young woman with a lock of copper-coloured hair hanging down over her face. The coroner had already come, filled out his forms and gone. We had to get some clothes back on Italia, but all her other clothes were in her luggage, which was in the back of my car. I wasn't her husband, I wasn't a relative, I wasn't anybody. The nurse who was giving me first aid had the same rights over Italia's body as I did, no more, no less. She raised her head, swiped the hair away from her eyes and tucked it behind her ear. I thanked her and got down off the bed.

I went into the hospital director's office, and from there I phoned a deputy prefect of police I'd operated on a few years previously. Everything got taken care of in less than an hour. A sergeant from the nearest police station showed up, a most accommodating man. He'd tracked down Italia's family, in the person of a female cousin. This woman, he said, had no objection whatever to my making all the arrangements for the interment of her cousin's body; she had, in fact, seemed relieved, particularly upon learning that I proposed to bear all the funeral expenses myself.

We were standing in the hall, the sergeant and I, and he looked at my bandaged hands. Then he said, 'What exactly was your relationship with the deceased woman?'

It was perfectly normal human curiosity, but wrapped in a uniform. I said, 'She was my fiancée.'

The sergeant had bright blue eyes. He made a grimace that looked like a smile and closed his eyes tightly, burying that blue light under wrinkles. He murmured, 'Please accept my condolences.'

Very soon after that, I had in my pocket an official document, covered with stamps, and in my arms a pile of Italia's clothes. I'd selected various items from her luggage. I'd walked to the car park across from the hospital and stood behind my car in the hot sun, bending into the boot and rummaging around in Italia's suitcases. Stop thinking, I told myself. Grab something and get away.

Corpses should be dressed by two people, but I wanted to do it on my own. When the nurse offered to help me, I shook my head and asked her to leave me alone. She made no objection. No one in that hospital, I noted, had dared make any sort of objection to me since the scene with the duty physician. The grief I was suffering from terrified and repelled all who came into contact with it.

Death has swift feet, Angela, and he comes running with great alacrity to take possession of what is his due. Italia was still, and she had no more temperature than the bed, the table or any other inanimate thing. Dressing her wasn't easy. I had to roll her to one side and then the other to get her arms into the sleeves of her blouse. For the first time, she gave me no help. And it broke my heart, because I knew she would have helped me had any trace of life remained in her at all. She would have lifted her arms, instead of letting them hang so heavily, and fall, and bang against the iron bed rail. It didn't hurt. At last, the blouse was on her, sleeves included, and the only task remaining was to get the buttons through the buttonholes. Now that she had taught me to love her, now that I knew I loved her – now she was leaving me.

I was looking at her nipples, one here and one there on the sides of her chest. Pale nipples, as transparent as larvae. By chance, while going through her things, I'd come across the little jewellery bag where she kept my toenail clippings, and I'd put it in my pocket. It was a soft camel-coloured velour bag. I hid it between her hands. *There you are, Italia; there are your jewels. You and these yellowed chips will turn into dust together.*

A man arrived. He wore dark glasses and a dark suit, and shiny shoes that resounded on the floor. He knocked on the door and, without waiting for a response, entered the room. This was a discreet but resolute person, one who knew how to behave around people in mourning. He looked into my expressionless face and perceived at once what kind of death he had come to deal with and what level of grief I was feeling. As he stepped over to the bed, his jacket opened, and I saw his black belt and its gold buckle. I was enchanted by that buckle. Its owner was a man of the old school, impeccably dressed, his gleaming pomaded hair slicked back flat against his round skull. The dark lenses erased his eyes, and his mouth was a slash in his face. He looked at Italia and considered her remains. Italia was beautiful, perfectly at her ease in death, fixed in a stony beauty without shadows, without cheapness. The man could not fail to notice that beauty, my child, or the distance that separated it from us. But this was the material he worked with, and I don't doubt that every dead person taught him something. He had the swift eyes of a seasoned tailor, of one who knows how to take measurements without a ruler. He did his job quickly. Italia was so thin that a child's coffin would have suited her; anything bigger was a waste of wood. I looked at her with his eyes, the eyes of an undertaker, who has to look very carefully. And then I felt a completely unexpected intimacy with this stranger. We were on the same frequency, two men united by a common thought, two faces turned towards a mystery. His was more accustomed to such contemplation than mine, but he still looked fragile, even behind the framework of the flawlessly pressed jacket and the impenetrably dark glasses.

He put his hand on my shoulder, a warm hand that didn't move. I'd been in need of that hand without knowing it. I could feel it doing me good. It was a gloomy, resolute southern hand, holding me to the earth. It seemed to say to me, We have to stay behind and forget, without trying to make sense of this darkness that comes over us. He made a broad sign of the cross, slashing the air. I stood next to him and followed his example, like a disobedient child before a priest.

We reached an agreement concerning the next several hours. It was still early, and a certain amount of time had to pass before the body could be transferred to the coffin. I was in no hurry; I wanted Italia to stay in my sight as long as possible. The sun was flooding the sky at my back, outside the window I hadn't dared look through again, and now the movements of things had ceased to interest me. I gazed at Italia's fixedness while the light was falling full on her, which meant that the shadow of the world was lowering itself into darkness. Later, in the bluish shimmer that filled every corner of the room, her flesh became blue-grey ashes.

I fell asleep sitting up, with my chin on my chest. And I dragged her along with me, blue as she was. I saw her, wet to the crotch, wading through the still, slimy waters of a docking basin, trudging towards a small vessel, perhaps a postal boat, laden with cargo. I heard the splashing sounds her movements made as she tried to get to that boat, which wasn't going to ride at anchor very much longer. She had some of her things with her. She was carrying a voile dress with a pattern of red flowers and pulling a floating table behind her through the shallow water; the dress was on a hanger, blowing in the wind. There was a chair on top of the table, an empty chair. She wasn't tired and she wasn't sad; rather, she seemed fervent, zestful, and in the gathering dusk, her hair looked like frogs.

Sometime after nightfall, a person came into the room and was amazed to find it in darkness. 'Where's the light?' he asked, and the hand accompanying his voice groped for the switch. I saw that hand, because you can sense things better when you're used to the dark. The man, it turned out, was a priest. He was short but not thin, and the ample skirts of his priestly robe trailed on the floor. His face was both gaunt and collapsing, free of colour, and given to a single expression, a kind of smile that was supposed to suggest the exalted level of beatitude he had attained but looked more like a sardonic and deeply insipid smirk. He approached Italia's bed and solemnly masticated an unintelligible prayer. There was nothing sacred about this priest's half-hearted blathering, and I thought I detected something sordid about him. He was, in any case, as insignificant as a lazy guard loitering in his sentry box, staring without interest at the crowd of people coming and going, as though he were looking at dust blown along by the sirocco. He gave the dead woman his blessing in a sequence of rapid movements, made a plaintive but barely audible sound and went away, leaving the light on in the room.

Came the dawn. I leaned out of my chair to the bed, rested my head on an elbow and looked at Italia from below. Her face was beginning to turn darker, as if the night had forgotten some shadows and left them on her face. In fact, the darkening was caused by her coagulating blood, the first sign of imminent decay. Instinctively, I looked at my arms to see whether there were such dark blotches on my skin, too. But my flesh looked unblemished in the dawning light.

When the undertaker came back, he had pushed his sunglasses on to the top of his head, exposing his eyes. The light in the room was icy, and his white shirt gleamed between the black lapels of his jacket. He wasn't alone; a boy was helping him. The coffin lay where they'd placed it, on the floor outside the room. 'Hello,' the undertaker said.

'Hello,' I replied.

He gave a satisfied nod, pleased with this response, because it meant that I was now capable of speech. I looked into his uncovered eyes, and I saw that he was conscious of the obscenity of his profession. He said, 'You'll have to leave the room.'

I went out and the coffin went in, together with the boy, also in jacket and tie, and a nurse who had come to assist them, a thin woman with shifty eyes.

Someone suggested a bar further along the road, close enough to walk to. It was next to a display of swimming pools – huge dusty sky-blue basins.

The old man behind the bar was intent on putting a deck of playing cards in order. 'What time is it?' I asked him.

'Six something.'

I drank a cup of espresso. Although I wasn't hungry, I did my best to force down a pre-packaged brioche that tasted like the plastic wrapping it came in. After two bites, I tossed the rest into a tall bronzed bucket that might have been an umbrella stand.

'See you later,' said the old barman, speaking to my back as I headed for the door.

As I stepped out, a bus passed by, ploughing the road silently, like a ship on the sea. The old fellow and I would not, in fact, see each other later; his coffee was an abomination. And I wouldn't be seeing this landscape again, either, this flat expanse of clay reaching to the horizon. This was where I'd thought I was going to live; this was where the adventure I'd believed in was supposed to begin. Now there was no wind, and the inert air was spread over the earth like cellophane as far as the eye could see, constraining the movements of every living thing. Italia's death reigned over that space all the way to the horizon, to the spot where the sun had risen. *Goodbye, my love. Goodbye.*

Pillowed on satin, she lay in her coffin. They'd tucked her blouse into her skirt and brushed her hair. The luxury of her surroundings revealed, by contrast, her humble origins. She looked like a country bride, or like the effigy of a local saint, fit for carrying in processions. I think they'd probably put something on her face, some cream or wax, because her cheeks sparkled a little. It was that very sparkle that made her piteous.

'She's missing a shoe,' the undertaker said.

I went back out to the car park and found the shoe – wine-coloured, with very high, very thin heels – where it had fallen off her foot the previous night. I put it back on her and looked at those twin soles, scuffed and darkened by who knew what roads. Those shoes made more of an impression on me than anything else. I thought about her gait, about the effort she put into walking, into living, about that little tenacity of hers, which had failed to do her any good whatsoever. The last part of her I touched was an ankle. After that, they closed her up.

We left the hospital. Since I didn't have the strength to drive – or the will, for that matter – I knew I'd have to make the trip sitting beside the silent man with the gold belt buckle. I locked my car and walked to the hearse. Before getting in, the undertaker took off his jacket and hung it up behind his seat, using a hook set into the upholstery on the other side of the glass that separated us from Italia's coffin. The jacket grazed the polished wood. The confident thought that this contact would be maintained throughout the trip appealed to me. I felt comfortable in the deep seats of that car, a machine as impeccable as its driver. A fragrance of sandalwood emanated from the upholstery and the dark brier of the dashboard.

We travelled down old roads, patched in many places and encroached upon everywhere by low-growing wild blackthorn and the suffering trunks of olive trees. Here and there, a palm tree had opened an unexpected crack in the asphalt. The vegetation in these parts followed no method; it simply rose up from the ground, as sporadic and confused as the buildings we passed along the way. Everything that stood out in that land-scape appeared arbitrary, ready to be pulled down and hauled off. I don't know, maybe all this reflected the spirit of the people who lived there, and maybe it was in that very arbitrariness that they saw order. I supposed one would eventually stop being surprised at chaos, grow accustomed to it, perhaps even discover in it a secret fascination. I looked out of the window. I had no sunglasses between me and the unsparing midday light, which laid bare everything it touched, exploring things in their smallest details. I reflected that we were, after all, on the way to a cemetery, and that this passage through purgatory was not at all disagreeable.

The undertaker drove without speaking. His hair was shiny with pomade, his shirt collar was immaculate and he showed no trace of perspiration. In such jumbled, disordered surroundings, his correctness appeared positively alien. He was driving quite fast, keeping his neck straight and maintaining his composure despite the repeated shocks. Our trip seemed to me like a journey out of life. The terrain, my travelling companion, my state of mind – everything was bound up together in the same consternation. And then there was that coffin behind me, sliding placidly over the felt carpet of the hearse as we sped around curves or bounced over the worst parts of the road. I imagined Italia's body rolling about in her excessively luxurious, excessively large casket. I'm not looking for pity; I'm not looking for anything, Angela, believe me. I don't even know why I'm going over all this again. It's like when a man drinks too much: He can't help pissing, and he pisses into a hole that carries away everything, or on to a wall that doesn't know him.

We drove past some houses built of stone, others covered with navy-blue tiles, and several working-class blocks of flats, rows of little balconies with thin railings. Modest lives were being carried on behind those burnished windowpanes. Everyone turned towards the funeral car and watched it as it passed; some touched their crotches to ward off bad luck, while others made the sign of the cross. The young boys playing football on whatever dusty spaces they could find turned and looked, and so did the women at their windows. Men planted in front of bars raised their eyes from the pages of their newspapers. It struck me that a lot of people seemed to be idling, but then I remembered that it was Saturday.

We passed a church with outside steps so steeply graded they seemed about to plunge into the street. A group of people wearing festival costumes stood on these steps. An emaciated woman with a little girl in her arms and a red cloth cap on her head followed our passage, rotating her upper body. When I met her eyes, they were alert and prickly with malevolent curiosity. The little girl's flounced dress was partly draped over the woman's arm, revealing the child's knickers. I stared at those little purple legs, dandled against that coarse body. In the state I was in, everything that passed before my eyes seemed to be a sign of something. And maybe this *was* a sign, the dim trace of an illicit destiny, whose only means of revealing itself, as far as I could tell, was to radiate promiscuously from every single thing I looked upon. It was as if the whole trip had been unreal – had been a dream, or an allegory. The little girl's face was buried where I couldn't see it, and her legs dangled down like inanimate objects . . . Maybe I frightened her, and that's why her mother was staring angry daggers at me.

In order to keep from plunging into my emblematic discomfort more deeply than I had to, I stopped looking all around and concentrated on a muddy little stream whose scanty waters poked along, bearing clusters of rubbish accompanied by clouds of gnats.

The silent man beside me was a consummate professional. When we passed through populated areas, he slowed down considerably, as if he wanted to provide the living with an opportunity to salute the coffin or say a prayer. The expression on his face changed; it became stronger, more purposeful. He was playing himself, in his melancholy role of Driver on the Last Ride, and he knew he was giving a memorable performance. But I detected an ironic streak in this façade. As far as he was concerned, I realised, it was always carnival time, and he was like a bad boy wearing a skull mask, brandishing a sickle and scaring passers-by. I assumed – I thought I could tell – that the black sunglasses obscuring his face served many functions. Now we were in a town, and he was driving slowly but inexorably through crowds of people. They flattened themselves against walls and ducked around corners as we passed them, cutting off the words in their mouths, capturing their eyes, making them bow their heads. We left them behind us like terrorised sheep.

Then, to my surprise, we reached the sea. I was sitting on my side of the car, resting my forehead against the window, and suddenly the sea struck me, entered my eyes and my nose. I glimpsed a motionless blue strip. A train passed, so close that I thought I was about to be run over, and I instinctively jerked my head away from the window. I hadn't realised it, but here the road ran side by side with the railway tracks, and there wasn't much space in between; some of the platforms were practically in the road. Then the train passed on, and the sea returned. Great cubes of cement were piled into breakwaters here and there along the coast. It was too thin – the waves had devoured it – and all that remained was a stretch of grainy sand, not very wide, wedged between the sea and the railway. On the other side of the car was an unbroken line of squalid buildings, multifarious in size and shape, with similar buildings crowded behind them and a forest of television antennas as far as the eye could see.

I should have called your mother, but I'd forgotten about both her and you. I'd stored the two of you away, and you were lodged in a part of my mind so remote that it hardly seemed like mine any more. I thought about Elsa as though she were the wife of a friend. As for you, I didn't think of myself as a father; I thought of myself as an orphan. My eye, reflected in the glass, stared back at me like the eye of some puzzled reptile.

We glided past a billboard that displayed a giant bathroom sink, complete with an imposing tap. This road was much wider than any of those that had preceded it. Glad to be on a smooth surface at last, the undertaker changed gears and put his big engine to work. Other cars sped along the road as well. There was no central reservation, and I pictured one of the oncoming vehicles travelling too fast and spinning out of control. It was a possibility, I thought, because people were so curious. As I saw all during the journey, everyone wanted to get close enough to the hearse to verify that it was already occupied. A driver could get distracted while trying to check our cargo and wind up crashing into us. Only fitting, I thought, for we were clearly part of death's victory parade, and it would have been sublime to die like that, sitting beside an undertaker in a hearse. For a while, I convinced myself that I was nearing the end that fate had reserved for me. As for my travelling companion, he appeared to know nothing about any of this.

Far from all premonitions, safe inside his big solid body, he drove on. His hands on the steering wheel were steady; dark lenses covered his eyes.

We stopped for petrol. He looked at the glass building beyond the pumps and asked, 'Would you like to get something to eat?'

She stayed in the car. It occurred to me that she'd stayed in the car the last time we stopped at a service-station restaurant, too. She'd been asleep, or pretending to be asleep, in the passenger seat. Later, when I turned from looking at the big blue brushes in the empty car wash and met her eyes, awake and watching me through the windscreen, I remember thinking that we wouldn't make it, and that I was about to lose her again. In the car park of a service-station restaurant, I'd realised she was going to die.

Having painstakingly, meticulously tucked his napkin into his shirt collar, the undertaker was eating. His chosen lunch consisted of a plate of cold rice and a bottle of mineral water. I watched him take his time. His calm was too studied – in fact, practically irritating. I attributed this trait to his character, but it appeared to be an advertisement for his profession, as well. Through his tiresomeness and his odd manners, he seemed to invite his neighbour to have patience, to await the inevitable end, which he epitomised in his laconic person.

No one sat down at any of the tables near us. I began to appreciate the advantages of travelling with a funeral director. I couldn't have asked for a better companion than this man, who brought his fork to his mouth without bending his neck or moving his head. I was having a fruit salad and a beer, drinking it straight from the cold bottle and looking out of the window at the hearse, which was parked under a shelter with a clay-tile roof. When I picked up my plastic fork and made a stab at my fruit salad, a dark-skinned grape shot up out of my dish and landed high on the undertaker's shirt, close to his collar.

This little mishap perplexed him. He'd taken his time and got his napkin tucked in just right, and now by pure chance I'd managed to strike him on the only unprotected scrap of his immaculate shirt. He pulled the napkin out, poured mineral water on it and rubbed the stain. I didn't even beg his pardon. I gazed at the dark body hair now showing through the wet cotton cloth of his shirt. His sunglasses lay where he'd put them on the table, with the earpieces open wide. His eyes were much smaller than I had imagined.

I picked up the beer bottle again and sucked it empty, right down to the noisy foam. He asked, 'Would you like a coffee?'

'No thanks,' I said.

He left the table and came back with a single espresso cup in his hand. After he drank the coffee, he put the unopened packet of sugar into the inside pocket of his coat. His sunglasses were still on the table, and he fumbled with them pensively, folding in their earpieces. I leaned against the window, looking out, partly supported by a non-functional radiator. Its tubes were covered with a layer of solidified dust.

'Was she your lover?'

This question was totally unexpected, as unexpected as the wind that began to blow, whistling around the clay tiles of the parking shelter where the hearse was.

'Why do you ask?'

I still hadn't turned to face him. The reflection of the beer bottle in the window spread a greenish glare over its grimy, anonymous surface.

'She wasn't wearing a wedding ring, but you have one on.'

'Maybe she never wore it.'

'No, women like *that* keep their wedding rings on their fingers.'

'She could have lost it.'

'They buy another one. They may have to economise on their household expenses or take out a loan, but they buy another one.'

Perhaps it would have been better if he'd persevered in keeping quiet. His voice was less impeccable than his silence.

'Did you love her a lot?'

'What's that to you?'

'Nothing. I was just making conversation.'

He picked up his sunglasses, sat up straight and examined the dark lenses against the light. He said, 'A year ago, I lost my wife.'

He put the glasses back on his face with a precise two-handed movement. The sturdy earpieces – very dark, but made from some kind of bone – slipped down behind his ears. He remained still, ascertaining that the glasses were correctly positioned, and then briskly moved his hands away. He was already on his feet.

'Shall we go?'

Afterwards, as he drove, he seemed to become sadder – or maybe that was me. The road looked like a stream of thick grey mud, rippling away from the oncoming hearse. 'I loved her very much,' I murmured. 'Very much.'

Sometime later, on a bleached-earth lane off the provincial main road, in the middle of a field, we came to a stop. The huge black car was hard to park. There was a big mulberry tree nearby. Leaning against its trunk – which turned out to be warm, much warmer than my back – I hung my head and cried. The undertaker stood next to me. At first, he tried to assist me, bending over me and putting his arm around my shoulders. 'Come, now . . .' he said. But then he drew himself erect again. I could hear his knees clicking as he straightened his legs. The wind slid into the tall grass around us and made a whistling sound like music. By that time, I'd told him everything – about my wife, Elsa, about you, our newborn child, and about Italia. And I wept for her, I wept every time I tried to pronounce her name. I simply couldn't do it; either I'd start sobbing in the middle of a syllable or I'd belch out fumes from the beer that was sitting on my stomach in a growing ferment.

From time to time, the undertaker flicked his eyes over parts of me. He was uncomfortable, but his discomfort was filled with affection and human sympathy. He looked at my grief-stricken mouth; he looked at my eyes, which were too red to be looked at. Then he drew back and turned to contemplate the wind-blown, musical grass, whose whistling continually rose and fell, fading away like eddies in a whirlpool. He lit a cigarette and smoked it in silence, then threw it on to the chalky lane. As he stamped the butt into the loose soil, he observed the torsion of his foot inside his black shoe. 'You die the way you live,' he said. 'My wife passed away like a leaf, without disturbing anyone.'

We climbed back into the hearse and spent the rest of the journey changing back into what we had been before, him with his tensed neck muscles and me with my forehead resting on the window. But inside us, in our dissimilar souls, we felt solidarity with each other. We were like two wolves that have chased a prey and lost it: they lie together in the dark woods, panting and weary, and they're still hungry.

By the time we arrived at our destination, the ambient air was crushingly hot. The village was perched on the sides and stump of a hill with a flattened summit that made me think of the crater of an extinct volcano. The bright yellow-ochre houses crowding the hillside looked as though they had been cut out of the sulphurous rock.

Women wearing their heavy traditional costumes, with black wool leggings, shawls and work shoes, were walking down the centre of the unpaved road leading to the cemetery. Instead of making the slightest movement to get out of the way, they stared at us incredulously, like goats. We crept into the parking area next to the cemetery gates. Other people were there, less exotic people, dressed in contemporary clothing and standing around an ordinary jalopy, but they stared at us with the very same stupefaction as the others, equally shocked by the sudden appearance of an unknown funeral car carrying a coffin with no flowers. The undertaker reached round into the back for his jacket. He said, 'I'm going to take care of a few bureaucratic matters.'

And he picked up his black leather case, which was stiff as a coffin.

I watched him walk past the two columns holding up the gates of the cemetery and unhesitatingly turn left. Do all cemeteries have similar topographies? Whatever the case, he moved about that silent place as though he knew it; in fact, the tremors in his legs increased, as when a horse recognises its stall. His head disappeared behind the white wall formed by the gravestones, which fanned out in all directions. The jalopy drove away in a cloud of dust. I got out of the hearse, stood behind it, with my back to the cemetery, and pissed, leaving a dark stain on the earth.

The undertaker came back, accompanied by a somewhat shorter man wearing blue work clothes. After exchanging a few words, they separated, and the undertaker walked over to me. 'They close at sunset. We have to find a priest.'

The coffin had already been let down, and the overturned earth rose in a mound beside it. The wind made the priest's vestments billow and stirred his censer, wafting the incense fumes our way. The cripple, who was waiting to be paid, had not moved. The undertaker had recruited him, and now he continued to stand there, supporting his body weight on the longer of his two legs and making an excessively disconsolate face, as if that, too, were part of the service he'd been hired to provide. The cemetery custodian was still there, as well. Together, we had lowered the coffin into the grave, and it had been no easy task. The undertaker took off his jacket when we started and didn't put it on again until the end. His sweaty forehead was covered with specks of dirt conveyed there by the swirling wind. But the muscular exertion had somehow helped my spirits. I felt calm, despite the hot wind fluttering around me. My hands had been the first to sprinkle earth on Italia's coffin, and now the custodian was swinging his shovel in a steady rhythm, scooping and dumping. My pain was still there, but diminished, dulled by exhaustion.

The cripple's face, framed by his shock of long blond hair, resumed its normal inexpressiveness. He looked like an onion lying in a field, unearthed and abandoned. The brotherly undertaker appeared to be at peace with himself; the sun was going down, and his work was done. As he breathed, the gold belt buckle under his belly vibrated a little. It had been a long day. He glanced up at the sky, his gaze sweeping across it with swift precision: yes, the darkness would bring him compensation. Italia was under the earth, and some of that fresh lumpy earth had passed through my hands, had rained down on her from my spread fingers. Now she was buried, Angela; my ephemeral moment of love was over.

I saw a dark shadow like the shadow of a bird. A rustic-looking figure was standing a few feet away from me, half hidden by the wall of above-ground vaults that divided the cemetery. It was an old man, but he was as small as a child. He stood there without moving, holding a hat in his hand. I didn't think he'd been there a little while ago, when I'd bent down for two handfuls of earth, but maybe I simply hadn't noticed him. He seemed to have come out of nowhere. His eyes met mine without curiosity, as if he already knew who I was. I turned away from him, but all the same, the memory of that look remained implanted in the back of my neck. Then I remembered the yellowing photograph Italia had in her room, the one of the young man. Her father, her first tormentor. I turned round again, this time with the intention of doing something, of going over to speak to him. But he wasn't there any more. There was only the sound of the wind, which was swirling around on the other side of the wall of vaults, and there was the encroaching black background, where you couldn't see a thing. Maybe it wasn't him; maybe it was just some curious passer-by. But I forgave him, Angela, and at the same time I forgave my own father, too.

No memorial marked Italia's presence in that cemetery. The undertaker had come to terms with the custodian for setting up a simple unornamented stone, but that wouldn't be ready for another ten days or so. The custodian passed me a pad of graph paper and a ballpoint pen and asked, 'What do you want on the stone?'

Pressing too hard, making a few holes in the paper with the pen, I wrote her name, nothing but her name. Now there wasn't anything left to do, so we all stared at the filled-in trench and waited for someone else to be the first to leave. The undertaker made the sign of the cross and moved away, followed slowly by the cripple. There was no gesture that I wanted to make, nor did I have any special thoughts, except for thinking that one day I'd remember this moment, I'd fill it up with something that wasn't there. I'd find a way to take what appeared utterly futile at the time and make it, in retrospect, quite solemn. I bent over and scooped up a little earth. I thought I was going to put it in my pocket, or perhaps let it trickle through my fingers like ashes. Instead, I shoved it into my mouth. I ate dirt, Angela, maybe without even knowing it. I was looking for a way to say goodbye, and I couldn't come up with anything more eloquent than a mouthful of earth. I spat it out, using the back of my hand to wipe away whatever was left on my lips, on my tongue.

The undertaker was on his way back from paying, with my cheques, everyone who had to be paid. The cemetery was now closed, and I leaned on the wall near the locked gates, waiting for him and looking out over the land that lay below us. It was dotted here and there with the fixed lights of houses and traversed by the headlights of moving vehicles. Night had completely fallen. I recognised his footfall behind me.

He leaned against the wall at my side, reached into the inner pocket of his jacket, and took out the packet of sugar he'd collected in the service-station restaurant. He opened the packet and poured its contents into his mouth. We were so close to each other that I could hear the sound of his teeth as they crunched the sugar grains, a grinding sound that gave me shivers. He moved his tongue across his palate, savouring the sweetness as it fused with his saliva. He looked below us where I was looking, over the precipice and down into the valley with the floating lights. 'I don't know,' he said.

'What?'

'It doesn't seem fair. Dying, I mean.' He swallowed the last of his sugar and said, 'But on the other hand, it does.'

I looked into the cemetery. She feels no more pain, I thought. And that was a good thought.

Ada's standing in front of me, very close. I'm looking out over that precipice, as I did fifteen years ago. You're down there in the darkness, one of those trembling lights. I don't know why I've brought you all this way, Angela. But I know I'm still leaning against that wall, and you're at my side; I'm clutching you like a hostage. *Here she is, Italia. This is my daughter, the one who was born back then. And you, Angela, raise your head, let her see you, and say to this lady, this queen, hello. She looks like me, doesn't she, Italia? She's fifteen. Her behind's a little big. She used to be skinny skinny, but for a year now, her behind's been a little big. It's her age. She's a girl who eats between meals and doesn't fasten her helmet. She's not perfect, she's not special, she's one among many. She's an ordinary girl. But she's my daughter, she's Angela. She's all I have. Look at me, Italia. Take a seat on this empty chair and look at me. Have you really come to take her from me? Stay there; I want to tell you something. I want to tell you how it was when I went back to the life I'd left behind. I had no more emotions; I felt no pain; I received no consolation. But Angela was stronger than me, and stronger than you. I want to tell you what it smells like to have an infant in the house: it's a sweet smell that sticks to the walls, that gets inside the walls. I'd post myself beside her cradle and gaze down at her sweaty little head. She'd wake up laughing and suck her feet. And she'd stare at me with the fathomless eyes of the newly born; she'd stare at me the way you used to. She had a beneficial effect, like a stove. She was a gift, brand spanking new. She was life, and I didn't have the courage to embrace it. An aeroplane is circling in the sky, preparing to land. A woman on that plane is weeping. She's fifty-three, somewhat heavier than she used to be, with a little bag of flesh under her chin. That's my wife. Her scent has grown old in my nostrils. She's looking at a cloud; she's looking at her daughter. Cut through that cloud, Italia, cut through it like a swan. Give me back Angela.*

'Doctor . . .'

I get to my feet, as though for the first time in my life.

'We're closing her up.'

'Vital signs?'

'Normal.'

My heart's about to jump out of my throat. I grab one of Ada's arms and cling to it, holding on to a last bit of silence, but soon I start sobbing into my hands, and I even wet my pants a little. And then, chaos; while my emotions swamp me, all the ambient sights and sounds come rushing back into my consciousness at once: voices, white coats, doors opening and closing. Alfredo's coat is spattered with blood. It's the first thing I see. When he takes off his gloves, his hands are white. Holding out those hands, he comes towards me.

'It took a bit longer than I thought it would. I had problems with the dura – it contracted. And there was excessive bleeding. I had a hard time making it stop.'

His surgeon's cap is soaked. He's got marks around his mouth from the surgical mask, and he's got the face of a madman. He speaks very quickly and gets mixed up. He says, 'Let's hope there isn't a diffuse axonal injury. Let's hope the brain compression the impact caused wasn't too severe.'

I breathe in assent. Then I ask him, 'What's your prognosis?'

'I told Ada to try weaning her off the respirator. We'll be able to tell better then, but it'll take a little while.'

Your bandaged head glides past me on the way to intensive care. The nurse pushes the trolley slowly and cautiously. Now you're inside these glass walls, and I'm looking at your closed eyes and watching the sheet over your chest move as you breathe. Your breathing's what I'm watching for. Ada's taken you off the respirator and removed the anaesthetic pump; she's trying to bring you a little closer to the surface so we can see what's happening. She moves around you, around your tubes, with special concentration. She's pale and drawn, and her lips are dry. 'Take a break,' I murmur. She obeys me reluctantly.

Now it's you and me again, Angela. We're alone. I stroke your arms, your forehead, all your exposed skin. Your head is resting on one of those croissant-shaped pillows. You've got to stay like that. Your neck muscles have to remain extended to avoid any compression of the venous circle. And your head has to lie higher than your heart. Your ears are brown from iodine solution. You've got some asphalt in your cheeks, but don't worry – those cinders work their way out by themselves. If there are any left, I'll remove them with the laser. As for your head, I'll buy you a hat. I'll buy you a hundred hats. Your friends will come and visit you – they'll think you look funny in that bandage. And they'll envy you because you'll get to skip school. They'll bring CDs and scatter them over your bed. They'll bring you a cigarette, too. I know who'll bring it for you: the short fellow, the little punk with the dreadlocks, the one who comes up to your shoulder. Is that the lucky boyfriend? I like him. I like his hair. I like everything you like. Look, I'll hire some skates, some Rollerblades. Black, with lots of wheels, like yours. I want to skate the streets with you on Ecological Sundays. I want to fall down; I want to make you laugh. There's a strange sobbing sound in your chest, so I'm going to hook you back up to the respirator. Don't move. But you *do* move. You squeeze my hand.

'Can you hear me? If you can hear me, sweetheart, open your eyes. It's me . . . It's Daddy.'

And you open them, open them with no effort, as though opening them were the simplest thing in the world. You uncover your black-and-white eyes and look at me.

Ada comes running up behind me. 'What's going on?' she says. She probably doesn't realise it, but she's yelling.

I don't take my eyes off you, and I feel myself smiling wetly. 'She's responsive,' I say. 'She squeezed my finger.'

'It might just have been a grasping reflex . . .'

'No. She opened her eyes too.'

★

260

Alfredo has washed, changed his clothes and combed his hair. He looks like an athlete who's just won a competition. He's wearing plastic bags over his street shoes. He says, 'Intracranial pressure, acute anaemia, cardiac arrest . . . I didn't think she was going to make it.'

'I know.'

'I could only hope.'

'You hoped well.'

He bends over you, stimulates you, checks your reactions. You open your eyes again, and this time I seem to recognise your funny, indolent gaze. Alfredo checks the medications on your chart. It would be better, he says, for you to be sedated again and then left alone for the first twenty-four hours. After that, he leaves the hospital in his typically brusque way, without saying goodbye to anyone. He goes back to his life as a separated husband, to his house, which a Philippine servant tidies up when he's not there. His colleagues in the intensive-care unit don't look up as he leaves; they're bent over the schedule sheets, discussing shifts. Ada alone follows him with her eyes, smiling at him. He wasn't on duty, and yet he came back to perform this operation. Maybe he did it because she was the one who asked him to.

I see your mother in the glass – her overcoat, her bag, her face. It's your mother, who hates hospitals, who knows almost nothing about how they work, who's never entered an intensive-care unit. A white plastic curtain is pulled to one side, and she's standing next to it, looking at you. Maybe she's been there for a while. I shifted my eyes away from you and discovered her, just by chance; at first, I thought she was a nurse. She's hunched over; her hair's dishevelled; she's old. You know what she looks like, Angela? You know what she looks like, with that nun's face? Like a mother outside a nursery, gazing in through the window. Exactly like that: a mother in her dressing gown, her breasts swollen and painful, looking at her newborn child, her little pink monkey. She's got the eyes of a woman with a slack, empty belly, examining the living flesh that has issued from her body. She's not sad, she's numb. And she

261

doesn't come in; she stays where she is. I get up and go out to her. When I embrace her, she's a bundle of tremors. And she's brought the smell of home into that desert of ammonia.

'How is she?'

'She's alive.'

I help her put on a white coat, a surgical mask, plastic bags for her shoes, a paper cap for her head. She bends over you and looks at you close up. She looks at your bandages, the electrodes on your bosom, the tubes in your nose and your veins, the catheter.

'Can I touch her?'

'Of course you can.'

One of her tears touches you first. It falls on your chest, and she blots it with a finger. 'Doesn't she feel cold, lying here naked like this?'

'The temperature in this room never varies.'

'So she can feel?'

'Of course.'

'She's not in a coma?'

'No, she's sedated. She's in a pharmacologically induced coma.'

Elsa nods, open-mouthed. 'Ah . . . that's what it is . . .'

I embrace her again. She seems small and misshapen. Fate has run over her like a bulldozer. She says, 'The whole time, I hoped the plane would crash. I couldn't stand the thought of seeing her dead.'

After that, she falls silent.

Now she's sitting next to your bed. She's recovered a little – she's not so afraid, not so stunned. She's like a vibrating jellyfish. The amniotic fluid you and she shared has somehow returned. I can sense the two of you floating towards each other in the silence. Her head may collapse on her neck tonight, but she won't let go of your hand. And tomorrow she'll know exactly what to do for you. She'll know better than me or Ada or anyone else. She'll be the one who'll take care of you, who'll recognise the signs of your recovery. She'll check the monitors and the drips; she'll feed you with a teaspoon, she'll help with your medications. She won't move from that chair. She'll lose weight at your side, and then she'll take you back home. And when your hair grows back, she'll cut hers to match. And this summer, I'll take pictures of you two with your short hair and sunglasses, like sisters.

I leave you to her. I leave you both, living, breathing and attached to each other, as you were in that clinic fifteen years ago. 'I'll be back soon,' I say, kissing her on the head.

Now I'm the one standing next to the plastic curtain and looking through the glass.

Elsa never asked me anything about my long absence; she acted as if I hadn't ever moved from her bedside. We put you in a carrycot and took you home. And when your cord fell off, we went back to that pine grove where we'd made love and placed the cord in the fork of a tree to bring you luck. I love her, Angela. I love her for the way she's been, and for the way we are: two old runners heading for a dusty finish line.

It's raining outside, but barely. The rainwater's practically evaporated, and it looks like damp dust motes in the air. I went to my locker and changed my clothes, took a little walk, and here I am in this modern cafeteria, crowded with tables that are always filled during lunch hours. Now the place is almost empty. I consider the sandwiches left over from lunch. I take a seat near the door, near the air. I'm wearing your ring on my middle finger. I got it on – I don't know when, but it went on – and now I can't get it off. It's still raining. It was raining when I made love to Italia for the last time, in a dark corner of this city. When it rains, I feel certain that, wherever she is, she regrets her life. But she was part of me, like a prehistoric tail; something mutilated by evolution, something whose aura I preserve, like a mysterious presence in the void. I'm hungry. A waitress is approaching the table to take my order. She's got a flat face, a striped apron and a tray under her arm. She's the last woman in this story.

THE POWER OF READING

Visit the Random House website and get connected with information on all our books and authors

EXTRACTS from our recently published books and selected backlist titles

COMPETITIONS AND PRIZE DRAWS Win signed books, audiobooks and more

AUTHOR EVENTS Find out which of our authors are on tour and where you can meet them

LATEST NEWS on bestsellers, awards and new publications

MINISITES with exclusive special features dedicated to our authors and their titles

READING GROUPS Reading guides, special features and all the information you need for your reading group

LISTEN to extracts from the latest audiobook publications

WATCH video clips of interviews and readings with our authors

RANDOM HOUSE INFORMATION including advice for writers, job vacancies and all your general queries answered

www.randomhouse.co.uk/vintage

www.randomhouse.co.uk